A life

On the surface, Jenny Dell appeared the model lady,
but nothing could have been further from the truth.
For her, every word and every act was a deception.
Until she met Brant Claremont, the Duke of Strachen,
and learned firsthand about love based on a lie.

"No matter how much any one of us pretends to be someone else, in the end we always are what we are."

"Ahh." For whatever reason, Brant relaxed. "Then you are a fatalist? You believe that we can never change from what we're born? That our destiny remains always the same, with no hope of growth or improvement?"

"No, no, no! It's not so complicated as that, Your Grace. I only meant that no matter how many changes you may make for the world to see, you are still at heart, or in your soul, the same creature you were born. That's what I *know*," Jenny said with conviction.

She did believe it. How could she not, when so much of her life was unabashed deception? If she didn't believe in herself independent of whatever new identity she'd concocted, why, then, she'd have nothing at all.

* * *

The Golden Lord
Harlequin Historical #672—September 2003

Miranda Jarrett

The Golden Lord

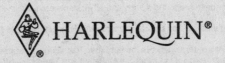

HARLEQUIN®

TORONTO • NEW YORK • LONDON
AMSTERDAM • PARIS • SYDNEY • HAMBURG
STOCKHOLM • ATHENS • TOKYO • MILAN • MADRID
PRAGUE • WARSAW • BUDAPEST • AUCKLAND

ISBN 0-373-29272-4

THE GOLDEN LORD

This edition published by arrangement with Harlequin Books S.A.

® and TM are trademarks of the publisher. Trademarks indicated with ® are registered in the United States Patent and Trademark Office, the Canadian Trade Marks Office and in other countries.

Visit us at www.eHarlequin.com

Printed in U.S.A.

Please address questions and book requests to:
Harlequin Reader Service
U.S.: 3010 Walden Ave., P.O. Box 1325, Buffalo, NY 14269
Canadian: P.O. Box 609, Fort Erie, Ont. L2A 5X3

Prologue

Harrow Public School
Middlesex
1788

The five boys sat cross-legged in a tight circle on the attic floor, the lantern in their center shaded so that just enough light filtered through to show the cards clutched in their hands and the hoarded heaps of coins before each of them. It was late, very late, and long past the six o'clock lock-up for the night, but no one would dare consider leaving this game.

Brant, as usual, had made sure of that. Through the sheer power of his personality, he'd made being asked to these clandestine games the most desirable invitation in the entire school, and the staggeringly high stakes that could gobble up a term's allowance in a single hand of cards only served to increase Brant's own mystique.

But why shouldn't it? Brant Claremont was the sixth Duke of Strachen, Marquess of Elwes, admired as much for his wit as for his daring on the cricket field. As an orphan, he had only a distant, disinterested guardian to answer to, and his two younger brothers had been sent so far away that there wasn't even a hint of fraternal competition. To the other boys in his form, Brant's life seemed as close to perfection as any mortal British male could wish for.

Only Brant himself knew otherwise. Still months shy of his sixteenth birthday, he already understood all too well the terrifying obligations that his wastrel father's death two years before had thrust upon him, along with the dukedom and a string of mortgaged, decaying properties.

Not that any of that mattered here in the chill of this drafty attic. Now Brant smiled as he leaned forward, the lantern turning his fair hair as gold as the guineas heaped before his crossed legs. He was winning, winning deep, and he did not want his luck to turn just yet.

"Your play, Galsworthy," he said, his voice deceptively languid. "Draw or show. Any time before Michaelmas will do."

The others sniggered nervously while the Honorable Edmund Galsworthy scowled down at his hand. "I say, Claremont, that's cutting it a little rough," he grumbled. "Not all of us are so deuced quick with ciphering as you are."

"That's why we call him the Golden Lord, Galsworthy," said another boy, obviously with a better hand of his own. "He can turn pasteboard cards direct into guineas if you let him. *Your* guineas."

"'Tis luck, no more," murmured Brant with a modest shrug, careful to mask his own excitement. It was luck, but it was also skill, coupled with the rare gift he had for recalling cards. He could sympathize with Galsworthy's dilemma—sympathize more, really, than anyone here would guess—but not now, and not with so much at stake. Nearly every shilling Brant won was sent off against his father's debts, while Galsworthy's mother was some sort of tin-mine heiress. The poor oaf could afford to lose almost in equal proportion to how desperately Brant himself needed to win.

"But you do know the rules of this game, Galsworthy," he said. "Laggards must forfeit, else the rest of us fall asleep."

"I'm considering, not lagging," snapped Galsworthy, his fingers leaving moist dimples in the edges of his cards as he studied the red and black figures one last time. Slowly he puffed out his cheeks and spread his hand on the floor for the others to see.

"There now, Claremont," he announced. "That was worth the wait, wasn't it?"

"Indeed," drawled Brant. He kept his expression unchanged as he fanned his own cards out on the floor in front of him. "I'd say I've won again, Galsworthy, and I— What the devil is *that?*"

Abruptly the door flew open, scattering cards and panicking boys as two large men thundered into the attic. Brant scrambled to his feet, stuffing guineas into his pockets as Conway, his boardinghouse monitor, caught him roughly by the collar of his coat while Parker, his tutor, gathered up the cards and loose coins as evidence.

"I'll give you all the devil you can handle, Claremont," growled Conway, yanking Brant's feet clear from the floor. "Least I will after Dr. Keel's through with you."

"Dr. Keel will have little interest in this," protested Brant as Parker now seized his arm. "This—this was harmless amusement, a mere game among gentlemen!"

"That's not what Dr. Keel believes," warned Conway

ominously. "Now walk, you cheating little weasel. *Walk!*"

Brant twisted, struggling vainly to free himself from the grasp of the two stronger, older men. He heard the tear of fabric, the sound of the sleeve of his superfine coat ripping away at the shoulder, and as he turned to look, one of the men cuffed his ear, hard enough to make him see bright flashes before his eyes.

"You—you have impinged my honor as a gentleman and—and as a lord, Conway!" he gasped, desperate not to show his growing fear as the monitor shoved him stumbling toward the dark attic staircase. Of course he'd felt Conway's wrath many times before—at Harrow even dukes were flogged regularly in the Fourth Form rooms—but never before had the monitor singled him out away from the others like this. "You cannot—cannot treat me like this!"

"I can treat you a deal worse if I please, Claremont," said Conway. Like most of the monitors, he was a hulk of a man, able to worry even a tall boy like Brant like a terrier with a rat. "And I would, too, if Dr. Keel didn't want you in his rooms directly. Now *walk.*"

This time Brant did as he was told, forcing himself not to panic, to order his thoughts as they half dragged him down the stairs and across the empty courtyard. Dr. Keel was a sensible man; surely he could be made to see this for the foolishness it was. Card-playing after lock-up was hardly the most grievous sin that took place at the school, scarcely worth this sort of melodrama.

But what if this wasn't about the card game at all? What if Dr. Keel or one of the tutors had finally discovered his blackest, most shameful secret? Was this the reason that Conway and Parker had stopped trying to hide their contempt for him? And what if this were only

*the first, stumbling step to his complete disgrace and
ruin, and a cell in the madhouse where he'd always
suspected he belonged?*

The headmaster must have been waiting for them, for
he answered the door to his study at once. To Brant's
surprise, he was still dressed as precisely as if it were
first dawn, instead of near midnight, but then there were
whispers that Dr. Keel never slept at all, nor needed to.

"Claremont," he said grimly, studying Brant from beneath the stiff curls of his wig. "Enter, pray."

For once Brant did as he was told and, with a final
shove from Conway, he slowly went to stand in the center of the bare floor before the headmaster's desk. His
heart pounding, he raised his chin and squared his shoulders in the torn coat, prepared to meet whatever disaster
came next. He'd only been in these rooms once before,
on the day he'd first arrived at the school, but from Dr.
Keel's glower, he knew better than to expect the same
welcoming hospitality this time.

"Claremont," the headmaster repeated more ominously. "Given all the blessings that your birth has
showered upon your head, I'd looked for more from
you."

Brant took a deep breath to steady his words and his
nerves. Despite the chill in the room, he was already
sweating, his legs itching to carry him from this room
and to run as quickly as they could away from this mess.

"I am sorry, sir," he began. "And you are right. At
such an hour, so long after lock-up, I should have been
either asleep or preparing tomorrow's recitation, instead
of allowing myself the indulgence of a mild amusement
among friends—"

"Is that what you believe your time here at Harrow
is to be, Claremont?" interrupted Dr. Keel incredu-

lously, his brows bristling together with astonishment. "Your indulgence and amusement?"

"No, sir, not at all," said Brant hastily, realizing he could not afford another such misstep. "I should hardly presume—"

"You should hardly *presume.*" The headmaster paused scornfully, as if struck silent with shock, and shook his head. "How can you venture such a statement, Claremont, when all you have done since you have arrived here is *presume?*"

"I am sorry, Dr. Keel," said Brant again. "But if I could—"

"Could *what,* you sniveling little creature?" demanded Dr. Keel, his voice ringing with his scornful anger. "Is it the list of your iniquities that you wish to hear? Is that the kind of recitation that would please you most?"

"No, sir," said Brant wretchedly. He tried to remind himself that he was a Claremont, a peer of the realm, while Keel was no more than a lowly public school headmaster, but the agonizing weight of his secret and the dread of its discovery smothered any self-defense. "No, sir, not at all."

"But you will hear them, Claremont, because it pleases *me,*" insisted the headmaster, rapping his knuckles impatiently on the desk. "I have kept tallies of what Mr. Conway and the others have reported to me. Because of your rank and the position you shall hold in the world after leaving this school, I have looked away. Most wrongly, it now seems to me, considering how often you have been caught in your *amusements* after lock-up."

Ah, thought Brant with bleak resignation, now would

come every last misdemeanor that Conway had caught him doing, and that he'd already been duly punished for.

"You have been apprehended fighting with boys from other boardinghouses," intoned Keen righteously, "swimming naked at night in the pond, gaming and gambling at every opportunity, and consorting intimately with the lowest sort of chits from the village tavern. Then there is the contempt you have repeatedly shown to this school and its scholars by your inferior work."

In spite of his resolution to stand tall, Brant caught his breath, clasping his hands behind his back to hide their trembling. Here it was, the end at last.

"You have done well enough with your recitations," continued the headmaster, "well enough to have kept you here by your tutor's mercy. But from your first day, your written work has been an unfailing mockery of learning. Why, an African monkey with a pen in his paw could do better than these!"

He swept a sheaf of papers from the desk, brandishing it before Brant. "And now come these. What am I to do with you, Claremont? Have you any answers to share with me by way of enlightenment?"

Keel tossed the papers back onto the desk with disgust, and Brant closed his eyes against the awful proof of his shame. He didn't have to see his examination papers to know what gibberish was scrawled across them or what that gibberish proved. He already knew.

He was no Golden Lord, but an imbecile duke, an idiot from his cradle. *That* was the truth. No matter how he tried, concentrating until his head ached with the effort, he could not make sense of the letters that others so effortlessly saw as words. No such troubles plagued him with numbers—certainly not at cards—and if a page were read aloud to him, like a nursery story, he'd comprehend and recall every line with ease. Throughout his life he'd contrived scores of little tricks and feints to hide his deficiency, and he'd done well enough to keep his secret, even here.

But to read and write like a gentleman was as impossible for him as flying through the clouds. Awake at night, he imagined that inside his skull his brain was a fraction the size of a normal man's, woefully shriveled and defective.

And now, it seemed, the rest of the world was about to learn the truth, as well, and scorn and pity and mock him for the half-wit that he'd always been.

"Speak, Claremont," ordered the headmaster, his voice booming through Brant's private dread. "I await your suggestions for me."

Slowly, Brant opened his eyes and met Keel's gaze, determined to savor what might well be his last few moments as a rational gentleman. "I have no suggestions, sir."

"None?" Scowling, Dr. Keel thrust out his lower lip and leaned toward Brant. "You surprise me, Claremont. You have taken these other boys sufficiently into your confidence to pick their pockets clean, and yet you have no notion of what I should write or say to their fathers?"

"Fathers, sir?" repeated Brant uncertainly, not following at first. What had the other boys to do with this?

"Yes, Claremont, their fathers," said the headmaster furiously, once again reaching for the sheaf of papers. "I have had these six letters in the past three days. The accusations are all the same. Hundreds, even thousands of pounds lost to you whilst gaming!"

"'Tis luck," said Brant slowly for the second time that evening, and what else could it be, to spare him in this marvelous, unexpected way? "Purest luck, sir."

"'Tis conniving tricks and cheats," said Keel, thumping his fist on the edge of the desk. "I do not care if you are a peer, Claremont. No true gentleman would win as often as you do."

"But I do not cheat, sir," protested Brant. He didn't cheat, not only because it was dishonorable and ungentlemanly, but also because he didn't need to. "I never have, not once."

"Don't compound your iniquities by lying to me," said Keel sternly. "Tonight's game shall be your last here. I will not let you turn Harrow into a veritable Devonshire House of gaming. You are a sharpster, Claremont, a shark who preys upon the trust of your fellows for your own gain, and I shall not tolerate it any longer, or you, either."

"You are sending me down, sir?" asked Brant, striving to keep the growing, giddy joy from his voice. "I am to leave Harrow?"

"As soon as is possible," said the headmaster disdainfully. "By tomorrow noon at the latest. Until then I shall instruct Mr. Conway to keep the others in your house away from you. By your actions, you have demonstrated that you are no longer a young gentleman worthy of Harrow. I shall recommend to your guardian that a private tutor might continue with your preparation for admission to university."

But Brant knew there had never been a question of him going to one of the grand universities at Cambridge or Oxford. His father's estate was simply too impoverished to afford such a luxury, any more than Brant could expect to make a Grand Tour of the Continent like other peers his age. The disinterested solicitor who served as his guardian had explained it all with perfect clarity: when Brant left Harrow, his education was done.

No, he was done *now*. He scarcely listened to Dr. Keel's final admonitions, too amazed by how swiftly one world was closing against him and another beckoning with possibilities. But outside in the shadows of the empty courtyard, returning to his boardinghouse for the last time, he could look up at the stars overhead and laugh with relief and exhilaration and a kind of fierce, wild joy.

He was a fifteen-year-old orphan with scarcely a shilling to his titled name. He could recite much of Homer, Aristotle and Shakespeare from memory, but he could no more read nor write than the commonest plowman. He had neither friends nor family to guide his choices and ease his path, and his two younger brothers were half a world away, if they even still lived. All he had to make his way was his title, his charm, his face and a gift for card-playing.

But he was free. *He was free.* Now, finally, he was done biding his time with school. Now he could make his own future and fortune, and keep the pledge he and his brothers had made to one another so long ago.

And best of all, his secret and his shame would now be safe forever.

Chapter One

Bamfleigh, Sussex
June, 1803

Jenny Dell was exceptionally good at doing things silently and in the dark. She had to be, or else she never would have lived as long, and as grandly, as she already had.

Without so much as a candle to guide her, she now hurried across the dark chamber, her bare feet as quiet as a cat's paws. While the innkeeper and his wife had been all kind welcome when she and her brother had first taken the house's best rooms, Jenny knew that same welcome could turn as sour as vinegar wine if they realized she and Rob were leaving them now, in the middle of the night, and quite forgetting the nicety of settling their reckoning.

Jenny was sorry about that, for she'd liked this inn and the rooms that overlooked a pasture filled with sweet-smelling pink clover. But Rob had had his reasons, even if he hadn't explained them to her just yet.

Once he did, he'd be sure to remind her that there was always another inn or grand house waiting over the next hillside, filled with more folk eager for the amusing company of two genteel young persons like Jenny and Rob, and willing to share their own good fortune in return. And where, truly, was the harm in that?

Swiftly, Jenny pulled her three gowns from the clothespress and folded them into her little traveling trunk. Though limited by their travels, her wardrobe was always of the latest fashion, costly Indian muslins with silk ribbons, fine Holland chemises, the softest Kashmir shawl. Rob didn't believe in skimping when it came to clothes. "Quality knows quality," he'd say, and indeed Jenny did find it easier to play a lady when dressed like one. Rob was clever about such matters, just as their father had been before him. She shouldn't forget that, especially now.

Somewhere in the inn a clock chimed three times and Jenny quickened her pace. The last of the men in the taproom had staggered home and the rest of the inn might be sleeping, but Rob would soon be waiting for her on the high road with the chaise. She closed and locked the trunk, and threaded a twisted bedsheet through the leather handles with well-practiced efficiency. Cautiously she pushed the window open—here, as at most country inns, the best rooms came with the most privacy—and tossed the bundle of her traveling cloak, stockings and shoes onto the grass below. Next went the trunk, lowered carefully down to the ground to avoid making too loud a noise when it landed.

She took two deep breaths to steady her racing heart, then clambered out the window, swinging down off the sill to drop into the grass. She untied the sheet from the trunk's handles, gathered up the bundle of clothes and shoes, and ran barefoot across the sweet-smelling clover, her long, dark braid flopping over her shoulder and the trunk thumping awkwardly against her leg. The road wasn't far, and even on this night with only a sliver of a moon, she easily spotted the hired chaise waiting in the shadows.

"Did anyone see you, pet?" asked Rob as he took her trunk and pulled it up into the chaise.

"Nary a soul," she said breathlessly, climbing up onto the seat next to her brother. "Everyone was safely abed. Now will you tell me why we had to flee tonight, and so sudden?"

"Because we had no choice," he said, no real answer at all. "Because we had to."

Jenny frowned impatiently. Most everything they did was because they *had* to, wasn't it? Their existence was precarious enough without Rob keeping the details from her like this.

"Here I thought we were doing so well with Sir Wallace," she said. "The way he sought your opinion on those fusty old books in his library, I was sure we'd be snug there for at least a fortnight, and leave with a bit of gold in our pockets for your trouble, too."

"We were." Rob pulled the horse away from the tall weeds he'd been grazing and snapped the reins across the animal's back to hurry him along. "I'd expected us to be invited as guests to Wallace Manor this very day."

"I know," said Jenny. "You've warned me before that we were perilously short of funds."

"Well, yes." Rob sighed, both for the shortness of their funds and the peril attached. "But there were certain, ah, complications that made it better for us to move along tonight."

"Mrs. Hewitt?" guessed Jenny, pulling on her stockings and shoes as the chaise began moving faster. "Was she your complication?"

"Yes, and a powerfully difficult one, too." Rob scowled. "All the time she'd been saying she was a lonely widow and coaxing me along, she'd neglected to tell me she'd another beau, a great, strapping grenadier who appeared out of the wainscoting. And I must say, Jen, he did not like my competition."

"Did he call you out?" asked Jenny anxiously. She knew Rob always carried a pistol, a beautiful French-made gun that he'd won gaming, though he kept it hidden because he knew she didn't approve. "You did not fight a duel, did you?"

"What, over Mrs. Hewitt?" asked Rob indignantly. "Faith, Jen, grant me more wit and judgment than that!"

Jenny shook her head, wiping the dirt from her fingers with her handkerchief. Although the name stitched on the linen was Corinthia, instead of her own—left from a highly profitable sojourn in Bath last winter when they'd posed as the Honorable Peter Beckham and his sister Miss Corinthia Beckham—she'd liked the Bruxelles lace edging too much to toss it away, even if it meant she'd kept the handkerchief far longer than she'd kept the name.

"So that is why we're leaving now," she said with a certain resignation, tucking the handkerchief back into her bodice. "So that you won't have to defend your honor and Mrs. Hewitt's virtue."

None of this was, of course, anything new. Although Rob was twenty-five and clever as could be, he still had not one whit of sense regarding women, and if he continued to follow after their father, he never would. With his bright blue eyes and curling black hair, her handsome brother attracted the fair sex like flies to honeycomb. In that first glow of fliration he could always find some special feature or comely grace in every female he met, whether old, young or in-between. He was the most charming of rascals, for he honestly loved each new woman in turn, almost as much as they loved him.

Now Rob sniffed, wounded. "I'd always thought, Jenny, that you preferred to have me as a live coward, instead of an honorable corpse."

"I do," said Jenny quickly, patting her brother's arm to reassure herself as much as him. "But I'd also rather you kept your breeches buttoned in the process. Now I'll just have to pray that she didn't pox you as a parting gift."

"What could I do, Jen?" he asked forlornly. "The dear little widow played me false. If only she'd been true! You know I would have been as happy as the cows in that sweet clover near the inn if I could but spend the rest of my days with her in Bamfleigh."

"You would not," said Jenny matter-of-factly. "You're just the way Father was. You like variety too much ever to be faithful. You'll never stop your roaming."

"For the right lady, I would," he said confidently. "And you will, too, Jen, though with a gentleman, of course. You're too young now, but I'll wager five guineas that the first time you fall in love, you'll be as moonstruck as every other Dell since Noah trundled down from the ark."

"I'm nineteen, Rob, more than old enough to fall in love if I pleased," she said wearily. This wasn't a new conversation between them, either, nor was it one that Jenny particularly wished to revisit. "It's more a matter of being sensible than too young. Just because I'm a Dell doesn't mean I must be a ninny about men."

Rob answered only with an incoherent grunt, and they fell into an uneasy silence that seemed to match the rocking haste of the chaise through the night. With a sigh, Jenny drew her shawl over her shoulders and propped her feet on the curved top of her trunk, letting both time and distance speed by in a leafy blur.

Rob would never understand her, or that she could want something different from life than he did himself. How could he know that the pastoral existence near the clover field that he'd described in jest was far more appealing to her than the charms of any mere lover could be? Her own snug cottage, a hearth that was hers without any fudging or dissembling: *that* would be her paradise. All her life she and Rob had spent roaming, first with her father and then by themselves, and wistfully she tried to imagine living in one place long enough to be able to call it home.

"I only hope, Jen," said her brother at last, as if the conversation had been continuing all along, "that when you do fall in love, you have the decency to do it with some rich old codger who'll put us both in his will."

Jenny grumbled. "Oh, yes, so we'll all three live happily ever after."

"Don't scoff, Jen," said Rob easily, sorry proof that he'd been considering this all along. "It's as easy to fall in love with a rich sweetheart as a poor one."

"And don't you scoff, either, Rob," said Jenny sharply. She would flirt, and smile, and flatter, and beguile, yes, but she would *not* seduce, and though she'd yet even to attempt the last with any man, when she finally did, she wanted it to be because she loved him and not because her brother had told her he was rich. "I'll play whatever role you wish, short of *that*. Didn't

we agree ages ago that I'd never be the bait for one of
your codger schemes, not when I must—''

"Hush," said Rob sharply, lowering his voice. He
turned to look over his shoulder, his hair blowing back
across his forehead. "Do you hear another horse behind
us?"

"What, on the road at this hour?" She turned around,
as well, holding on to the back of the seat as she peered
into the night.

"It's that infernal idiot grenadier, I know it, still looking for his satisfaction and my head." He slapped the
reins again, urging the horse into a faster pace. "Blast
the man for being such a prideful idiot!"

"We must be close to the crossroads to London," said
Jenny, her heart racing as the chaise's tall wheels rocked
precariously over the rutted road. "Couldn't we turn
south, the way he wouldn't expect us to go?"

"The devil knows what he's expecting," said Rob
grimly. "But I don't want him getting at you, too."

"He'll have to catch us first!"

"Which, given that he's on horseback and we're stuck
in this ancient rattletrap with a hired nag, is entirely possible. Now, see that stand of trees beyond the next hill?
I'm going to slow, and as soon as we've ducked below
the hill, you're going to jump out into the grass. You
can hide in the trees and wait there, and I'll come back
and fetch you as soon as I've lost him."

"I will not!" cried Jenny indignantly. "I'm staying
with you, Rob, and I'm not about to go leaping like a
frog from a running chaise!"

"And I say you will," ordered Rob, concentrating on
controlling the horse. "For your own good. You'd be a
hindrance, pet. This idiot believes I have defiled his

woman, and I don't want to give him even the remotest chance to wreak his vengeance on you.''

Alas, Jenny understood. Most likely Rob *could* wriggle his way free more readily without her there in the middle. He'd done it before, and those other times, too, she'd been left or sent to wait elsewhere while he did it. She didn't want to be a hindrance, nor, to be honest, did she wish to be defiled by an idiot grenadier, either.

''But what if he hurts you?'' she protested. ''What if you're left bleeding somewhere? However will I find you again?''

''Because I always find *you* first, little sister.'' He still smiled fondly. ''Now come along, you're only going to have the one chance. How different can it be from jumping out a window?''

''You're a bully, Rob Dell,'' she said, cautiously leaning over the side to gauge the drop to the ground.

''Only if you're a coward, Jenny Dell,'' he answered. ''Which I know for a fact you're not, being my sister.''

''What you should know, Rob, is that I'll challenge you to a duel myself when this is done.'' They were just cresting the hill, the chaise slowing as Rob had promised. She rose unsteadily in the swaying coach, slung her skirts over one arm, and bent just long enough to kiss Rob on the cheek. ''God be with you, you ninny, and mind you keep yourself clear of that man's pistols.''

Then, before she could be afraid, she jumped.

The ground came up harder than she'd expected, the waving grass not nearly as soft as it had looked in the moonlight. She stumbled forward and rolled twice from the force of her landing, then sat upright, gasping, to wave at her brother. Looking over his shoulder, he waved back, reassured, then snapped the reins. The chaise rattled off, over the next hill, and Jenny was alone.

And better she should stay that way, too, she told herself firmly, and not be found by the side of the road by the idiot grenadier. She scrambled to her feet and began to run back up the hill toward the safety of the copse of trees. Their branches were low and gnarled, making her duck and dodge into the shadows, as perfect a hiding place as Rob could ever have picked. Overhead a tawny owl hooted crossly at being disturbed, and with a grin Jenny looked up, trying to spot him through the leaves as she hurried deeper into the brush and trees.

But she didn't see the owl, and she didn't see the low-slung branch, either, as she crashed her forehead into the rough bark.

And then saw nothing more.

This was the time of day that Brant liked the best. The new morning had scarcely begun and the old night was just fading away while the stars and moon stubbornly remained in the sky, the dawn no more than a glow on the horizon. The birds had already begun to chatter and soon the field workers would start trudging across the meadows, but for now Brant felt as if he had the world completely to himself, or at least the large green corner of it that belonged to Claremont Hall. With his dogs for company, he rode along the borders of his lands every morning at this time, regardless of whether the summer sun was going to shine warmly on his back or winter clouds threatened snow and wind sharp beneath the brim of his hat.

Although riding his property like this would strike most of his fellow peers as unnecessary at best, and at worst, laughably medieval—the ducal lord of the manor!—Brant had worked too hard to rescue Claremont Hall from his father's creditors to take his own possession of the estate lightly. As often as he might go up to London, he always came back here. He loved this place, and he took great satisfaction in seeing the improvements he'd been able to make in it. Besides, at this hour, all things appeared wonderfully possible to him, especially on a perfect early summer morning like this one.

"Here, Jetty, Gus, here!" he called as his two black retrievers bounded ahead of him. "How many more rabbits can there be left to chase?"

But the dogs didn't return as they usually did, instead racing off into a copse of trees not far from the road. Brant whistled for them, and when they still didn't appear, he sighed and swung down from his horse, looping the reins around a branch.

"Must be a righteous big rabbit," he grumbled. More likely the pair had stumbled upon something deliciously, foully fragrant only to dogs, and were busily rolling in it. He pushed aside the branches, letting his eyes grow accustomed to the faint gray light as he searched for the two dogs. But this time when he whistled, it was with surprise.

The dogs had discovered something, true enough. Jetty and Gus were sitting on either side of the too-still body of a woman, lying facedown in the old leaves. Hurrying to her side, Brant prayed it wasn't a girl that he knew, a serving girl from the Hall or the daughter of one of his tenants. He believed in taking responsibility for whatever happened on his land, even tragedies such as this.

But as soon as he knelt beside her, he could see from the fine muslin of her gown and the soft wool of her cloak that she was a lady, no farmer's daughter, and that the small, pale hand that lay curled on the dried leaves had never seen hard work. Yet lady or not, there was no question that trouble had found her: the skirts of that white muslin gown were grass-stained and streaked with dirt, her once-neat hair a tangle down her back. Worst of all was the raw, ugly bruise on her temple, swelling just below the neat curve of her brow.

Gently, Brant smoothed her hair away from the bruise and touched his fingers to the side of her throat, searching for a heartbeat. At least the girl still lived; he hadn't been sure. He'd little knowledge of practical physicking, and he wasn't certain what his next step should be to assist her. His experience with pretty young women—and he now could see that, beneath the dirt and bruises, this one was very pretty indeed—was generally of a far more lively sort.

Jetty whimpered, prodding at the woman's arm with his nose.

"Stop that, Jetty," ordered Brant softly. "She's suffered enough without you adding to it."

But the dog's wet nose had already roused her, and with a groan she shifted, flopping onto her side. Her eyes fluttered open and she grimaced with pain, pressing her hands to her temple.

"You'll be all right, miss," said Brant. "You have my word on it. Can you tell me what pains you?"

Gingerly she touched the bruise. "Only my head."

"You're certain?" he asked cautiously. When he'd first seen her lying in the leaves, he'd been sure she'd been abused and abandoned by some man.

"It's my head. I should know." She squinted up at him from beneath her hands. "You're not the dreaded idiot grenadier, are you?"

"I don't believe so, no." The poor girl had been

struck on the head and was entitled to speak nonsense. "Do you think you can try to sit upright? That must be the first step toward moving you to a more comfortable place."

She nodded, and he slipped his arm beneath her back to help raise her. She was a little bit of a thing, more fragile than he'd first realized, and once again he thought of how fortunate she was not to have been more badly hurt, whatever misfortune had befallen her. As soon as he could take her back to the Hall, he'd call the surgeon to come make sure she was as well as she claimed. He always wanted to help those too weak or flawed to protect themselves, especially if the rest of the world had abandoned them—exactly as this girl seemed to have been.

She gasped as he lifted her upright, her eyes closed and her hand still pressed to her temple. With his help, she sat there, not moving. Then to his surprise, she opened her eyes and smiled. With her face so close to his, the effect was dazzling, if dizzying.

The dawn was beginning to reach even into these shadows, and he could now see the details of her features: round cheeks and a dimpled little chin, a surprisingly strong nose softened by freckles, pale eyes that turned up merrily at the corners. She was too elfin to be considered beautiful, but too appealing for him not to smile back.

"There," she said, her voice thick, almost sleepy. "I did it, didn't I?"

"You did, indeed," he agreed, shifting so that her beguiling little mouth wasn't as temptingly close to his. He'd never been the kind of man who took advantage of such opportunities with women, and he wasn't about to begin with now, while her wits were so addled. "Rest a moment, and then we'll try standing."

"Very well," she said, reaching out to ruffle Jetty's ears. "I like your dogs."

"They like you, too," he said. Without a shred of shame, Jetty was making blissful growly noises, his eyes unfocused and his tongue lolling from his mouth in canine ecstasy. "That one, there, is Jetty, and the other is Gus, shortened from the far-too-grand Augustus. They were the ones who found you here, you know."

"Then I thank them for their trouble," she said, wobbling to her feet. "And I thank you, sir. You see I'm mending already."

"Don't be too hasty, now," he cautioned, doubting she'd be standing at all without his support. "No need to go running off just yet. Can you recall your name, or how you came to be here? I'm not going to send you on your way until you can tell me both. Besides, you likely have family or friends worrying about you."

Her face lost its sunniness and she looked away. "I— I do not know my name. I suppose it must be my poor foolish head again, but I—I don't know it. Perhaps if you told me your name, I—I could recall my own."

"Forgive me," said Brant gravely. "I should have introduced myself to you before. I am the Duke of Strachen, and you are standing upon my land, not far from Claremont Hall."

"Oh, my," she whispered, not listening to him as, instead, she pressed her palm over her bruise. "Perhaps I should not have stood so soon, not when…when—ah, how my sorry head does ache!"

She swayed back against his arm and he caught her just as her eyes closed and she went limp against him. She was as light in his arms as he'd guessed she'd be.

But he still didn't want to subject her to the long walk home and her head jostling against his shoulder with each step, nor could he imagine a comfortable way to carry her on the horse for the same reason. Gallant knights in old romances might carry their ladies fair on a charger like that, but in modern reality, it simply didn't work.

With concern he looked down at Jetty and Gus, thumping their tails on the ground as they gazed up at him. If he was to be a modern-day gallant knight, then this was what he had for faithful squires. Lucky him.

"Home," he ordered, hoping that at least for this once, they'd decide to obey. *"Home!"*

And for once the pair did do as he'd asked, racing off across the open field toward Claremont Hall. They were that loyal to him, or perhaps, like him, already that besotted with the nameless girl. But when the dogs returned to the Hall without him, the men in the stables would be sure to come looking, and he counted on the dogs leading them back here. Until they did, he'd simply have to wait.

Carefully he sat on the ground beneath the trees, cradling the girl in his arms. She looked pale to him, and her breathing had grown so shallow and faint that she once again seemed lifeless.

He'd given his word to her that she'd be all right. It was a promise he now could only hope to keep.

Chapter Two

For the first few hazy moments when Jenny woke, she was convinced she'd gone directly to Heaven—especially if Heaven was filled with clouds as soft as feather beds to lie upon and as sweet-smelling as a field of lavender, and all of it wrapped up inside the snug, dark cocoon of heavy velvet bedcurtains. She was clean and warm and dressed in a comfortably too large nightshift, with her hair neatly braided into plaits over her shoulders. She was still too sleepy to question how she'd come to this state, but awake enough to relish the blissful peace of it.

She yawned happily, stretching her arms over her head. Happily, that is, until a sudden bolt of pain drilled into the side of her forehead, a pain that was very much the opposite of Heaven. Her yawn turned to a gasp as she pressed her hand to the spot and tried to recall exactly how she'd come by this hideous, throbbing lump.

She'd been riding with Rob in a hired chaise, and because they were being followed by an idiot grenadier—she remembered her brother's description quite clearly—she'd jumped into the grass, meaning to hide and wait for Rob to return for her. That part of remembering was easy.

But from there, however, things became confused. Somehow she'd struck her head, or had it struck for her. After that, she'd awakened to see two black dogs and a handsome gentleman kneeling beside her, his face showing such concern that she'd almost laughed, or would have if her head hadn't hurt so much.

But as soon as she'd felt the warmth of his kindness and the strong, sure way his arm had circled her waist to hold her steady—why, then laughing had been the last thing in her thoughts. Then, even as her head had throbbed, she'd found herself wondering what it would be like to lean forward and kiss him, from gratitude and curiosity but mostly because she'd wanted to, pure and simple.

Even the memory of it now made her flush with shame at her own lack of judgment. She'd been absolutely no better than Rob, perhaps even worse, and the man hadn't even been a rich old codger. Wherever had her good sense fled? If longing to kiss a stranger just because he'd been nice to her wasn't proof of how hard she'd struck her head, then nothing was.

She groaned again, this time with frustration. She knew there were more things that she should be remembering, important things, yet still they stayed stubbornly out of her grasp, hovering in a hazy fog. She'd have to remember, and soon, because she'd have to leave wherever she was to go find Rob, the way they'd planned, so that—

"Here she is, Dr. Gristead," whispered an older woman's voice outside the bedcurtains. "Poor little creature, she's barely stirred since we put her to bed this morning."

The poor little creature must be her, realized Jenny just as the bedcurtains were pulled back with a scrape of steel rings along the rod. After the darkness of the bed, her eyes were unaccustomed to even the single candle's light, forcing her to squint up at the two strange faces staring solemnly down at her: a ruddy gentleman in spectacles and an oversize physician's wig, and an older woman dressed in gray with a large ruffled housekeeper's cap that was, in its way, the solemn equivalent to the man's wig.

"Ah, miss, you're awake at last," said the woman, beaming happily at Jenny with her hands clasped over the front of her apron. "How pleased His Grace shall be to hear of your recovery!"

His Grace? Into exactly whose bedstead had she tumbled, anyway? Uneasily, Jenny pulled the sheet a little higher beneath her chin, as if a length of linen would be enough to protect her. The young gentleman beneath the trees must have brought her here—to his father, or uncle, or perhaps just the nearest local worthy known for charity. But "His Grace" meant a duke, and she'd no experience at all with dukes. Although she and her brother had brushed with their share of lesser aristocrats, trying to cozen a lord as high-born and powerful as a duke was more of a challenge than they'd ever attempted.

Now she looked from the doctor to the woman, and smiled faintly, too cautious and bewildered to answer their question. Silence was often the best friend that she and Rob had in a difficult spot, and this certainly qualified as that.

"She's hardly recovered yet, Mrs. Lowe," said the gentleman. He took Jenny's wrist, pinching it between his thumb and forefinger, and frowned ominously. "The beat of her heart is still erratic, and the pallidity of her complexion indicates a continuing ill balance of the vital humors. Attacks to the cranium such as this can often prove fatal, Mrs. Lowe, especially to young females like this one.''

"Goodness," exclaimed Mrs. Lowe, drawing back a step as if fearing contagion. "To my eyes, Dr. Gristead, she seemed much improved."

"In medical matters, one cannot rely on sight alone," said the physician sagely as he held the candlestick over Jenny's face. He cleared his throat before he began to speak, raising his voice as if she'd trouble hearing, instead of remembering.

"Pray attend to me, young woman," he said. "I am Dr. Gristead, and this is Mrs. Lowe, the keeper of this fine house. You have been struck insensible, and have lost your wits. You have, however, had the great good fortune in your infirmity to have been taken into the care of His Grace the Duke of Strachen. Are you properly grateful for his mercy?"

What Jenny *was* was properly dumbfounded. A little vagabond like her, fallen into the care of His Grace the Duke of Strachen! How Rob would marvel at such great good fortune, and how far this could surpass their last situation, there with Sir Wallace and his musty old books! Merciful gratitude might seem like a simple enough question to a man like Dr. Gristead, but Jenny wanted to be sure she said and did the right thing, especially where a generous old duke was concerned.

"Yes, sir," she murmured at last, sinking lower on her pillows in a puddle of meekness. She was glad they'd braided her hair; the plaits would make her look younger and more innocently pitiful. "I *am* most grateful, Dr. Gristead."

The doctor grunted, pleased with her response. "Very

good. You are progressing, indeed. Perhaps now, young woman, you can recall your name and tell it to me, as well as the place of your home.''

''My name?'' repeated Jenny hesitantly, stalling. Of course she knew her true name—Miss Jenny Dell—just as she knew that she'd been born in Dublin, not far from the theater where her parents had met and performed together. But neither she nor Rob were in the habit of telling their real names or history to anyone. For now, until Rob found her and decided what they should do next, it seemed wisest for her simply to...*forget* for a bit longer.

''Your name, young woman,'' said the physician, his mouth growing more grim with each passing second that Jenny didn't reply. ''Even your given name will be an assistance to us.''

''But we know the young lady's name already,'' whispered Mrs. Lowe. ''I told you before that—''

''She must tell us herself, Mrs. Lowe,'' said Dr. Gristead sternly. ''Otherwise it is meaningless.''

''What is meaningless, Gristead?''

At once Jenny recognized that voice: the gentleman who'd rescued her, and as he came to stand between Dr. Gristead and Mrs. Lowe, she willed herself to look even more languid and weak. He was dressed for dinner, doubtless with the duke himself, in a beautifully tailored dark suit and a red waistcoat with cut-steel buttons and embroidered dragons.

And, oh, my, he *was* handsome. She hadn't forgotten that. The candlelight made gold of his hair and deepened the blue of his eyes to midnight. His features were regular, his nose straight and his chin squared, but to her disappointment she saw none of the warm kindness or concern in his blue eyes that she'd remembered. Instead, his smile now seemed distant, impersonal, almost aloof, as he gazed down at her.

"Are you feeling better, miss?" he asked. "If anyone can wrest you back among the living, then it's Gristead here, though he's hardly pleasant company while he does it."

The physician's frown deepened, as if to prove the gentleman's words true. "She still does not appear to know her name or any details of her situation, Your Grace."

Jenny gasped. "You—you are the Duke of Strachen?"

"Ah, Gristead, mark how she does know what's important!" exclaimed the gentleman she now realized must be the very duke himself, his gaze still so intent on Jenny that she felt her pale cheeks warm. "You should know who I am because I told you myself, there under the trees this morning."

Her flush deepened. Already she'd misstepped, and all she'd spoken was a single sentence to the duke. The *duke.* How had this man become a duke, anyway? Oh, her head still hurt far too much for sorting out puzzles like this one! Dukes were supposed to be old and gray and dozing in their places in the House of Lords. They weren't supposed to be young and appallingly handsome and wear dashing silk waistcoats with Chinese dragons.

"I wish to thank you for your *largesse,* Your Grace," she said finally with a wan smile. "Largesse" was one of those words that Rob always made sure to use: it was fulsomely French, and sounded much more impressive and flattering to the largesse's possessor. "You have been most kind to me, and I promise not to take advantage of your hospitality any longer than is necessary."

"You shall remain here at Claremont Hall as long as

is necessary," he declared with a lordly sweep of his hand. "You'll stay until you are quite recovered or your friends or family have fetched you away."

"Or until you tire of me, Your Grace." She sighed sadly, taking her hands away from her forehead to better display her bruise—which, if it looked even half as hideous as it felt, would be an undeniable way to prove she'd no business going anywhere. "I won't burden you, Your Grace. I'll leave myself rather than do that. I'm not your prisoner, and you can't keep me here against my will."

Most gentlemen—especially the gentleman she remembered rescuing her this morning—would have made a gallant protest against her even considering leaving, but not this duke.

"You're not my prisoner, sweetheart, no," he said evenly, his expression not changing even a fraction. "But since you met your misfortune on my land, you *are* my responsibility, until someone else comes forward to claim it, and you."

"But to be a mere tedious responsibility!" She sighed dramatically. She hoped he wasn't truly as chilly and arrogant as he seemed. Chilly gentlemen were never generous, and again she wondered sadly what had become of the kind gentleman with the dogs.

"Tell me for yourself, Your Grace," she continued, striving to sound pitiable enough to rekindle that well-hidden kindness. "How should you like being deemed no more than a charitable obligation?"

"Consider before you speak to His Grace, young woman!" scolded the physician, his brows bristling severely beneath the front of his wig. "You are unwell, true, but that is no excuse for such...such *familiarity*.

His Grace would be perfectly within his rights to send you to the almshouse!''

But the duke himself did not seem to agree. Instead, for the first time, his smile seemed genuinely amused as he studied her with new interest—interest enough that Jenny felt her cheeks blushing all over again.

"Oh, don't frighten the lady, Gristead," he said softly. "And you don't listen to him, Miss—Miss—now whatever am I to call you if we don't know who you are?"

"But indeed we do know her name, Your Grace," said Mrs. Lowe, eager to help. "This was tucked in her shift when we undressed her earlier."

Jenny let out a little sigh of relief as the attention shifted away from her, even if only for a moment. The woman was holding a folded handkerchief out to the duke, and she'd turned it so the letters stitched in red thread in one corner were neatly facing toward him for his convenience. But the duke was far too important to bother to read the name for himself, brushing the handkerchief back toward the housekeeper with an impatient flick of his hand as he looked once again at Jenny.

"Tell us all, Mrs. Lowe," he said with that same smile seemingly for Jenny alone, as if the request were more of a secret jest between the two of them. "Enlighten us as to the lady's name."

"Corinthia, Your Grace," volunteered Mrs. Lowe promptly. "It's stitched right there, plain as can be. A lady's name on a lady's handkerchief. It's next to new, likely from her having so many of the same, the way ladies do. You can see how fine the linen is, Your Grace, and this lace trimming—that's the kind the French nuns used to make in the convents over there, what can't be bought now for love or coin."

"All that knowledge from a single scrap of linen, Mrs. Lowe?" The duke studied the handkerchief and shook his head with wry amazement. "I must take care with my own belongings, lest you begin spinning tales about my cravats. But if 'Corinthia' marks her linen, then Corinthia her name must be. Would you agree, Miss Corinthia?"

"I—I suppose it must be so, Your Grace," said Jenny, marveling at how much the housekeeper had concluded from the single handkerchief. None of it was right, of course, but every wrong guess helped build her credibility as a true-born lady. "My name must be Corinthia."

"It's a start, Miss Corinthia," said the duke as he idly smoothed the ruffled cuff on his shirt, "Or perhaps I should rather address you as Lady Corinthia, the way Mrs. Lowe so desperately desires?"

"The given name is sufficient to begin inquiries, Your Grace," said Mrs. Lowe firmly. "Discreetly, so as not to upset her family any further. Although a lady's name must not be made common, surely there cannot be too many Corinthias gone missing in Sussex last night."

"That would be most kind of you, Your Grace," murmured Jenny. To the best of her knowledge, there hadn't been *any* Corinthias gone missing last night, but Mrs. Lowe's discreet inquiries would serve to let Rob know where she was, and that she was safe. For that matter, she wished she knew if and how he'd escaped the jealous grenadier, and as she thought of her brother, the sum of her family, she felt a single and quite genuine tear slide down her cheek to splat upon the sheet.

"There now, Your Grace, you've made her unhappy," said Mrs. Lowe, reaching over to blot away the tear with Corinthia's handkerchief. "The poor creature might not be able to recall her home or family, but she still can pine for them."

Not that the duke cared.

"Tell me, Miss Corinthia," he said. "Are you hungry?"

"You cannot, Your Grace!" sputtered Gristead indignantly before Jenny could answer. "Given this young woman's perilous condition, it is not wise for her even to consider eating!"

"And I say it is unwise for her not to," said the duke with the easy assurance of someone accustomed to always having his own way. "Especially when I'm so hungry myself. Mrs. Lowe, have a table brought, so I might dine in here with the lady. What would you like, Miss Corinthia?"

"Tea, if you please," she said, realizing she was in fact very hungry, indeed. "And toast, with jam, if that is possible."

"Anything is possible at Claremont Hall," declared the duke. "You've only to ask. Isn't that so, Mrs. Lowe?"

"Yes, Your Grace," said the housekeeper, already backing from the room to begin fulfilling his orders.

"But, Your Grace," protested the physician again, his chins quivering over the top of his neckcloth. "The young woman is my patient and—"

"Clearly she is out of danger, Gristead," answered the duke, "and I'm sure you have other patients to see, as well. You can be sure we shall send for you if there is any change."

After such an obvious dismissal, Gristead could only bow a red-faced farewell and follow the housekeeper from the room.

And leave Jenny alone with the duke.

"So," he said, pulling a chair closer to the bed. "Here we are, Miss Corinthia."

"Yes, Your Grace," she said softly. "Here we are, indeed."

Indeed, indeed, she thought glumly. It wasn't just the setting, or the fact that they were alone together, for her unconventional life often tossed her in and out of riskier situations than this. No, what worried her now was how she'd become so acutely aware of the man beside her, of each gesture and word he made. Every detail of him fascinated her, from the way his light hair slipped across his forehead, to the small wavy scar along his jaw, to how his fingers rested lightly on the arm of the chair. He hadn't so much as hinted at touching her, yet still her heart was racing and her palms were damp, merely from being here with him, and that—*that* was what put her at such risk and made her feel so uncharacteristically vulnerable.

"You are improved, aren't you?" he asked with concern, misreading her silence. "I can call Gristead back if you need him."

"Oh, no, Your Grace," she said quickly. "I am much better, truly."

"I'm glad." He leaned back in the chair with his legs stretched comfortably before him, his elbows on the arms of the chair and his fingertips pressed lightly together in a little tent over the red waistcoat. "But you're anxious about being here alone with me, aren't you?"

"Perhaps." She smiled, ordering herself to put aside her giddiness and concentrate, *concentrate*. If she didn't, she could very well find herself in that county almshouse or even the gaol. "My position is not an enviable one, Your Grace. I've no sense of who I am, my head aches abominably, and I am undressed and lying in a strange bed, unchaperoned, with a strange man beside me. Isn't that just cause for anxiety?''

He grinned, clearly pleased by her answer in ways she hadn't intended. ''Not if you trust me as a gentleman.''

''Which is exactly what I keep telling myself, Your Grace.'' She slid her shoulders up higher against the pillows until she was almost sitting, being sure to keep the sheets tucked modestly under her arms. ''You are a gentleman, a great lord, a man of honor and integrity, and therefore worthy of my trust. Besides, if you'd wished to take advantage of my position, you would have done so already.''

''Ha,'' he said, still smiling. ''That doesn't sound like you trust me at all.''

''But I do,'' she insisted, though there was something to his smile that warned her against trusting him at all. ''I must. What other choice do I have, being that I'm a charitable obligation?''

''I thought we'd already agreed that you were my guest,'' he said. He swept his arm through the air, encompassing the entire room. ''A lowly charitable obligation would not be put into a bedchamber such as this. My guests, however, are.''

She seized on that. ''Have you many guests, Your Grace?''

''Almost none,'' he said with a careless shrug. ''My brothers, their wives and children. That's all.''

''All?'' she asked, surprised. Most people with grand houses in the country entertained an unending stream of guests for their own amusement as well as for hospitality's sake. ''I should think a lord like you would have an enormous acquaintance!''

''Oh, I do,'' he said easily. ''But I prefer to see them in London, where they are more manageable and less demanding. I would rather keep Claremont Hall just for me, not them. Here I must please only myself.''

It was very hard for Jenny to imagine a gentleman as elegant as this one living alone among the Sussex fields as a veritable hermit. ''Then you must be the prize of every squire's daughter in the county.''

He grimaced. ''Which is precisely why I avoid all contact with the local gentry. I'm certain my neighbors judge me the worst kind of inhospitable recluse and spoilsport. I don't care. I have more than my fill of society when I am in London.''

Jenny's smile widened, this time with unabashed relief. She couldn't begin to guess how far Claremont Hall was from the inn she and Rob had fled in Bamfleigh, or from poor, abandoned Sir Wallace and his library, either. But if the duke didn't believe in speaking to his country neighbors, then she should be safe enough here, hiding in plain—or rather, grand—sight.

''You are amused that I am a recluse?'' he asked dryly.

''No, Your Grace,'' she said, twisting the end of one of her braids through her fingers. ''I simply do not believe it.''

She meant it as lighthearted teasing to relieve the tension between them, no more, but he didn't laugh the way she'd expected. Far from it.

''No?'' he asked, the edge to his voice a warning that made no sense. ''Would you rather believe my interest in this estate is mere country playacting, like the French queen with her beribboned dairy cows before the Bastille fell?''

''No, no,'' she answered quickly. She didn't want to offend him, especially over something as foolish as this. ''I only meant that no matter how much any of us pretends to be someone else, in the end we always are what we are."

"Ah." For whatever reason, he relaxed. "Then you are a fatalist? You believe that we can never change from what we're born? That our destiny remains always the same, with no hope of growth or improvement?"

"No, no, *no!*" She shook her head, then winced and pressed her fingers to the bruise again. "It's not so complicated as that, Your Grace. I only meant that no matter how many changes you may make for the world to see, you are still at heart, or in your soul, the same creature you were born. That's all."

He nodded solemnly. "Then you are a fatalist, if that's what you believe."

"That's what I *know,*" she said with conviction. She did believe it, too. How could she not, when so much of her life was unabashed deception? If she didn't believe in herself—Miss Jenny Dell!—independent of whatever new identity Rob had concocted for her, why, then, she'd have nothing at all. "But you don't agree, do you?"

"On some days I would," he said lightly, "and other days I wouldn't. Look, here's our dinner at last."

Mrs. Lowe reappeared, leading a little parade of servants. Two footmen came first, carrying a narrow dining table already set with a pressed cloth, followed by more footmen and maidservants bearing cutlery, candlesticks, napkins, even a porcelain bowl full of pink and white flowers, as well as a silver tea service and several covered dishes, each fragrant with wisps of steam.

The table was placed between Jenny's bed and the duke's chair, and as one of the footmen lit additional candles, she was able to see more of the details of how well His Grace treated his infrequent guests. She made such appraisals automatically, almost without thinking, for her father had trained both her and Rob in how much such niceties could reveal about their owners' personalities as well as the depth of their fortunes.

The bedchamber was large and square in the old-fashioned way of country houses, but the furnishings were in the latest London style, delicate and airy, fit for any fine lady. So was the table being set before her: costly new porcelain rimmed with gold, damask linens so spotless she doubted they'd ever been used, and double-weight sterling for the spoons and forks, also so new that the ducal crest engraved upon each one was still crisp and sharp.

In fact, to Jenny's surprise, everything seemed new. In her experience, titled folk tended to surround themselves with ancient bric-a-brac and gewgaws that had been in their family since at least the days of the Conqueror, another way they separated themselves from jumped-up merchants and mill owners. She'd never expected to see so much that was fresh from the shops in the house of a peer.

But because of the quality of these belongings, new or old, Jenny could come to a most cheerful conclusion: that the handsome Duke of Strachen must be rich as Creoseus, and, even better, that he didn't mind spending the fortune he so obviously had.

Yet at once she reached a second conclusion, less cheerful, more startling, and terribly disloyal to Rob. As pleasing as her brother would find the duke's title and wealth, she herself would selfishly trade it all for the return of the smiling country gentleman and his two black dogs.

Clearly the bruise to her head must be more serious than it felt.

"Here you are, miss," said Mrs. Lowe, plumping Jenny's pillows herself. One maidservant poured her tea and handed her the cup, while another solemnly buttered triangles of toast and spread strawberry jam exactly to the crusts. The duke's fare was considerably more substantial, and while Jenny's toast and tea were just what she'd asked for, she still looked longingly at his dinner: a ragoo of oysters, veal Florentine, roasted artichokes and forced mushrooms, with the wines to go with it all.

Yet though everything was perfectly presented, the servants did not remain to attend while she and the duke dined, the way servants in most such households did, but once again left them alone together. Had this been prearranged for her sake, wondered Jenny uneasily, or was it simply another way that His Grace chose to reinforce his solitude here in the country?

"The toast agrees with you, Corinthia?" he asked at last, sipping at his wine. "You feel more fortified, in spite of what Gristead predicted?"

Jenny smiled, and nodded, prepared to watch every word she spoke. Most gentlemen that she and Rob met were elderly and too enchanted with her youth and beauty to ask inconvenient questions. She could hardly expect the duke to be like that. "Much better, thank you, Your Grace."

"I am glad to hear it," he said, his eyes too serious to match his smile. "Do you think now you can speak of the grenadier who did this to you?"

"The—the grenadier?" she stammered, confused. "I do not recall any such man, Your Grace."

"You did," he said, swirling the red wine in his glass. "When I found you this morning, that was one of the first things you asked. Was I the idiot grenadier?"

Abruptly, Jenny set her saucer down on the table before her. "I told you, Your Grace. I have no memory of such a question, or of any such man, either."

He tapped his fingertips lightly against the glass. "I'm not asking this to shame you, Corinthia. Pray note that for your sake, I waited until we were alone before I did. You certainly wouldn't be the first lady led astray by some villain in regimentals."

"But I wasn't," she insisted, trying not to panic as she wondered what else she might have mumbled in those first confused minutes this morning. If she'd spoken of Rob as well as the grenadier, or perhaps worse, climbing from the window of inn, then this ruse was done before it had begun. "I would know if I had."

"Why, when you cannot recall so much as your own name with any certainty?" he asked with unquestionable logic. "Someone brought you to that remote corner of my land, Corinthia. You didn't walk there, at least not in the kidskin slippers you were wearing this morning."

"Is that more of Mrs. Lowe's deciphering, Your Grace?" asked Jenny, her chin tucked defensively low against her chest. "Or did you determine the state of my slippers for yourself?"

"Be reasonable, my dear," he said. "If this scoundrel is still prowling somewhere nearby, I need to know, not only for your sake, but for that of the wives and daughters of my tenants. He must be prevented from doing this again."

She looked down, dodging his scrutiny, her hands betraying her nervousness as her fingers pleated the edge of the sheet into a tight little fan.

Think, think, think! You don't need Rob to tell you what to do here. Be your own lass, Jen. You know what chances to take, how to turn this inside out and around to your own advantage. When this blue-eyed lord asks

*you to remember, remember first that you're clever, too,
Jen, every bit as clever as he!*

She took a deep sigh, soft and breathy, then began her
gamble.

"You have two dogs," she said softly, still not meeting his gaze. "I remember them finding me. Gus and
Jetty, isn't it?"

"Yes," he said with such gruff pride that he might
have been another dog himself, instead of their master.
"Gus and Jetty, the greatest pair of canine rascals in
Chrisendon."

"Oh, but they weren't rascals to me," she said, now
looking up from under the fringe of her lashes. "Not at
all. They're large, lovely, black dogs who licked my
hands to rouse me where I lay, and made little worried
noises over me until you came, too."

"Rascals," he murmured again, but the way his expression warmed with affection proved she knew she'd
made him forget about the grenadier. Here, at last, was
the man she'd remembered.

"Not rascals," she said, that warmth in his face giving
her the courage to go on. Now it wasn't a game or a
ruse. Now it was the truth, and infinitely more risky.

"They were gentle and kind to me, your dogs were,"
she continued, more wistfully than she realized, and for
the first time her smile was genuine, as warm as his own.
"Rather like you were then yourself, Your Grace."

But, instead of returning her smile, the warmth vanished from his eyes and, beneath the elegant clothes, his
whole body tensed warily against her. She recognized
uncertainty when she saw it, just as she recognized the
defensiveness that went with it; but why should either
be in a man like this, a peer whose entire world bowed
to his wishes?

"Who *are* you?" he demanded hoarsely, as if she were the one threatening him.

"I don't know," she whispered, stunned by his reaction. "Who do you wish me to be?"

"No." He shoved back his chair and rose, and in three long strides was already at the door. "Damnation, *no.*"

And before she could ask him to explain, he was gone.

Chapter Three

He'd not made such a blatant misstep—or such a fool of himself—in years.

Brant stood at the tall, darkened window of the library where he'd fled, and swore again. As a rule, he wasn't a man overly given to swearing, but this time he knew he deserved every single oath he could muster, and a few more that he invented spontaneously.

The girl had done nothing at all worthy of his idiocy. Without a murmur, she'd gone along with his inane impulse to dine together. She'd made a brave best of his attempts at conversation, and she'd answered his questions as well as her poor battered head permitted. That bruise must have pained her abominably, yet she hadn't complained once. She hadn't been able to remember her own name, but she had recalled Jetty and Gus, which was far more than a self-centered dunderhead like himself could reasonably expect from any woman in her situation.

She had, in short, behaved as perfectly as any true lady would, with grace, charm and wit, and an astonishing degree of loveliness. At least he could be objective about that. In London he'd known scores of famous beauties—actresses, titled ladies, courtesans—who'd never have the kind of innate appeal this girl displayed with her braided hair, upturned eyes and, yes, even with that great violet blossom of a bruise on her temple.

So why, then, when all she'd done was to mistake him for what he wasn't, had he turned on her like some raving Bedlamite?

He groaned and swore again. At least if he were in Bedlam, he'd be safely under lock and key, unable to offend the rest of the world.

He felt something bump against his leg and looked down to see Jetty beside him, panting happily just to be at his side. With a final halfhearted oath, Brant reached down to ruffle the dog's ears.

"We broke the rules, didn't we, old Jetty?" he said softly. "Claremont Hall's always been for us bachelors alone. You know the arrangement, the same as I. No females permitted, not ever. You shouldn't have found that young lady beneath those trees, and I shouldn't have brought her back here, so I could make a right flaming ass of myself."

The dog gave a sympathetic low growl in the back of his throat, turning to look toward the doorway and the approaching footsteps that he'd heard before Brant.

"Good lad," murmured Brant as the knock finally came on the door. "You've saved me from doing it again before another witness. Isn't that true, Tway?"

The small, pale man in the black suit and snuff wig only bowed slightly over the salver full of letters in his hands. "As you say, Your Grace."

Brant smiled, oddly comforted by the man's predictable reply. If anything at Claremont Hall would be unaffected by this young woman's appearance, it would be Tway, his manservant, secretary, steward and unflaggingly loyal salvation for the last ten years of Brant's life. His brothers made sport of Tway, noting how his colorless face must have been pinched from old tallow candles, or wagering over what disaster would befall Tway's mouth if he ever actually smiled. Yet Brant never joined in their jests. Deep down he trusted Tway more than he did either of those same brothers, and with good reason, too. How could it be otherwise, when Tway was the one man alive who understood his shameful secret?

"Your correspondence, Your Grace," continued Tway, raising the salver a fraction higher, as if the neatly piled letters were an offering. "Do you still wish to make your replies now, or shall I put them aside for tomorrow?"

"Now," said Brant without hesitation, dropping into an armchair with Jetty settling at his feet. He'd forgotten that he'd set aside this time for business, but the task of answering the requests and queries would help shift his thoughts from the girl. The same easy comprehension of the patterns, percentages and probability that made him so successful at the gaming table had carried over into investing and speculation, even into ungentlemanly trade, and earned him the wealth to match his peerage. "I doubt that there's anything in there that will improve with age like a wheel of cheese."

"Very well, Your Grace." Tway nodded, setting the tray on the desk. He reached for the first letter on the stack and held it open before him, the corners pinched daintily between his thumbs and forefingers. "This first is from Mr. Samuel Lippit of the Pennyworth Mines."

"Doubtless, Lippit is unhappy about my suggestions for improving the mine." The Welsh tin mine was one of Brant's newer business ventures, an experiment that seemed likely to cost him dearly before it turned a profit. "He has always seemed disinclined to make such investments, regardless of the returns they will produce."

"Precisely so, Your Grace," agreed Tway. "Shall I commence?"

"Please." Brant, his legs more comfortably before him as Tway began reading the letter aloud. This was how he and Tway conducted all his correspondence, from detailed arrangements regarding his investments to the most intimate *billets-doux* from lady friends in London. In the beginning, Brant had claimed a weakness of the eyes prevented him from reading and writing, but he was sure that Tway had long ago deciphered the truth for himself. Yet nothing was ever said between them on the subject, any more than there was further discussion about the nearby cottage that Brant had provided for Tway's aged mother. It was, in Brant's opinion, a quite perfect arrangement.

Now Brant closed his eyes to help concentrate on the words that Tway was reading and to compose the proper response to dictate, the way he'd done countless times before. But, instead of that well-organized response, the only thing that kept stubbornly drifting into his thoughts was the girl's elfin face, the way her tip-turned eyes had glowed when she'd challenged him, how their expression had softened when she'd asked after his dogs, how she—blast it all, she did not *belong* there, or here, or anywhere else at Claremont Hall!

"Forgive me, Your Grace?" asked Tway, his pen stilled over the letter. "I do not believe I heard you properly, Your Grace."

"You damned well heard more than enough," said Brant in enough of a growl to make Jetty's ear perk.

"Have there been any replies to our inquiries about the young lady?"

The corners of Tway's thin-lipped mouth turned down with disappointment. "No, Your Grace. Not yet. But I should expect some response by dawn."

"You're not blathering it all over the county, are you?" demanded Brant with concern. "She's a lady, you know, not some circus wire dancer with her face pasted on broadsides to the walls of stableyards."

"Of course, Your Grace," answered Tway, his voice determinedly soothing. "I have supervised every inquiry myself, Your Grace."

"Mind you, no interfering sheriffs or magistrates, either." The girl had already suffered enough without becoming the centerpiece of some sort of county scandal. Hell, for all he knew she already was—a rebellious daughter, perhaps, or an eloping heiress. Anything was possible.

"No, Your Grace. The lady's name shall remain untrammeled by the public."

"Very good, Tway," said Brant, taking another deep breath. "I am reassured."

But he wasn't, not at all. He had always considered himself the model English gentleman where ladies were concerned, endlessly polite yet coolly distant. He was a peer, a man of the world. Yet here he was, fussing over this girl and her welfare as if she truly *mattered* to him, and the harder he tried to stop, the more willfully his foolish brain seemed drawn back to her. And having his dinner brought to her bedside, pretending there was some sort of friendship or intimacy between them—what manner of nonsense had *that* been?

He really was behaving like a witless ninny, and though he stopped his fingers from drumming on the arm of his chair as soon as he realized he was doing it, he wasn't fast enough to escape Tway's notice.

"Her family shall be found, Your Grace," Tway continued in that same calming tone that Brant, in his present humor, could only find infuriating. "You may be sure of that. And might I say, Your Grace, that I am certain her family will be much gratified by your concern for her welfare?"

"You may say no such thing, Tway," said Brant irritably. He'd taken the girl in because he couldn't very well have left her there beneath the trees, not because he wished fame for doing good. Surely, Tway of all men should realize that. "You'll ruin my reputation if you spread drivel like that."

Unperturbed, Tway dipped his pen into the ink and waited expectedly over the half-written letter before him. "You were advising Mr. Lippit on the matter of reinforcing the north shaft with new timbers for the safety of the miners working within it."

Tway was right, of course, in his characteristically roundabout way. What Brant needed to do was to focus on the work before him, on his genuine obligations. If he didn't wish to make a babbling ass of himself again, then he'd have to be sure to keep away from the situations where it happened. Hadn't he learned that in his first year in London? Didn't he know by now that no woman—any woman—could hold a lasting place in his life, not if he wished to keep his secret and his sanity? Hadn't he long ago decided never to wed and risk passing along his shameful disability to an innocent child?

He should be trusting his own hard-won experience, not his dogs. No more amusing himself with this girl in the guise of concern, and no more cozy bedside suppers as if she were his mistress, instead of an uninvited temporary guest.

He studied the stack of waiting letters with new resolve. "What else is there besides Lippit?"

"Lord Randolph and Lord Andrew wish your support for their bill, Your Grace," continued Tway. "The overseer from your estate in Northumberland seeks approval for certain improvements, a gentleman inventor wishes you to invest in his new steam engine, and the usual ladies request the honor of your company for the usual invitations."

Brant nodded with new determination. Surely that should be enough to make him forget a dozen girls with winsome smiles. "That is all, Tway?"

"Not quite, Your Grace." He slid the last letter from the bottom, tipping it so that Brant could see the familiar seal for himself. "As was previously arranged, Your Grace, Captain His Lordship Claremont and her ladyship will be arriving here in a fortnight for the christening in the chapel, as will Lord and Lady Revell."

Blast. How in blazes had he forgotten that particular obligation? When, soon after Valentine's Day, his younger brother George and his wife had produced the first legitimate child in the next generation of Claremonts, Brant had expansively offered to have the boy baptized in the family chapel, with all due pomp and ritual. He was vastly fond of George and his youngest brother Revell, too, and delighted that both his brothers had finally found so much happiness in the last year, both with new brides. Besides, George's son was now the heir to Brant's title, at least until the unlikely event he sired a child of his own.

So what could explain why he was suddenly feeling

so damned melancholy about such a joyful family celebration?

What do you wish me to be…?

She couldn't have guessed the truth, and yet she had. How could she know that all his life he'd wished himself to be other than the sorry creature he'd been born?

"You need not concern yourself, Your Grace," Tway was saying, for once misinterpreting Brant's silence. "Most certainly the young lady will have been reunited with her family before then. You can be sure that she shall be quite gone from Claremont Hall before Captain His Lordship arrives."

"Quite," said Brant softly. There was no useful reason to correct Tway's misconception, any more than there had ever been any lasting purpose to trying to change himself, no matter how hard he tried. "Now pray, return to Lippit's reply, or we shall be at this until dawn."

Jenny lay awake for what seemed like an eternity, listening until she was sure the rest of the household was fast asleep for the night. She slipped from the bed, wrapping the coverlet around her shoulders as a makeshift shawl, and padded barefoot across the darkened room to the window. Cautiously she pushed aside the heavy curtains a fraction, peering down along the walls to the house's other windows. All were as dark as her own, and with relief she pushed the curtains more widely open. The window's sash was latched but not locked, and she easily slid it open.

The clean night air rushed into the closed room, sweet with the songs of night birds and the scent of the lawns and the flower gardens, and she breathed deeply. That alone helped lessen the ache that still throbbed in her head; she'd always preferred the outdoors anyway, and hated feeling trapped in a closed-up house, particularly one where she'd already made such a mess of things, and without even trying, either.

With the coverlet bunched around her shoulders, she swung her legs over the sill. A narrow balcony ran along the facade beneath the windows, and though there was no doorway from her bedchamber, it was simple enough for Jenny to slip down to the paving stones and hurry along to the end of the balustrade, keeping close to the wall and away from the moonlight.

Anxiously she scanned the shadowy fringes of the trees and bushes, waving the coverlet back and forth as she searched for a sign from her brother. The few times they'd been separated by chance before, Rob had always reunited with her, one way or another, by the following night, and together they would then plot their next step. Rob would know exactly how to soothe this duke that she'd only been able to insult. She wasn't even sure *how* she'd insulted him—asking a man what he'd like her to be had always been one of her standard questions, making them puff up and preen that she'd be so obliging when all she was really doing was learning more about them for Rob.

But tonight no matter how hard Jenny studied the gardens, there wasn't a sign of her brother's cheerful face popping from beneath the hemlocks, no false owl's hoot calculated to catch her ear. She twisted her hands inside the coverlet, her apprehension growing with every second. It wasn't like Rob to abandon her like this. Surely even given her accident, she must be easy enough for him to find, especially if the duke in turn was seeking information about her family in the most worrisome way imaginable.

No. The only answer—the answer Jenny desperately didn't want to accept—was that the irate grenadier had caused Rob more trouble than he'd expected. With another worried little prayer for his safety, she leaned over the edge of the stone wall, hoping against hope to finally spot her wayward brother.

"Ha, so it is you, Miss Corinthia, surprising me again," said the duke behind her, so suddenly that she gasped with surprise. "Here I thought I was the only ghost to patrol this walk."

Jenny turned to face him, thankful that the moonlight would hide her guilty flush. At least she hadn't been interrupted calling Rob's name, or far worse, with Rob himself here on this walkway with her.

"Your Grace," she said with a little dipping curtsy inside her coverlet cocoon. "I should say you are far too much of this world for me to mistake you for a ghost."

"Flesh and blood and bone, you mean." He held his hand out toward her to judge for herself. "I can assure you I'm real enough."

She didn't have to take his hand to know that. He had shed his jacket and unbuttoned his waistcoat, and the neck of his shirt was unbuttoned over his throat and a good deal of his bare chest. His sleeves were carelessly shoved above his elbows and his hair was no longer sleekly combed but rumpled and tousled, the way she'd remembered from when he'd first found her. He looked comfortably disheveled, too, more relaxed and also somehow much more male, as if a veneer of gentlemanly propriety had been shed along with the stiffly embroidered evening coat.

Had he forgiven her? she wondered warily. Heaven knew dukes could do whatever they pleased. Was this

his way of showing that he was willing to overlook whatever unwitting misstep she'd made earlier?

"I trust my eyes to tell me the truth, Your Grace," she said, hugging the coverlet around her shoulders. "I could scarce mistake a gentleman as imposing as yourself for some wandering specter."

"Ah," he said lightly, lowering his hand to the balustrade as his gaze never left her face. "So much for the magic spell cast by moonlight. Are you feeling better, then?"

"Thank you, quite." She nodded, nervously smoothing her hair back behind one ear. How could she not be nervous, considering how carefully she'd have to tread with him? "Your Grace, please let me ask your forgiveness for…for whatever I said before that…that disturbed you so."

He frowned. "Nothing disturbed me," he said, "and so there's no reason to apologize. Shouldn't you return to your bed?"

"I'm not sleepy," she said. "When I asked you what you wished me to be, Your Grace, I meant nothing wrongful by it. I only meant that because I could— *can*—recall nothing of my past, it seemed reasonable enough to look forward, to the present and the future where for now you are the only constant."

"I can send for a sleeping draught from Dr. Gristead if you wish." His looked down at his fingers resting on the moss-dappled stone, considering. "You are my guest. That is all. I have asked for no such grand gesture as to make me the center of your universe."

"It's fresh air that I sought, not sleep," she said, "much the same as you did yourself. And I intend no grand gesturing, Your Grace. Rather, it's the one practical thing I can seize for myself. If I have no other past, then I must make do with what I have in the present. And that, you see, is you.''

Oh, Jenny, Jenny, that was awkwardly phrased, and to what purpose? Think, lass, think! Think of what Rob would say, how many useful details he'd be learning of the duke and his circumstances in this precious time alone together, while all you can do is to babble on like some giddy green serving girl!

"I haven't even tried to sleep yet," the duke was saying, still looking away from her. "You see how I haven't changed my clothes since supper. From habit I seldom see my bed before three or even four."

"Fine gentleman often don't, Your Grace." She'd learned that from her father, who'd freely embraced gentlemanly habits—gaming, drinking and other such late-night amusements—without the income to support them. "I'd scarce expect you to keep farmer's hours and rise with the cock's crow."

He smiled at her, something so unexpected that she felt a shiver of startled pleasure ripple down her spine.

"But I do keep farmer's hours," he admitted, "especially here in the country. I find I can accomplish all manner of things when the sun is down. Some nights I simply don't sleep at all."

"But that's not good for you, Your Grace!" she protested, gliding over the nighttime accomplishments. Those were best left without inquiry, at least while she wore only a coverlet and a nightshift and most especially while she was feeling so giddy in his presence. "Perhaps you should be the one to ask for a sleeping draught."

"I think not." He shrugged carelessly, a simple gesture filled with potent charm. "I've been like that as long as I can recall, at least since I was boy at school. Besides, if I'd been snoring away yesterday morning, the way you'd have me do, then I wouldn't have gone out with Jetty and Gus, and I—rather, they—wouldn't have found you.''

She ducked her chin contritely. ''I should thank you again, Your Grace, if you would but allow me.''

''Which I won't, because it's not necessary.'' He tapped his palm on the balustrade and smiled again, the kind of smile meant to end their conversation as definitely as a period did a sentence. ''Now whether either one of us plans to sleep or not, Miss Corinthia, perhaps it would be best if we each returned to our separate—''

''No—that is, not yet!'' She gulped, wondering desperately what had become of all her well-practiced poise in such positions. She was supposed to be *good* at this. ''That is, the evening is so fair, and I am not tired, and you aren't, either, and…and—''

''And so we should remain here together awhile longer?''

She nodded vigorously, relieved he'd understood despite her dithering.

''Even if this must seem a, ah, compromising situation for a young lady like yourself?'' he asked, more bemused than scandalized. ''Swaddled only in bedclothes, your feet quite bare, alone in the moonlight with a wicked old rogue like me?''

She made a little puff of indignation. ''I never said you were wicked, *or* old, *or* a rogue!''

He laughed, and roguishly, too. ''I'll admit I'm gratified by that, even though I shouldn't be. You know there are others who would judge me with far less sympathy in these circumstances.''

''*I* wouldn't. Besides, who else will ever know?'' she asked, sweeping one arm, draped with a coverlet wing, to encompass the rest of the sleeping household. ''Who is there to see us, Your Grace, or even to miss us when—oh, please, you are not married, are you?''

"I?" he asked, a question to her question and no answer at all. "Why?"

"Because I should like to know, Your Grace," she explained. "Not because I have any *designs* upon you, but because while being your guest is one thing, being the guest of you and your lady wife would be quite another altogether."

"Ah," he said. "So you would expect her to have come inspected you by now?"

"Well, yes." Jenny smiled wryly. "I don't believe any wife worth her salt would lump me into the same category as a stray puppy."

"And here we had a straw-filled basket and a dish of warm milk all ready for you in the stable, right beside Jetty and Gus!" He chuckled, but the smile didn't last and even in the moonlight she could see the fresh wariness in his expression. "But tell me. Why does my being wed seem so damned inevitable?"

"Because of who you *are*, Your Grace," she answered promptly, with another little curtsy for emphasis. "You're not like common folk, free to marry or not as we please. Dukes must marry their duchesses, to produce the next generation of heirs to your lands and titles and goodness knows what else."

"But I'm not married," he protested. "Never have, nor likely ever shall."

"No, Your Grace?" she asked curiously. "How... how *remarkable*."

Of course Rob would judge it not only remarkable but remarkably lucky. It was always easier to win the confidence and trust of a lonely bachelor, to gull him without a wife to ask suspicious questions about where his money was going. That was the situation here, as Rob would see at once, and one he and Jenny had worked often before.

And yet for Jenny it wasn't the same at all. How could she lump this duke into the same hamper with the other fusty old bachelors with bad teeth and ill-fitting wigs that she and Rob had known?

"'Remarkable'?" he repeated, still guarded. "You consider it so remarkable that I have never inflicted myself upon some poor woman in matrimony?"

"No," she said. "Rather I think it remarkable that no woman has inflicted herself upon *you*. Surely you must have a trail of broken hearts to your credit."

"I can assure you there's not a one," he said, his wariness fading, as if she hadn't said what he'd been dreading after all. "You flatter me to believe otherwise, miss, but if you knew me better, you'd realize that I'm hardly the great prize you seem to think."

She frowned. Of course he was a prize. He was a *duke*.

"But let us speak of you, instead," he continued. "Are you some fortunate man's wife?"

"Oh, no," she answered promptly, her thoughts still on the question of prizes. "I'm most certainly not married."

He paused, letting her answer hang between them for so long that now she was the uneasy one.

"You've remembered that much more, then? Enough to make you sure there's no worried husband scouring the countryside for you?"

"There's not—there can't be—because I would *know*," she said softly, and as she did, she realized how much she meant it, too. "If I loved a man enough to marry him, nothing would make me forget him."

"That's a rashly romantic thing to say," he scoffed. "If you've been struck hard enough to have forgotten the name you've had since birth, how could you possibly remember your lover's, instead? Here, give me your left hand."

Before she could refuse, he'd claimed it for himself, holding her fingers up into the moonlight.

"There now, that's more logical proof," he said. "No wedding ring."

She pulled her hand free, rubbing the empty finger where he'd touched it. "My ring could have been stolen by Gypsies."

"Then thieves would have taken the gold hoops from your ears, as well," he countered. "Besides, a ring worn day and night, such as a wedding ring, would have left its mark upon your finger."

Gemini, he was quick at this sort of banter, quick as Rob! "All that proves is what I said before. That even if my head cannot say for certain if I've a husband or not, my heart—my soul!—would never forget."

He wrinkled his nose as if he'd smelled something foul. "Rubbish," he declared. "Only poets and over-wrought young girls believe that."

"Then you do not believe in love, Your Grace?"

He sighed with world-weary resignation. "I believe that men and women can find a thousand ways to amuse one another in bed and out of it, and call it love," he said. "And I believe in the useful partnership of marriage for producing children, if it brings reasonable happiness and contentment to both the husband and the wife. But as for Cupid's darts and boundless souls and all the rest of the established claptrap—no, I do not believe in that, for it doesn't exist."

She frowned, perplexed. The duke was claiming to be

exactly the opposite of her brother, who could fall in love with a donkey if she fluttered her lashes at him. "Then you have never been in love for yourself, Your Grace, have you?"

"I have generally tried to govern myself by reason," he said with a solemnity at odds with his disheveled hair and unbuttoned shirt. "I've always tried to avoid being ruled by my passions."

"If you can say that, Your Grace, then you simply haven't met the special one who'll convince you otherwise," she suggested. "I know that must be the case with me. I have yet to find any gentleman that pleases me enough to love. But I shall. I know it."

"Ah, and so we are back where we began," he said softly, his half smile now unexpectedly bittersweet. "Here we are, with your heart able to recollect more than your head."

"I suppose we are, Your Grace." She drew the coverlet more tightly around her shoulders. Ordinarily she would have laughed and tipped her head to one side in the well-practiced way that gentlemen found so charming.

Yet this time didn't feel ordinary. Perhaps it was only the bruise on her forehead, or perhaps it was the moonlight addling her wits and making her see things in his expression that weren't truly there. This time, just this once, she wished she didn't have to do what she'd practiced. She longed to be able to explain what he said, to ask if that bittersweet half smile meant that he, too, still longed to find the love that didn't seem to exist.

But he was the grand Duke of Strachen, while she was no more than an invented girl named Corinthia, not even real. Her sole purpose in being here in this house—and only from purest luck at that—was to be pleasing enough that the duke would think kindly toward whatever scheme Rob would decide to invent. Tonight's moonlight would never matter as much as the money—a loan, an investment, or a gift—that Rob would coax from the duke's pocket, especially not after she and Rob vanished one morning, off into the next set of false names and identities.

No, better to smile than to dream, and far, far better to keep her wits sharp and keen than to go longing for something that couldn't be changed. The moment she began thinking with her heart, instead of her head was the same moment the luck would end, and she and Rob would find themselves taken up and tried as common criminals, with transportation or the gallows as their final reward.

That is, if Rob ever *did* return to find her....

"You are cold," the duke was saying with concern. "You're shivering."

"No, Your Grace," she said quickly, forcing her smile to be winning even as she began inching back toward her window. If she'd shivered, it had been from the reminder of the gallows and her fears for Rob, not a common chill, and certainly not from anything that he could remedy. "Only...only more weary than I first thought."

He took a step toward her, his hand gallantly outstretched to offer support. "Then let me guide you back to your rooms. There are, you know, easier paths than hopping through the window."

"The window does well enough for me, Your Grace." Tonight she was the one running away, not him, but it was the wisest course—the only course, really—before she blundered and said or did something that couldn't be undone. Far better to retreat now, until morning, when she could meet him with a clear head in the bright, un-magical light of day.

Lightly she pulled herself up onto the windowsill before he could stop her, the coverlet billowing around her bare legs.

"You were right before, Your Grace," she said breathlessly. "We should say good evening now and part. Good night, and pleasant dreams. Good night!"

Chapter Four

Brant rode slowly through the misty rain, his collar turned up and his hat pulled down against the damp, the two dogs loping along ahead. This was the other side of June mornings, with the green grass blurring in a hazy mesh with the gray sky, soft and wet and peculiarly English, and usually as irresistible to Brant as a bright, cheerful dawn. While his brothers might have sailed as far as they could across the world and away from these fields, to him there could never be a more lovely place in every season and weather than the rolling lands around Claremont Hall.

At least that was how he'd felt on every other morning before this one. Now the clouds could part before the most beautiful rainbow in all creation, and he'd scarce notice in his present mood. The girl had been under his roof for only the briefest time, yet already his entire household was in a blasted turmoil of distraction.

A branch of wet leaves slapped across his cheek and he muttered an irritated, halfhearted oath at his own inattention. And that was the whole problem, wasn't it? If he were honest—which, as a gentleman and a peer, he generally aspired to be—his household was functioning perfectly well, the way *they* always did. *He* was the only one who wasn't. The girl smiled, she wept, she sighed, she sunk languidly back against her pillows with her hair in childish pigtails, she flashed him a glimpse of a charmingly plump calf gleaming silver-pale in the moonlight, and now he was a hopeless, useless muddle of inattention.

Inattention to everything reasonable and productive, that is. To her, this lost country waif without a memory, he was attending all too well.

He'd told himself sternly that it wasn't the girl herself, but the mystery she represented. He didn't like mysteries. He liked things ordered, arranged, neat in their proper places, the way he'd remembered them to be. He took it as a personal, rankling challenge that this girl didn't seem to belong anywhere. He wasn't even convinced that Corinthia was her true name, and she didn't seem to be, either. And Brant didn't like guessing games. He needed to *know*.

Which was why he was now heading toward the squat Norman tower of St. Martin's, and the rambling timbered cottage nestled beside it that served as the parsonage. While his father had neglected the church just as he had everything else, Brant's luck and success had provided a new roof that didn't leak, new bellows that didn't wheeze for the small pipe organ, even new leading for the windows so the wind wouldn't whistle through the cracks during the psalms every Sunday. He'd even granted the living to a local man from the county, instead of to one of the better-connected applicants.

It wasn't that Brant was particularly pious, or eager to make a great show in this life with an eye to the next, especially not here in the country. Rather he assured himself that such improvements were simply one more responsibility of his title that had been neglected too long by his father, and another way to help keep his tenants happy and, ultimately, the estate happily profitable, as well.

Ordered, arranged, neat, with everything exactly as it should be: it all made perfect sense, didn't it?

"G'day, Your Grace," called the oldest Potter boy, racing from the house, not bothering with a coat as he hurried to take the reins of Brant's horse. Jetty and Gus bounded around the boy, their tails whipping as they snuffled happily at the interesting new smells on his trousers.

"And a fine, wet morning to you, Simon. Is your father at home?"

"Aye, Your Grace, that he is." With open admiration the boy stroked the white blaze on the horse's long nose as Brant swung down from the saddle, and the horse whinnied contentedly in return. "Shall I put this fellow in the stable for you, Your Grace? If it pleases Your Grace, I can rub him down proper, too, and give him a bit to eat."

Brant nodded. A sympathetic appreciation for horseflesh was always a fine quality in a boy, especially if the horse agreed. "Let him drink first, Simon, and let these two rascals have a sip, too. But mind you, if you spoil Thunder—that's his name, you know—if you spoil Thunder too much, he won't want to carry me back home."

"Oh, no, Your Grace," answered the boy so solemnly that Brant chuckled. "Thunder will be ready the minute you call for him, and Jetty and Gus, too. You can rely on me, Your Grace."

"Thank you, Simon. I shall." Brant turned toward the house so Simon wouldn't see his smile. Yes, all *was* well with the world, so long as the bond between boys and horses and dogs remained this strong. Too bad that wasn't what had brought Brant here; his grin had disappeared by the time he reached the parsonage's heavy oak door.

He'd scarcely begun to knock before the door flew open, with Mrs. Potter herself eagerly waiting on the other side. Clearly, Simon hadn't been the only one to see him arrive.

"Do come inside, Your Grace, do!" she ordered, bustling aside with a harried curtsy. She was a county girl herself, the daughter of one of his tenant farmers, and even her giddy rise through the social ranks to become the reverend's wife hadn't given her airs or changed her cheery good nature. With four children of her own and a good many more from the parish running in and out, she was everyone's mother, her thick sandy hair always slipping from beneath her starched cap and small sticky handprints pressed perpetually into the hem of her apron. "I won't have it said that I've let His Grace the Duke wait outside on my step in the muck and the wet!"

"As you wish, Mrs. Potter." Obediently, Brant stepped inside, shaking the raindrops from his hat before he let her take it. "Simon told me your husband is at home."

"Of course he is, Your Grace!" She beamed, neatly smoothing the damp beaver felt of Brant's hat with her sleeve before she set it on a chair with the greatest care possible. "He's working on his sermon, Your Grace, same as he does every week at this time, but for certain he'll see you."

Briskly she ushered Brant back to the back parlor, where Reverend Potter was toiling over his next sermon. And he *was* toiling, his broad back bent and his brow furrowed and his shirtsleeves rolled up to spare them from the ink, with books propped open around him for inspiration. Seeing how tightly the quill was clutched in Potter's ink-stained fingers, Brant could secretly sympathize all too well with his agony—not, of course, that he'd ever be able to confess his own miserable weakness, or find any comfort in commiserating. He was the Duke of Strachen, wasn't he?

Mrs. Potter loudly cleared her throat. "Attend me, my dear. His Grace is here to see you."

At once Potter looked up, startled, and groped for his coat as he jumped to his feet.

"Ah, ah, Your Grace, forgive me, please!" he exclaimed as he thrust his long arms into his coat sleeves. "I've never a wish to keep you waiting, but my sermon—you see how it is, how lost I can become in the writing of it. My meager talents are seldom worthy of the divine challenge ''

"It's of no matter, Reverend," said Brant as he moved more books from a chair to sit. "Once again I've come to consult your knowledge of the neighborhood."

"Yes, yes." Potter smiled with satisfaction; he was on more comfortable ground here than with the sermon. Little escaped his notice in his parish, and he'd helped Brant before to solve small problems among his people before they grew to large ones. "I'm always delighted to be at your service, you know. Ann, please, tea for His Grace. Now it's not a problem with the Connor girl, is it? You know her mother was so pleased you'd found a place for her up at the Hall."

"No trouble at all from that quarter," said Brant, unwilling to be distracted. "Have you heard of any military men in these parts?"

"Military?" The minister frowned. "A regiment quartered in this county?"

"A lone soldier, I'd say, passing through on leave. Most likely an officer, a grenadier." Brant made a little tent of his fingers, tapping the tips together as he remembered how the girl had spoken of such a rascal. "Have you heard of any such man visiting family or friends, or perhaps stopping for a can of ale at the tavern?"

Potter shook his head. "I cannot say I have, Your Grace. Not that I know of everyone's comings and goings, to be sure, but I would have heard of such a man. Even the children in the schoolhouse would have spoken of a soldier in uniform. But is the man dangerous, wanted for some crime?"

"Perhaps," said Brant, purposefully vague. Although he trusted Potter and his reticence, for the sake of the girl's good name he'd keep what little he knew of her to himself as long as he could. "I have certain suspicions, that is all."

"I'll send word the instant I learn anything." Potter sighed. "I know the Bible counsels us to be welcoming to strangers, Your Grace, but I agree that there are times when it is perhaps the wisest course first to question those we do not know."

Ann Potter returned with a tea tray, setting it on the table between the two men. "So you have settled what's to be done with the young lady, then?"

Brant looked up sharply. He'd come here looking for news, not to volunteer it. "The young lady, Mrs. Potter?"

"Aye, Your Grace." Her round face flushed, but she didn't back down, folding her hands tightly over the front of her apron. "The confused young lady what's at the Hall. You scarce had to ask, Your Grace. We understood, and we should be quite happy to have her here to stay with us, as long as she needs.''

"Then you have misunderstood me, ma'am," said Brant briskly, surprised that she'd even consider such an arrangement. The girl would stay at Claremont Hall for as long as was necessary, and that was an end to it. "There is no reason for the lady to be moved here with you. All her needs are being tended sufficiently at the Hall.''

"Oh, for certain they are, Your Grace," said Mrs. Potter quickly. "I never dared think otherwise!"

"I never thought that you did, Mrs. Potter," said Brant with a heartiness he didn't quite feel. "Not a woman of your impeccable character."

"But *that's* just what I did mean, Your Grace!" she exclaimed. "That's why the young lady should be here and not at the Hall. We're more humble here, true enough, but we're also the most respectable haven a lady could wish for."

"What my wife is attempting to say, Your Grace, is that a family situation might be more, ah, more proper for the lady," said Potter, striving awkwardly to be both deferential and diplomatic. "A family, Your Grace, rather than the household of a, ah, single gentleman."

Brant arched a single brow of disbelief. "Mine is hardly an ordinary household, Potter."

Balefully, Potter shook his head. "Forgive me, Your Grace, but you make me speak plain. Preserving the lady's good name may depend upon more than, ah, more than your rank."

"Be reasonable, Potter." Brant's disbelief was growing by the second. His actions toward the girl had been nothing, absolutely nothing, but the most decent and honorable. The moonlit image of her last night, her sleepy eyes and bare feet and her shoulders wrapped in the coverlet from her bed, rose suddenly in his thoughts and just as quickly he shoved it aside. He'd done nothing wrong there, either, doubly nothing, really, considering all the potential the situation had offered.

"Listen to yourself," he continued. "You're acting as if I'm some great rapacious ogre, sweeping the maiden away to my mountain lair!"

But neither the minister nor his wife smiled at his exaggeration, their expressions so dutifully solemn that Brant realized that this was exactly what they believed of him, and what they feared, too. No matter how scrupulous he had been about keeping his amusements in London separate from his life here, well-traveled gossip still seemed to have managed to blur the distinction he'd carefully tried to maintain.

He sighed, meeting their disapproval face-to-face. Exactly what drivel had they heard? It could have been any number of things, really: he wasn't a devil, not by London standards or those at Court, but he wouldn't qualify as a saint, either, especially not here in Sussex. But from the Potters' disapproval, he'd wager more on the devil, and restlessly Brant sighed again.

He didn't owe them an explanation. He didn't owe one to them, or to anyone else, either. He was the sixth blasted Duke of Strachen, wasn't he? By birth and by right he shouldn't give a tinker's dam for the opinions of anyone else in the world other than his own lordly self and, perhaps, His Majesty. The rest of England could believe he sprouted horns and a forked tail for all it should matter to him.

But damnation, matter it did, and always had, one

more way that he was a sad, sorry pretender to his own title.

"It's not as if the girl's alone at the Hall with me," he began again. "Consider the size of the staff attending to me night and day. You know we couldn't be alone even if I wished it."

"It's not my place to know what you wish, Your Grace," said Mrs. Potter primly. "I only know what I know for myself, Your Grace, and what Mr. Potter tells me."

"Then you can also know what I tell you as the truth, Mrs. Potter." Brant rose slowly to his feet, striving to sound ducal, instead of merely defensive. "The young lady is my guest, not my mistress, nor my prisoner, either. I am taking all possible steps to bring to justice the villain who has reduced her to this sad state, and to reunite her with her family and friends. In the meantime, she will receive every comfort toward her recovery, for as long as she is in need, and if that is the stuff of scandal, why, then so be it."

Potter bowed, an ungainly duck of reluctant surrender.

"So be it, indeed, Your Grace," he said, absently twisting one of the horn buttons on his black waistcoat with his fingers. "Because it is your wish, it shall be so, and I'll not question you again."

"Thank you," said Brant stiffly, wishing he felt more as if he'd won. Mrs. Potter presented his hat and he took it, as clear a sign as any that his visit was over. "Good day to you both."

Potter bowed again, his wife dipping a neat curtsy at his side. "Good day to you, Your Grace. I shall be sure to report to you if I hear of anything useful to you."

He followed Brant out onto the step, standing silently with him until Simon brought around Brant's horse, with

Jetty and Gus following. He took the lead from his son,
holding the bridle steady as Brant mounted, the two
black dogs weaving in and out between them.

"May God go with you, Your Grace, and guide you
in all things," he said as Brant gathered the reins into
his hand. "And mind, Your Grace, that a wise man will
know how to look into his own heart and question himself even when others do not."

Brant nodded curtly, not answering as he wheeled
Thunder around and rode away past the church, but the
minister's words were already burrowing deep into his
thoughts. He dug his heels into the horse's sides, furiously urging him faster, harder, than was wise on such
a wet morning, and letting the leaves and branches lash
against him.

*A wise man will know how to look into his own heart,
and question himself....*

Ah, but Brant knew already what kind of questions
were inside his heart, didn't he? Dark questions he'd
carried all his life, heavy as lead in his chest, and heavier
still from having no answers.

But those weren't the questions that Potter had meant.
He'd meant those that involved the mystery girl, the one
with the elfin eyes and moon-pale skin, sleeping even
now beneath his roof, questions that were almost laughably easy to answer. By holding himself apart from anyone who could learn and thus betray his flaws, by keeping brief company only with the most superficial of
women, he also managed to respect and honor the ladies
who needed respecting and honoring. And was there any
lady more needy than the one he'd found beneath the
trees?

Yet Potter's cautions still gnawed at his conscience.
She amused him, he'd grant that much, and she was

deuced charming in an unusual way. She was obviously
well-bred, yet without a speck of false coyness in her,
and he could only imagine what a delight she'd be when
she wasn't suffering from a sore head. He smiled at the
memory of how she'd asked him to stay in the moonlight
and how happy he'd been to oblige. He'd never told any
other woman about how he stayed awake most of the
night working, but then, no other woman had ever
seemed interested, particularly not one dressed only in
bedcovers. And if she'd lingered another minute or so,
he was quite sure he would have kissed her.

Perhaps he wasn't as distanced from the girl as he'd
claimed. Perhaps he was treating her like one more stray
dog. Duke or not, what if he truly wasn't doing the best
for her? Perhaps Potter was right and this was the question he should be asking himself.

But the answer to such a question wasn't in *his* heart,
was it? This one was the girl's to answer, not his. He'd
tried to do everything in his power to make her feel safe
and secure, and if she still didn't, why, then it was up
to her to tell him so, wasn't it?

He nodded, reassuring himself. This was reasonable,
logical, even gallant, letting the girl decide what was
best for her. This was common sense, if only a scrap of
it in the whole wretched mystery. And if Brant's unruly
conscience insisted that it was cowardly, not reasonable,
that he was once again twisting matters to escape the
sorry truth: that he was the vulnerable one, the one who
felt the whole careful facade of his life begin to quake
whenever this lost girl smiled.

And he could not—*would* not—let that happen.

Jenny sat in the chair before the fire, her back cush-
ioned with a silk-covered pillow, her legs wrapped

snugly in a soft blanket, and a cup of orange-laced tea cradled in her cupped hands. Light rain drilled against the tall windows, making her feel all the more cozy and warm here inside this beautiful room with pink roses in porcelain vases, gold-framed looking glasses, and the plushest of Aubusson carpets beneath her feet. If this was how a duchess lived every day, then it must be the most agreeable existence in the world, and with a happy sigh of pleasure, Jenny stretched her toes toward the glow of the fire.

Happy and pleasing and cozy, yes, but not hers to savor. She wasn't a duchess, nor ever likely to be one, and if she wanted to be allowed to stay in this room even a day longer, she'd work to do.

"Is His Grace still abed?" she asked Mrs. Lowe. Jenny understood the hierarchy of servants. The housekeeper herself had brought Jenny her tea, and was now smoothing the sheets on her bed—as sure a sign as any that she was eager to chat. What other reason could there be for Mrs. Lowe to linger here with her over low tasks better suited to the parlor maids?

"His Grace abed?" Mrs. Lowe turned with a pillow in her arms, all smiles. "Oh, my, no, miss! His Grace is never one to sleep late into the morning. He's been awake and about for hours now, and off riding, too, same as every day."

"Even on such a miserable morning as this?" asked Jenny with surprise. The duke had told her as much himself, but she hadn't believed it, not really. Why should a duke trade his feather bed for a chilly, uncomfortable ride that had no purpose?

"Weather makes no difference to His Grace, miss," said Mrs. Lowe with an odd pride in her master's heartiness. "As long as that horse of his can put one foot before the other, he'll be off."

Strange how easily Jenny could picture him doing just that, his blond head bent into the rain with an unducal determination that seemed at odds with his ruffled shirts and fancy waistcoats. She'd already learned that much of him, that he took his obligations seriously, and that once he'd decided to do something, he wouldn't let himself be distracted or deterred until it was done.

"Fancy," she murmured politely. "But then, His Grace did tell me he stays awake most of the night, too."

The housekeeper nodded. "That he does. He scarce needs to sleep at all."

"Gentleman's hours, I suppose." She hoped Rob would take his care finding her here if he came by night, what with the sleepless duke prowling the house. "They say the fine folk in London day up until cockcrow, gaming and dancing and drinking."

"They say that His Grace does just the same in London, too, that he'll sit at the card table the whole night through with the pile of his winnings before him growing bigger with every hand. Not that you'd know it from how he lives here." Mrs. Lowe gave the pillow an extra punch for emphasis before she placed it back on the bed. "Here at Claremont Hall he's the most sober man you can imagine, full of industry, and working nigh every hour with Mr. Tway."

"Truly?" asked Jenny, surprised again. The gaming she could accept without question, but a lord who worked at anything was even more remarkable than one heedless of bad weather. "On what does he work?"

"Trade and commerce," answered the housekeeper promptly. "That's what Mr. Tway says it is, miss. The sorts of things more usually done by merchants in countinghouses. He's interests in mines and factories and sailing ships and goodness knows what else. Mr. Tway says His Grace is monstrous clever, with a finger in every pie that might bring him a penny.''

''Mr. Tway says that?'' Jenny wasn't exactly sure who Mr. Tway might be, but if he was so familiar with the duke's finances, then he must be some kind of secretary or banker: the kind of man who could be either an ally for her to charm into compliance, or a zealous enemy who'd see through her and Rob at once.

''Aye, aye, and Mr. Tway would know, having been with His Grace since the beginning.'' Mrs. Lowe's voice dropped to a confidential whisper. ''When the old duke—His Grace's father—when he died, Claremont Hall wasn't fit for nothing, he'd let things go so bad, not a stick of furniture left inside and every blade of grass outdoors mortgaged to the skies. A wicked devil, the old duke, with wicked habits and not a minute to spare for his poor motherless sons. It was the shame and the scandal of the whole county. He's gone to the devil where he deserves, that's for certain.''

But Jenny was more interested in the current duke. ''You mean to say that His Grace has made his own fortune, as if he weren't a peer at all?''

''Oh, aye, all three of them boys did, miss.'' Clearly this was the favorite part of the housekeeper's story. ''His Grace, and his two younger brothers, Lord Revell and Captain Lord George Claremont. Left without a farthing—less that that, when you consider the old duke's debts—yet each made good in his own way, His Grace the best, and still a young man, too. That's why they call him the Golden Lord, from having made gold from nothing.''

''What a remarkable achievement,'' said Jenny, and it wasn't simply an idle remark, either. She was impressed. One of her father's favorite beliefs—and his favorite excuse—had been that no true gentleman ever worked, yet here in this duke was certain proof to the contrary. She'd never met anyone who'd grown so astonishingly prosperous by his own cleverness and luck, especially not one who was also a peer *and* alarmingly handsome in the bargain. It didn't seem quite fair to have so many blessings showered upon a single person.

Yet what must it have been like to have had so callous and uncaring a father? Her own father had been a cheerfully self-indulgent rascal whose only lasting legacy to her and Rob had been their vagabond life, but she'd never doubted he'd loved them both with fierce, endless devotion until his death. The security of that love had always warmed her wherever they'd wandered, and she wouldn't have traded the memory of it for any peerage.

She thought again of last night, of how confident the duke had been that he would never wed. He'd tried to seem as if he were too rational for love, but Jenny had sensed a sadness, a longing for more, hidden beneath his claims. Was his father to blame for that, too, poisoning any notion of a loving family? Had the old man robbed his son of that chance of happiness along with his inheritance?

With a little shake of her head, she frowned down into her teacup. What was she thinking, turning all soft and sentimental over the sufferings of a *duke?* No matter how many debts his father may have left him, she doubted he'd ever gone to sleep hungry or laid his golden head upon anything harder than a feather-stuffed pillow. What could he know of hard times?

No, she must stand firm and forget whatever mistaken connection she'd felt to him in the moonlight. She wasn't some giddy schoolgirl, after all, swooning over a

handsome Drury Lane hero. She must be firm. She could
understand his reasons for doing things, of course, but
to understand with too much sympathy could be disas-
trous, the same sort of trouble that Rob tumbled into
with all his lady friends.

"Is it your head again, miss?" asked the housekeeper
with concern. "Shall I send for Dr. Gristead?"

"No, thank you, no," said Jenny quickly. "I was only
thinking of how difficult it must have been for His Grace
to have such a father."

"True enough, miss, true enough, and I wouldn't—
oh, Your Grace, good morning!"

At once Jenny twisted around in her chair, her heart
racing with anticipation. Of course the duke was there—
no, *here*, when she least expected it. Already he was
striding into the room to stand before her, his neckcloth
and hair still wet from the rain and mud splatters on his
riding boots, and once again catching her by surprise,
blast him, popping up from nowhere like a conjurer's
trick and no doubt overhearing her gossiping about his
past with Mrs. Lowe.

Yet still her idiotic heart raced, thumping on at a
breakneck pace that had no rhyme or reason to it.

"Good day, Your Grace," she somehow remembered
to say as Mrs. Lowe sank into a curtsy beside her.

Double, triple blast, *she* was supposed to do that, too,
and swiftly she rose from the chair. But while last night
the coverlet had been a gracefully makeshift cape, now
it tangled around her ankles as she stood, hobbled, and
the result was not pretty. Instead of a neat sweeping
curtsy, all she could manage was an ungainly bending
from the waist, with one hand grasping the chair to keep
herself from toppling forward onto the muddy toes of
his boots.

"If you are still unwell, miss," he said sternly, "then why the devil are you not in bed?"

So that was how it was to be, she thought, fighting disappointment she'd no right to feel. She didn't even have to look up at his face to realize that she was being graced with the cross-tempered duke this morning and not the charming one from the moonlight. She knew she should adjust and make herself more agreeable, more accommodating, the way that Rob would advise. After all, perhaps the duke's moodiness wasn't his fault at all, but came from being unloved by his father, or from having to earn his own fortune, instead of merely inheriting it.

She *knew* all of this. Yet whether because the remaining ache in her head was making her contentious, or because she simply felt that, after last night, he'd no right to be so surly toward her, she discovered she'd no wish to be either accommodating or agreeable in return. She didn't give a fig for his reasons. If he could be as changeable as the weather, why, then, so could she.

And, instead of meekly sitting back down, she kicked her feet free of the coverlet and stood as straight and tall as her limited height would allow, her arms crossed over her chest. Because he was so much larger, she'd have to look up to meet his gaze; instead of granting him that small victory, she chose to study the ends of his damp neckcloth, the crumpled linen impaled with a pearl stickpin.

"I am not in my bed, Your Grace," she announced, "because I am feeling much improved, thank you so very much for inquiring."

He growled like one of his dogs, so crossly that she felt instantly vindicated. "Then why are you not properly clothed? A bed coverlet over a shift is hardly decent dress for a lady."

Rebelliously she thought of how he hadn't objected last night. "It is perfectly proper dress for a lady in the privacy of her bedchamber, Your Grace. Unless, of course, a gentleman decides to intrude upon a lady without warning."

"How can it be intruding when the lady's bedchamber is part of the gentleman's house, and therefore mine, not yours—I mean, hers?"

Instantly, Jenny looked up, too indignant now to worry about the niceties of meeting eye to eye, no matter how close they were standing to each other. His blond hair was still dark with the rain, spiking around his face in a way that seemed to accentuate the sharpness of his mood; no soft moonlight now.

"*And* therefore, Your Grace," she said, "is everything within the gentleman's house his to do with what and when and how he pleases? Does being the gentleman's guest, within the gentleman's house, mean that the lady must now regard herself as the gentleman's property, at his constant disposal?"

His expression darkened. "Damnation, I was speaking of your clothes, not—not your *person!*"

"Forgive me, Your Grace," interrupted Mrs. Lowe with another more nervous, curtsy, "but the lady has no other clothes than that coverlet. The laundress is still washing what the lady came in, bleaching the stains. Even that shift is borrowed from one of the parlor maids."

"Then see that she has others, Mrs. Lowe!" he said, waving his hand through the air with an impatient, imperious sweep. "Surely there must be shops in Chichester that can supply a proper lady's wardrobe. Send to them now, Mrs. Lowe, so the lady will have no further excuses."

"I've not used my lack as an excuse, Your Grace, but

an explanation," answered Jenny warmly. "A match to the explanation I hope will come from you, unless you intend to force this new clothing upon me."

He opened his mouth to answer, then changed his mind, turning instead toward the housekeeper. "Mrs. Lowe. Leave us. *Now.*"

The housekeeper scurried away, closing the door behind her and leaving them alone together. With his hands clasped behind his back, the duke stared down at Jenny, neither moving nor speaking, and for the next instant she considered whether she should be afraid. After all, she scarcely knew the man, or his temper. He was a great deal larger than her and likely a great deal stronger, as well, and yet in the face of all that she had quite willfully provoked him for the simple reason that he had provoked her first.

With a restless little gulp, she stretched her arms out to either side and shook the coverlet over her hands before she folded them protectively—or was it defensively?—across her chest like wings. No matter how great a fool she'd made of herself, she wasn't going to back down, which she supposed meant she wasn't afraid of him after all: a heartening realization, if only her heart would slow down enough to notice, if only—

"Are you unhappy?" he asked suddenly. "Is anything not as you wish it to be?"

This she hadn't predicted, and she looked at him warily. Even though her anger had faded, she still could feel the tension swirling between them, a palpable force simultaneously pulling them together and pushing them apart.

"I have only one wish, Your Grace," she said, raising her chin, just remembering to reply the way her ruse demanded. "I would wish to know who I am."

"No," he said, an unexpected urgency in the gruff-ness of his voice. He took a step closer, so close that she could see the fading splatter of drying raindrops on his coat and smell the scent of his soap on his new-shaven jaw. "I meant here, in this house. Would you find another situation more satisfying for your recovery?"

She waved one hand to encompass the luxuries of the bedchamber. "What situation could possibly be more agreeable than this, Your Grace?"

He shrugged restlessly, as if the notion weren't really his. "A smaller place, a cottage, perhaps with a family. The minister of this parish has offered to shelter you."

"A parsonage, Your Grace?" Dull, deadly dull, especially without him, though she tried to keep that from her voice.

But in response, his mouth twisted just enough to show that he thought it would be monstrously dull, as well, and Jenny's hopes leaped.

"His wife is very kind," was what he dutifully said. "She would look after you."

"Instead of you, Your Grace?" she asked, tipping her head to one side. "That is why I should prefer to stay, you know. Not because of your grand house, or this feather bed, or the servants, but because of you. You are...you are *special*."

His expression had grown so fixed, so frozen, that was miserably certain she'd said too much. Yet still she blundered onward, unable to stop herself now that she'd begun.

"You pretend to be all world-weary and jaded, but you're not, not by half. You're better than that, though I don't think you see it in yourself. You've been so kind and generous to me, I could nearly weep from it, in a time when I'm sorely in need of kindness. But if you wish to be rid of me now, Your Grace, if you wish me to go, why, then I—''

''I never said I wanted you to leave.''

''That is true.'' Her smile wobbled. Everything *she* was saying was true, too, even if he didn't realize how rare that was for her. The coverlet slipped, taking the nightshift with it and baring her shoulder. She pretended not to notice, though she was certain he did, especially since it meant he didn't have to meet her eye. ''Mrs. Lowe told me you like to play games of chance.''

He nodded, his gaze still lingering over that bare shoulder. ''I do, but only if I can lessen the chance and my risk with it.''

''Which is why you wish to settle me upon the parson's wife, isn't it?'' Oh, she was on such dangerous ground here, ignoring all her experience and instincts for self-preservation, yet there was no place else she'd rather be than here with him. ''To lessen your risk?''

''You are a lady,'' he insisted with a doggedness she found charming. ''You're the one whose honor could be at risk, staying here with me.''

''You don't know for certain I'm a lady,'' she countered, taking the smallest step of willingness toward him. ''How can you, when I don't even know myself?''

''You are,'' he said gruffly. ''I would know otherwise. Damnation, you *are*.''

And then, before she realized it, his mouth was on hers, and he was kissing her, and oh, Gemini, she did not want him to stop....

Chapter Five

Brant was kissing her: against all better judgment, against all reason and common sense, he was kissing her, and without the slightest inclination to stop, either.

Why would he, when she was so soft and yielding in his arms? She tasted like no other woman he'd kissed before, with a heat that glowed with eagerness, not worldliness. That was what made her so irresistible: the rare sense of innocence without coyness, the joy of discovery unclouded by guilt, and so strong she seemed to vibrate with it. He drew her closer, feeling the warmth of her body beneath the coverlet as one of her braids slipped over his wrist and teased his nerves like a rope of silk. Wanting more, he pushed the coverlet further down her arm, relishing the velvet of her skin beneath his fingers. He slanted his mouth and deepened the kiss, forgetting almost everything else except the pleasure to be found in the mouth and body of this single small woman.

Almost everything, but not quite. When his hand impatiently slid further inside her nightshift, seeking more of that lovely soft skin, she gasped, a surprised, shuddering catch in her breathing that he felt through her body and in her kiss. It lasted only as long as it took for one breath to replace another, but that sigh was enough to jar his sleeping conscience awake.

Abruptly he broke the kiss, though he kept her in his arms.

"Ah, Your Grace," she whispered, her eyes heavy-lidded with desire and her lips still parted in a dreamy, unfocused grin, tempting him all over again. "Where did you go?"

"Not nearly as far away as I should have," he said, his voice a husky growl of frustration as he forced himself to lift his hands from her waist. He wanted her, wanted her badly, and his body was having a difficult time understanding why his head was suddenly being so damnably honorable. "Hell, I could be a thousand miles away from you, sweetheart, and it wouldn't be far enough, not by half."

She pulled the coverlet back around her shoulders and touched her fingertips lightly to her lips in wonder, not enticement, yet still more than enough to make him want to groan aloud. "Is that intended to convince me to flee to your parson, or make me wish to stay here with you?"

"You should know that yourself," he said gruffly. "Ladies always do."

He'd purposefully kept clear of ladies, but he'd seen—and avoided—enough to recognize one. By her speech, her manner, even how she stood and held her head, she was a lady, bred, born and educated. But none of the young ladies he'd been introduced to in London or elsewhere would have kissed him so freely, or with such delicious enthusiasm. Why wasn't she wailing about her offended virtue, or perhaps slapping his face with a righteous palm? Why, instead, was she gazing up at him now with the same kind of pleasurable bewilderment that seemed to be befuddling him?

"Ladies always know what's right to do," he continued. "And recall that you *are* a lady."

"So you have told me, Your Grace," she answered, her voice a low, breathy whisper. "Just as you are a gentleman. But, Gemini, when you kiss me like that, I don't seem to know anything at all, it felt that grand."

Kissing her had felt powerfully grand to him, too, not that he was about to confess it.

"That doesn't matter," he insisted, though of course it did. "I cannot take advantage of a lady in your—your present confusion, and ruin you."

"I suppose I must not wish for that, should I?" She smiled wistfully. "But tell me, Your Grace. What if I've taken advantage of you, instead?"

He gulped and barely managed to turn the sound into an undignified throat-clearing. But he couldn't help it: how else was a gentleman to respond to a question like that?

"Damnation, it isn't possible," he said finally. "Ladies ruining men. No."

"I didn't really think it was," she said with a little squeak of frustration that seemed to mirror his own. "But I suppose as a lady, all I must do is receive, and not expect to give anything in return, even when I kiss. Not that I've ever wished to before this."

"You mean not that you can remember," he said firmly, to himself as much as to her. It had been a single, impulsive, unwise kiss. Damnation, it had been nothing more, nothing else, even if he could not stop looking at her mouth, how her lips were still red and swollen from his, fair begging to be kissed again. "And none of that nonsense about your heart remembering, either. You're such a pretty little creature, you've likely had scores of suitors.''

"*That* I would know," she said softly, almost regretfully, her eyes now clear and free of that earlier hazy joy, "and I haven't. But if that is the reason, Your Grace, that you need to send me away to the parson, why, then I must—"

"Hold there, sweetheart," he interrupted sharply. He'd never intended to send her away, nor had he meant to hurt her, either, not like this. "I didn't say that I would—now what in blazes is *that?*"

"It's someone at the door, Your Grace," she whispered, prompting him as if he truly didn't recognize the sound of the knock.

He stared at her, incredulous. "I'm not an idiot."

"I never thought you were, Your Grace," she said, her tone properly meek and soothing, though her eyes seemed to say something far more rebellious. "All I did was answer your question."

With astonishing efficiency she wrapped the coverlet around herself and dropped back into her chair. Balancing the teacup in her hand, she once again looked genteelly fragile, as if nothing at all had happened between them, and certainly nothing like that single kiss. "If you please, you should ask them to enter."

"If *I* please," he grumbled. More proof that she must be a lady, to recover her poise this fast. She was also likely one equal to him in rank, because no one else would dare speak to him with such impunity.

But blast, the worst part was that he liked her all the more for it.

"You don't have to admit them, Your Grace," she said mildly, sipping at the tea, which by now must have been as chill as the rain outside. "Isn't that one of the prerogatives of being a duke? Being able to impose your will on whomever you please?''

"You make me sound like some damned pagan dictator," he growled as Tway's polite knock came again. And of course it was Tway; Brant could identify the man's precise rap anywhere. "Enter, blast you!"

Noiselessly, Tway opened the door, adding a bow in a single seamless motion.

"Your Grace," he said, unperturbed by his reception. "I have news for you and, perhaps, Miss Corinthia."

The girl's teacup clattered down upon the saucer. Her eyes were round, her whole body so taut with expectation she almost looked afraid. At once Brant went to stand behind her chair, there if she needed him. To his surprise, she reached back and took his hand, her fingers tightening anxiously around his.

"What manner of news, Mr. Tway?" she asked breathlessly. "What have you discovered about—about me?"

"Not you precisely, miss," admitted Tway. "But it is news that might lead to that, yes."

"Then out with it, Tway," ordered Brant. He liked the trust that came with her fingers in his and he wanted to be worthy of it. "Don't keep the lady waiting."

"As you wish, Your Grace." He bowed again and drew a scrap of paper from the pocket of his waistcoat. "Here are the facts as I learned them this morning. On the night before His Grace found Miss Corinthia, there was an altercation between two men behind the Black Lion."

The girl turned and looked up at Brant. "The Black Lion is a tavern?"

"A foul local inn on the London road that survives only because the keep bribes the stage drivers to stop," said Brant dryly. "The constable sends one of his men there each night, just from habit. There's so many fights in that stableyard I cannot believe one more would attract any notice."

"On account of the combatants, Your Grace," answered Tway. "They weren't like the Lion's usual customers, and their disagreement seemed to be an old one, begun far from the tavern's taproom. A young gentleman, the others said, and a great bluff officer, a grenadier by his uniform."

The girl gasped and her fingers tightened into Brant's. Of course, he thought: a grenadier was one of the few clues to her past that they had. Hearing this must be bringing back other details, some perhaps that she wished she hadn't recalled, and he gently pressed her fingers in reassurance.

But what if that little gasp came from concern for her lover? What if she feared for his safety in this tavern-yard brawl, if her love for him made her tremble over his risk or suffering?

And why should any of that make Brant feel as decidedly unhappy as he was now?

"Forgive me, miss," Tway was saying. "I did not intend to distress you. If you prefer, I can tell this to His Grace in private and not—"

"No," she said, shaking her head. "Go on. I need to hear this. Oh, pray, go *on!*"

"As you wish, miss," said Tway quickly. "The event itself was nothing remarkable, the usual bluster and scuffling, battering and bruising, doubtless fueled by strong drink. The grenadier was taken to the gaol by the constable, where his superior retrieved him last evening to rejoin his regiment before I could learn more than his name."

He glanced down at the paper in his hand, reading the name. "John Parker, miss, or so he told the gaoler. A large man with a ruddy complexion and fair hair, perhaps thirty years of age. John Parker of Bristol. Is that a name that is familiar to you, miss?"

She let out a sigh so long that Brant realized she'd been holding her breath.

"No," she said forlornly. "It does not. But what of the other man? The one you said was a gentleman?"

"That's what the others said he looked to be, miss," said Tway, frowning down at the paper, "though I have no proof, nor name for him, either. None could even agree upon his appearance in the dark beyond that he was younger and quicker, and dressed like a gentleman. The moment the two were separated, he seemed to vanish clean away into the night, not to be seen again."

Brant snorted, now reassured that she'd have nothing to do with such rascals. "Of course he vanished. What gentleman wants it known he was scuffling with some drunken soldier in the Lion's stableyard?"

"At least there were no pistols, Mr. Tway, and no serious wounds," she said faintly. "A scuffle, as His Grace says, not an affair of honor."

"After a fashion, it was, miss," said Tway, and if such a thing were possible, Brant would have sworn the man blushed. "It was said that they were fighting over a lady, miss, and I judged it worth considering that…that…"

"That they were fighting over *her?*" asked Brant incredulously. He refused to imagine that this girl, sitting here dressed in demure white linen, could be the centerpiece of anything this sordid.

But the girl herself was nodding solemnly. "It is not impossible, Your Grace," she said. "You said I'd mentioned a grenadier when you first found me, didn't you? Mr. Tway was only following the clue I'd given him. What a pity that the two men themselves are gone and beyond asking more!''

''They're not, if you wish it,'' said Brant with a duke's unthinking assurance. He was accustomed to making things right: if she wanted this, why, then, it would be so. ''They can be found and brought here, if you believe it might help you learn who you are.''

''But I know the name of the lady in dispute, Your Grace,'' said Tway quickly. ''Mary Hewitt. The two men were unfortunately quite free with it during their dispute. I have already begun inquiries to learn more of her and her family, where she resides and if she has, ah, lately departed that place.''

Brant knelt down beside the girl's chair, his face level with hers. He almost felt as if they were back at the beginning of their first meeting, beneath the trees—except that now when he gazed at her mouth, he knew what it was like to kiss it, and knew, too, that he wanted very much to kiss it again.

Damnation, how had such a simple bit of kindness grown so wretchedly complicated?

''Tell me, lass,'' he said gruffly. ''Could that be your name? Mary Hewitt?''

She pulled her hand free of his and, instead, twisted it tightly into the other in her lap. She looked back at him without blinking, her eyes enormous and her face pale. She was trying hard not to show it, but he was certain something was frightening her, frightening her badly. But what was it about so simple a question that could do this to her?

''You can tell me if you are,'' he coaxed. ''I won't think any differently of you one way or the other.''

"What happened to being called Corinthia?" she asked in a soft, miserable voice. "That was the name on my handkerchief. Why would I be this Mrs. Hewitt, yet carry a handkerchief with another woman's name?"

"Perhaps your sister's named Corinthia, or your mother," suggested Brant. "Maybe the laundress confused your linens with another lady's. It's all a guess at this point, isn't it?"

"But I'm no widow, Your Grace. How could I be, when I've told you before I've never loved?"

Brant waved his hand, dismissing her objection. "You could still have been wed without love. There's plenty who do, for better or for worse."

"But not I." She lifted her chin a fraction, her small jaw set with unexpected determination. "I am sorry to disappoint you, Mr. Tway, but I cannot possibly be this Mary Hewitt that you have found."

"Oh, lass," said Brant ruefully. Her reasoning seemed flimsy enough to him, all emotion and this maddening love talk, especially when she had so little else to go upon. Yet despite his own reliance on hard facts and numbers, things that couldn't wobble one way or the other, he still found it hard to question her maddening illogic. Instead, she fascinated him because she was so different from anyone else he'd known, and especially from himself. Besides, how could he fault her, when those same impulsive emotions of hers had led them both into that infernal kiss?

Not that Tway had any such constraints. "But if you do not object, miss, I intend to continue my inquiries to their conclusion," he said. "I do not like to leave matters incomplete. If you are not Mrs. Hewitt, as you are convinced, why, then there will be no harm done. And there is always the possibility that such information, however wrong, may still lead us to your proper identity."

She shook her head. "I don't wish to squander your time on a pointless errand, Mr. Tway, not on my account."

"Nonsense," said Brant. "It's not pointless, not at all, and certainly not that way because of you. Besides, it's Tway's duty. That's what he's here for, you know."

Tway bowed, but the girl didn't smile in return, as both men had expected.

"Mr. Tway," she said. "If you please, I should like a word alone with His Grace."

Tway bowed again, this time in acquiescence, and left the room, quietly closing the door after him.

Yet she didn't speak as Brant had expected, instead sitting very still with her hands clasped, lost in her own thoughts. He wished she'd be outspoken and merry again, the way she'd been before Tway had interrupted, but he hadn't a clue how to bring that side of her back. With a sigh of frustration, he rose and looked past her to the windows.

"The rain has stopped," he said finally. "With luck we'll have sun by dinner."

She nodded. The fear he'd seen in her eyes earlier was gone now, replaced with a kind of sad resignation. "The farmers shall be happy, I suppose."

"Well, yes," he said for lack of anything better. "The barley needs sun as well as rain."

"Indeed." He could see her swallow, the nervous little convulsion sliding along her pale throat. "What if Mr. Tway does discover who I am? What if you learn more of me than you wish to know?"

He nodded gravely, for the thought had occurred to him, as well. Not that she'd any deep, dark secret to her past—he was a fair enough judge of character to doubt that she'd much to hide at her age—but he dreaded discovering a much more likely one: that she already belonged to another man who would, most certainly, wish her back.

"I've seen much of the world, both good and bad," he said slowly. "I'd venture that there's little about you that could shock me still."

"But there could be," she insisted. "You don't *know*."

"Neither of us do, do we?" He wished he could reassure her better; he wished he could do the same for himself, as well. "Until you remember, or Tway learns you are Mary Hewitt, or Corinthia, or even the damned Queen of Sheba, then I'll just have to accept you as you are."

That was all he longed for himself, wasn't it? To be accepted as he was by the world, no matter how deficient, how wanting, he might be? Couldn't it be the same for her, as well?

"You'll accept me as I am. I cannot ask for more than that, can I?" At last she smiled up at him, and he felt as if the sun had already burst through the clouds. "But, Gemini, what a sorry bargain that must be for you, Your Grace!"

"I'll accept that, too," he said, feeling himself grinning like an idiot in return, and in relief, too. He'd wanted her happy, and now she was, though he wasn't exactly sure that he'd had anything to do with the change. But he'd take it; he'd take it. "And while we are alone together, I would rather you do away with my title and simply call me Brant."

"Very well, then. Brant." Her smile turned wistfully lopsided, one dimple left like an uncertain question mark. "So you will not send me away to the parsonage, after all? You'll let me stay here with you regardless?"

He'd forgotten entirely about finding her a haven with the Potters. No wonder, too. She'd never looked lovelier or more guilelessly innocent there in the cool light of the last rain shower, her face turned up toward him, her cheeks once again rosy and her lips parted expectantly. Yet deep inside he felt a twinge—only a twinge—of his gambler's instincts, the kind of unconscious warning to be wary, to be sure, and not to be tricked by things that might not be as they seemed.

With her fingertips, she brushed away a stray wisp of hair from her forehead, wrinkling her nose sheepishly, charmingly, as if he'd caught her being less than perfect, and the warning twinge receded. How could she be anything other than exactly this?

Gently he reached out to touch the unruly little wisp she'd pushed aside, the hair curling around his finger in a way he found surprisingly intimate. Other women he'd known had not wanted him to muss their hair, or spoil the elaborate arrangement of curls stiffened into place with sugar water or pomade. But this girl only chuckled when he touched her hair, soft and unruly, just like her.

"I never did want to send you away," he said softly, "to the parsonage or anywhere else. Stay here as long as you wish, as long as you must. Stay here with me."

Obediently, Jenny stood on the low stool in the center of the room, her arms stretched out for the woman measuring her width and length and breadth. The mantuamaker from Chichester and her assistants were fluttering around her like a flock of plump cooing pigeons, so overwhelmed to be summoned here to Claremont Hall by the duke himself that they wouldn't dare risk their good fortune with a single disagreeable word.

Ordinarily, Jenny would have welcomed their attentions. She'd always liked dressing well—first her father and then Rob had always spoiled her in that regard—and the current fashions with their gauzy muslins, high waists and tiny sleeves and melting-candy colors, flattered her small figure. Now left with nothing but a single grass-stained gown and not the faintest notion of what had become of her traveling trunk with the rest of her clothes, she had every excuse for a new wardrobe.

Yet as the mantua-maker began to drape and pin pink-sprigged muslin around her body, Jenny found it difficult even to notice the new gown taking shape, let alone enjoy herself. How could she, after this morning?

The risks surrounding her here at Claremont Hall were growing by the minute. She'd been relieved to learn that Rob was unharmed and that he'd managed to escape both the jealous grenadier and the local constable. Surely by now he'd discovered in turn that she was here, and Jenny had no doubt he'd soon appear on the doorstep in some new guise calculated to impress the duke.

But that had been the only good to come of the morning. She'd pretended to have lost her memory several times before—it was one of her brother's favorite ruses, being one that always garnered so much sympathy—but not once had anyone tried to hunt down her true identity with the determination that Mr. Tway had shown. She'd tried to discourage him as strongly as she could without betraying the truth herself, but neither he nor the duke had wavered. Tway would persist in his inquiries for her sake, and there was nothing more she could do to stop him.

And what would he find? That she was not at all the

born lady that the duke so firmly believed, but instead the feckless daughter of Irish actors? That she was an adventuress, bound to wheedle and charm His Grace as she plucked his pocket as deeply as she dared? That she traveled in the company of her rascal of a brother, leaving behind a merry trail of false names and unpaid bills?

Or that their uncertain future that could prove considerably less cheerful, including prison, transportation, even the gallows?

Tway wouldn't have to look too deeply. Rob had certain rules—never revisit the same place, never write letters, never take too much, leave when things were still rosy and with a plausible excuse for being called away and heartfelt promises to return—but he'd never worried overmuch about covering their past adventures. In fact, he never worried much at all, the same way that their father hadn't. Worrying had fallen to Jenny's lot, a murky and inescapable inheritance, and ah, how she was worrying now.

Because the worst of what had happened this morning had nothing to do with Tway's inquiries. She'd discovered it all by her own foolish self.

What *was* it about the duke that made her behave so freely, so irresponsibly, as if she truly were a wholly different woman? No, not the duke, but Brant. He'd asked her to call him by his given name, and she'd happily obliged, treasuring the significance of such an intimacy. All gruff and self-conscious, he'd somehow manage to smile at her, and she'd melted inside. She'd kissed him, kissed him into a happy, heart-thumping delirium, and her only regret at the time—and likely his, as well—was that they'd been interrupted. She'd barely recovered in time to coax him into letting her stay here, but by then the most shocking damage had been done between them, damage that would have stunned her brother.

She'd forgotten everything about who she was, and she'd told Brant how she felt about him. She'd told him the *truth*.

Sadly she wondered if he'd believed her, let alone recognized the significance of her little confession. And how fast his own feelings were bound to change once he heard Mr. Tway's report!

She groaned aloud at the thought, making the mantua-maker pause anxiously, pin in hand.

"Forgive me if I have pricked you, miss," the woman said contritely. "I do try to take care, but sometimes a pin will slip and—"

"You didn't," said Jenny quickly, forcing herself to smile as an assistant held a mirror for her to view her reflection. "My thoughts were elsewhere, that was all. But now I can see that the gown will be very beautiful. The pink truly was the best choice, as you suggested."

"Thank you, miss," said the mantua-maker, dropping a slight, pleased curtsy at the compliment. "But it is your grace and beauty that give life and honor to my humble work. Ah, how you will please His Grace!"

Jenny smiled wanly. For now, Brant would be pleased, the way most men were by the sight of young woman prettily dressed at their indulgent expense.

For now, yes, but how much longer?

Standing to one side of her drawing room window, Mary Hewitt watched the pale man climb into the chaise waiting at the end of walk to her cottage. Dressed all in black, he'd seemed more like a solicitor, or even a minister, than anyone in the employment of the Duke of Strachen.

At least that was what this Mr. Tway had claimed to be, asking his questions and prying into her personal affairs as if he'd every right. Mary was still trembling with outrage, her handkerchief twisted into a tight, damp knot in her sweating hands.

Surely these last days had been the most dreadful of her life. To think that a respectable young widow like herself should be so humiliated, so shamed, for the amusement and titillation of her neighbors here in Bamfleigh—why, it was nearly beyond bearing, and it would serve them all if she expired right now, leaving them to answer to their Maker.

It had begun innocently enough, even with promise. She'd met Mr. Richard Farquhar and his sister Jane one evening at Sir Wallace's house, which was the most well-bred and refined company one could aspire to here in Bamfleigh. She wouldn't give a bent shilling for the sister, a sly, saucy little thing, in Mary's opinion, but Mr. Farquhar had been the handsomest gentleman there, and so charming and amusing that Mary had been flattered into near giddiness when he'd volunteered to turn the pages for her when she played the pianoforte. By evening's end she'd strolled arm in arm with him through the romantic shadows of Sir Wallace's conservatory, she'd confessed how lonely she'd been since her poor Herbert had died, and if she'd allowed a kiss, why, what lady wouldn't, in such circumstances?

Richard had come calling here to her cottage the next morning. Though he modestly hadn't bragged about himself the way most men did, she soon had determined all she needed to know: that his parents were gentry in the north; that his fortune was as handsome as his face and that his prospects were even better; that he hadn't married because he sadly hadn't yet found the right lady to stand by his side for eternity.

She'd only known Richard three days before she resolved that she must be exactly the lady he needed. She'd married her first husband for security, an older man chosen by her parents; the second time, she meant to please only herself. And could there be a more attentive, more ardent gentleman than Richard Farquhar? Even Sir Wallace noticed, making jests about Cupid's darts and gallantly offering to give Mary's hand away to his friend if necessary.

It had been the most blissful time of her life. Until, that is, one morning John Parker had come marching back into her tidy little world in his bright red uniform to spoil everything—*everything!*

Mary sniffed furiously, striking her fist against the window frame with frustration. She'd met John Parker two years ago, walking along the sands at Brighton. She'd been a new widow then, her mourning still fresh and keen, while John was facing death as well, on his last leave before being shipped off to the French war. The spark between them had flared bright and fast and without regret. He was sure he would die, and she was just as certain she'd never see him again in this life.

But, instead of that romantically melancholy ending, he'd had the audacity to reappear in her garden last week as if he'd every right to be there, and every right to her person, as well. She'd rebuffed him; he'd persisted. Of course John had been there when Richard had called, the introductions polite but frosty.

She'd expected Richard to become her gallant knight, her savior, and drive the unwelcome interloper away. She'd even dared hope he'd feel driven to make his claim to her permanent and ask for her hand.

But he hadn't. He hadn't acted one bit like the gentleman he'd claimed to be. Instead, he'd backed away from John Parker like some skinny whelp with his tail between his legs. He hadn't been brave or gallant, and he hadn't been as wealthy as he'd led her to believe, either, disappearing from the inn with that sly-faced sister of his like a pair of worthless Gypsies in the night. John Parker proved no more constant, running off on the same night, though at least he'd paid his reckoning.

Now Mary would never, ever forgive Richard, not as long as she lived. He'd left Mary without so much as a letter of farewell, and left her, too, to face the humiliation of being *jilted*—she, Mary Hewitt, pitied and laughed at by the same people who'd begged to dance at her next wedding!

Yet just when she'd thought her affairs could sink no lower, this Mr. Tway had popped up upon her doorstep, telling her that her shame had spread even farther. Her two lovers had brawled over her in the courtyard of a wretched tavern, dragging her good name through that sordid mud for the amusement of drunkards and wastrels. It would be in the papers by week's end; her reputation was as ruined any woman's could be. There was nothing left for her to do but close up her cottage and flee to her sister in London until the scandal faded.

One fat tear of self-pity slipped down Mary's cheek. Only one. She didn't want to cry anymore. What she wanted was to make Richard Farquhar suffer as much— no, more!—than she had, and that priggish Mr. Tway had just given her the means. In the midst of the rest of his story, he'd let slip that Richard's sister was now living with the Duke of Strachen at Claremont Hall as his guest. His "guest." Ha. Mary knew what that meant. How such an arrangement had happened, Mary couldn't guess, but she knew how it would end, because she'd be the cause of it.

The tear dropped from Mary's chin and she smiled with grim determination. Some said she was most fortunate that Richard Farquhar had taken no money from her. But he had stolen away her hopes and dreams and her good name with it, and for that he—and his sister— would be made to pay.

Chapter Six

With Jetty and Gus snoring on the carpet before him, Brant sat in the well-worn leather armchair at the desk in his study, tallying the long rows of figures one more time. The tall windows were propped open, letting in the sweet scent of the first grass being mowed on the west lawn, but Brant was too lost in his numbers to notice.

It was a strange quirk of his mind that though he could not begin to transform letters into words, he had no difficulty at all with ciphering. He could swiftly complete the most complex operations in his head, without pen or paper, just as, at the gaming tale, he could tally the points and figure the odds of a particular hand appearing in a game of cards. It was enough of a talent to prove he wasn't the total imbecile he feared in his blackest moods, but he also always found a kind of comfort in the numbers, their absolute right and wrong bringing a certainty that was impossible to find anywhere else in life.

These particular numbers held his interest even more than usual, for they were the basis of a proposal for a new venture for him, an expedition to discover new veins of coal and other minerals in the American states.

The first reports from his partner in Virginia seemed endlessly promising, but the trick would be to interest other investors on this side of the Atlantic. While the ducal imprint on Brant's writing paper did carry great persuasive power, he'd also arranged a meeting in town with several City men for the following week, and he wanted to be able to convince them with projections of every possible profit. He'd memorize the other facts, the names and places, with Tway's help so no one would notice he didn't refer to any notes.

But this time, the numbers didn't seem to be enough. As hard as Brant tried to concentrate, his thoughts kept turning to a balance of a different sort.

Of course it was the girl. Again.

He swore softly to himself, tracing his finger over the numbers as if that would make him concentrate on that other than her. At least now he'd admit it wasn't just her beauty that attracted him. He'd known plenty of women who were much more beautiful, and he hadn't felt this way toward them, especially not after kissing them. No, there was something more with her, something much stronger, and he wished to hell he could pinpoint what it was.

He couldn't read or write, and she couldn't remember. Could it be because both of them were flawed that he was so drawn to her? He struggled with the possibility, fighting its undeniable allure. He was exceptionally generous with his material wealth, but he'd never given much of himself to anyone. Always he'd kept the same careful facade in place like well-bred, charming and slightly bored armor, protecting his wretched secret tight inside. While Tway likely had guessed the truth, Brant had never volunteered it, never daring to trust enough to share its burden with another.

And she wasn't the same as he, not really. Someday she would remember her past and who she was. Someday she would once again be whole, complete, while he never would. She would leave because she wouldn't need to stay, while he'd always be lacking, and always alone. With another oath of frustration, he crumpled the sheet of paper into a tight ball and hurled it across the room.

At once the heads of the two dogs popped up with their ears cocked, Jetty growling sleepily for good measure.

"It's nothing, you foolish beasts," muttered Brant. "Only your half-wit master."

"And me."

He jerked around in his chair to face the voice, twisting so fast that he nearly rocked the chair over. Oh, hell, he thought as he somehow managed to stand. Now she'd judge him an oaf as well as an idiot.

Because of course *she* was one who was there, waiting in the gap of the half-opened door. Not Tway, or Mrs. Lowe, or any other of the vast army of servants: only the one person he didn't want to see him tripping over his own feet.

"I knocked," she said, unperturbed or at least pretending not to notice his oafishness. "Twice."

"I was working," he said. "I didn't hear you."

"I know," she said. "Else I wouldn't have interrupted you. All I wished was a book, you see. I didn't expect to find you here, as well."

Yet she didn't move to leave now, and he was infinitely glad she didn't. He hadn't seen her at all yesterday, claiming his work as an excuse while he tried to distance himself from her.

It hadn't worked. If anything, not seeing her had only

made him think of her more, not less. This morning she seemed older, more poised, more his equal, and it took him a moment to realize it was because, for the first time, she was actually dressed for day.

Gone were the braided hair and bare feet, the night-shift that slipped from her shoulders and the coverlet clutched around herself as a makeshift shawl. In their place were the new clothes he'd insisted she have, some manner of pink gown with the rest of the matching fol-derol, slippers and stockings and ribbons and such. Cor-seting, too: she was standing too straight for otherwise, her shoulders drawn back and her small breasts raised higher, rounder, in more blatant invitation.

Jetty lumbered to his feet, and when he trotted over to her, his tail thumping in happy greeting, she reached down to rub his ears.

"You're scowling black as night," she said, looking at Brant over the dog's head. "I *am* interrupting you, aren't I?"

"I was finished anyway." He took a deep breath, then let it out in a slow, soft whistle. Didn't she realize how damned distracting it was to have her bending over like that, her breasts practically spilling out of that infernal gown, and all for the sake of his oblivious dog? "Now that you're here, you might as well stay."

"Thank you." She straightened—mercifully—and tipped her head to one side. "But if I am not interrupting you, Brant, then why the black scowl?"

It wasn't so much of a black scowl as a grimace of confusion. How could she know she was the first woman other than a servant to ever see the inside of this room, his most private of sanctuaries? Next, to confound him more, she'd gone and used his given name. Even if she'd only done as he'd asked, it had been enough to make his insides do cartwheels with an alacrity that none of his London acquaintance would ever believe possible.

She was waiting patiently for his answer. Damnation, he supposed he'd have to give her one, even if nothing coherent was rattling about in his mind.

Except for how much he wanted to sweep her into his arms and muss all that pink gauzy stuff and kiss her into willing abandon.

"I didn't intend to scowl," he said finally, making himself look away from her and look back down at the papers on the desk. "I was, ah, preoccupied with my, ah, my reckonings."

"Mrs. Lowe said you were vastly clever with numbers," she said, nodding, accepting, so he realized he actually had given a sensible answer. "I should like to hear more, if you'll care to tell me."

"It will not interest you." It wouldn't, either. Brant knew that. The only other people who cared a fig for the schemes and investments he'd found so fascinating were City men. Everyone else found it tedious, if not outright vulgar.

"Let me decide that," she said, gracefully seating herself in the straight-backed chair usually occupied by Tway on the other side of his desk. Her hair had been tamed along with the rest of her, twisted and subdued into fashionable foolishness, and glumly he realized there'd be no more toying with her hair, no loose tendrils or renegade wisps. "I promise to tell you if I am bored."

"Would you, indeed?"

"Indeed, I *would*," she answered promptly, her blue eyes turning fierce, as if daring him to try. "Go on, tell me what it is on those papers that made you scowl and brood."

He sighed, tempted by his own enthusiasm for the

project to want to believe she'd be interested in it, as well.

"Your head seems much improved this morning," he said, hedging. "I don't wish to have the blame for a relapse put upon me."

"I am feeling much improved, yes." She lowered her small chin with cheerful determination, then looked up at him through her lashes. "That is, my head has stopped aching, but it remains quite stupid and empty."

"You still remember nothing?"

"Nothing of any real use, such as who I might be." Briefly her determination faltered and the cheerfulness with it, both done in by the frustration of her situation.

"It will come back," he said quickly. "I'm sure of it."

"I won't be sure until it *does*." She sighed ruefully, and he could see the effort it took for her to recover the cheerful determination. "Now. Brant. If you do not wish to tell me of your affairs, why, I hope you will tell me so directly, without making such sorry excuses that not even Jetty and Gus would accept them from you, not wrapped and tied around a mutton bone."

"The hell they wouldn't." He met her gaze without flinching; he liked a challenge as much as the next man, particularly when it was issued by a pretty woman like this one. Usually such challenges came over the faro table or a hand of cards, but if she wished to call his bluff with her boredom as the stakes, he'd take it.

He rested his elbows on the desk, leaning across toward her. "Very well, sweetheart. Let's see how long you'll last."

"Longer than you ever dreamed," she said. "Mind, I've precious little cluttering my head at present, so I'll have great endurance."

"Then I'll begin slowly," he said. "With the French making such a righteous mess of the Continent, I'm looking elsewhere for a new venture. I've formed a partnership with a Virginian gentleman to search for new minerals and ores in the western territories. He has the rights to the land, while I can provide the knowledge and experience and, if matters go as I've planned, the capital, as well."

She nodded, concentrating wholly on what he was saying. "A Virginian gentlemen? You mean this venture will take place in the America?"

"To the west of America, actually. Well beyond the formal boundaries of their states, out among the wild beasts and savages."

She shifted her glance sideways, skeptical, which, of course, she'd every right to be. "Why would anyone wish to go there, then?"

"Because of what's to be found." He swept his hand through the air, unable to contain his enthusiasm. "Here in Britain, everything's known, and has been since the Caesars. There's nothing *new* left. In America, it's *all* new, undiscovered."

"And waiting for you?"

"Waiting for anyone with the proper vision," he said. "Consider this. I own three copper mines in Cornwall. I could have left them as they were, earning a decent profit, but instead I've invested in new mechanisms for mining as well as improving conditions for the miners. It's common sense, no great secret. If your people are content, if they are given the best tools with which to do their work and paid fairly for their labor, then your profits are bound to rise, as sure as the sun in the morning."

She nodded again, her eyes reflecting back his own

excitement. "So you would do this next in the American states?"

"I would like the chance to try," he said. "I would begin with one mine, depending on what is most prevalent, and I would send the best men—engineers, managers—I could find to oversee the work. There will be nothing else to rival it on that side of the Atlantic, and I expect whole villages—towns!—could grow from this beginning."

"But you would use local miners from America, yes?"

"If I can find them," he said. "Otherwise I'll have them trained, any willing to work and earn a good wage. I've no wish to start my own colony. But only free men, you understand. My partner, being a Virginian, had first wanted to employ African slaves, for economy's sake. I would not have it, making him vastly unhappy with me. But I believe we have come to an agreement on that, too. All that's left now is to raise more capital, to divide the initial risk."

"And thus you will improve the region with industry, as well as lining your own pockets." She glanced down at the papers strewn over his desk. "Is that what you have written there? Calculating your profits to woo others to join you?"

He nodded, pleased that she'd understood this far, and slid the paper around for her to read. "You can see how the first years will be costly, but after that the profits are as close to a certainty as this life offers. The ore can be refined and sold in the American cities along their coast, or exported back to England, or anywhere else in the world."

She frowned a bit as she studied the numbers. "In vessels that you own, as well?"

He shrugged modestly. "I have shares in several shipping houses, yes. As the old adage states, it's unwise to put all of one's eggs in a single basket."

"What a wise old farmer you are," she teased. "But how all these schemes in the wilderness must vex your bankers!"

Brant smiled. "I let them be vexed. If I'm to be an old farmer, then I'm one with his shillings knotted in a mended stocking around his waist for safekeeping on market day. I watch after my own funds and let the bankers follow."

"But surely Mr. Tway must help, doesn't he?"

"With the bookkeeping, yes," he admitted, thankful she'd no notion of how much of a necessity Tway's neat penmanship was to him. "But the decisions are mine, wrong or right."

"I would say that they are more right than wrong," she said, glancing around the room, to the shelves full of leather-bound books and the Italian paintings in gilded frames on the walls. "When Mrs. Lowe told me you liked games of chance, I thought she meant only faro and such, not foreign ventures and shillings in your stocking."

"Ah, so I have bored you, after all," he said lightly, disappointed but not surprised. "I warned you, didn't I?"

"Oh, no, I am not bored," she said quickly, her eyes wide as she looked back to him. "Not at all. Rather I was thinking how unusual, how rare, such interests and talents are for a peer."

That made him grimace. He'd often wondered how much of his interest in finances had been driven by the ruinous necessity of his father's debts. If he hadn't been left so poor, or struggled with such a desperate need to prove his own worth to himself and the world, would he have been more like other noblemen and never strayed beyond the gaming tables? "How unusual, you say. Meaning that such interests make me damned dull for a duke."

"Meaning that you are a remarkable man, whether duke or thrifty farmer," she said softly, her smile lighting her eyes with sunny warmth. "Meaning that you are not like the others in the very best possible way, clever but honorable, too, and leagues away from being dull."

She might have been unabashedly flattering him, but something in that sunny smile made him doubt it and trust her honesty, instead. She didn't find him dull. She found him...*remarkable,* and he'd been remarkable being himself, not some contrived imitation of a high-bred, world-weary rake.

Not that she could realize how marvelous all this was to him. Slowly she leaned forward, toward him, and rested her elbows on the desk, putting herself within his reach. Then with nothing better to do with her hand while he watched, she nervously pulled at one of those artfully crafted curls, twisting it into a lopsided, drooping corkscrew that betrayed the risk she'd taken by coming here to him in the first place.

And as he smiled back at her and her tousled curl, he made a thoroughly stunning realization: that as much as he'd enjoyed playing her rescuer when he and the dogs had first found her unconscious beneath the trees, as much as he'd been happy to support her when she'd been so weak and faint she'd literally needed him, as deeply as he'd been touched by her wan, waifish face against the pillow—as much as he'd liked all that, none of it could hold a candle to the way she was now, with her eyes bright and clear, her interest in his work genuine, her expression still holding the edge of a challenge and that one bedraggled curl making her even more appealing.

"Is that one of the new gowns?" he asked, though of course he knew it had to be.

"I trust it meets with your approval." Her smile widened because he'd noticed. She plucked at the tiny sleeves, smoothing them over her shoulders, the gesture directing his gaze once again to the perilously low bodice. "The seamstress must have sewed through the night to have it done so fast."

"I'm sure her bill will make up for the lost sleep." What that seamstress should be doing is roasting for all eternity for creating such an infernal temptation for *him*. "But I like it. I like it fine."

"I'm glad," she whispered, pleasure making her cheeks blush a deeper pink than the gown. "I...am... *glad*."

Which led Brant to make a second realization: that if he were to kiss her now—which he wanted very much to do—she would not only permit it, she'd welcome it. And, once again, likely kiss him in return.

He wasn't sure who was challenging whom, and he didn't care. He shoved back his chair and stood, intent on joining her on the other side of the desk, on taking her into his arms and kissing her the way they both wanted. But in his haste, the buttons on the cuff of his coat caught the edge of the piled papers and sent them fluttering off the edge and to the floor at her feet.

"Oh, Gemini, Brant!" she exclaimed, trying to catch the sheets as they fell around her.

"Leave them," he ordered. "It doesn't matter."

But she was already crouching down to retrieve the

papers and rescue them from the two dogs who'd come bounding forward to investigate.

"Of course it matters, after all your work," she said, gathering up sheet after sheet and squaring them in her hands. "I wouldn't want—oh, my. Oh, Brant."

Slowly she stood, staring down at the sheet that had ended on the top, her expression as shocked as if the paper had burst into flame in her fingers.

"What is it, sweetheart?" What could she have possibly found in his reckonings to make her respond like this? "What in blazes is wrong?"

"It's this," she said unhappily, holding one of the papers out for him to see. "Oh, Brant, why didn't you tell me?"

But as he stared down at the paper in her hand, he couldn't tell her even now, because to his great shame and embarrassment he'd no idea what the scrabble of writing on it had said to her. He recognized the sheet as the kind of common stock, halfway to foolscap, that Tway used for every day, but beyond that he could not say if the writing was an inventory, a letter or a bill of lading. He'd spent most of his life bluffing his way clear of situations exactly like this, but now here with her, he found himself suddenly, horribly speechless.

"I know it must seem unimportant to you," she continued sadly, "what with all these grand ventures of yours, but to me—to me it could have meant everything."

"Everything on this desk is important," he said, a miserable, cowardly half reply that made him despise his weakness even more.

"Perhaps when it's on your desk, but not when it's here in my hands." She sighed and mercifully turned the paper away from him. "I never did believe I was this widow that Mr. Tway had found, but I still would have liked to have been told for certain.''

So that was it, Tway's notes from his trip to Bamfleigh. *Blast* him for leaving them on this desk, and double blast himself for forgetting to tell her outright!

"Damnation, I meant to tell you," he grumbled, though too angry with himself to sound properly contrite. "What purpose would it serve to keep it from you? The widow wasn't you, and that's an end to it, even to Tway. But when you came here and surprised me, the whole thing flew clear from my head."

She nodded, but clearly wasn't reassured. "Did Mr. Tway meet with Mrs. Hewitt himself or send someone else?"

"Oh, he rode down to Bamfleigh to meet her himself," said Brant, relieved that she didn't seem as cross with him as she'd every right to be. "When you know Tway better, you'll understand that he can't bear to leave any matter of importance to another."

"He didn't tell Mrs. Hewitt about me, did he?" she asked anxiously. "That is, once he could see she wasn't me, then there wasn't any need to tell her more, was there?"

"Oh, I doubt it," said Brant, surprised by her reaction. "Tway is as tight-lipped as they come, and I understand Mrs. Hewitt was too shamed by her own misadventures to volunteer much in return. And with good reason, too. You recall the battle at the Black Lion. Tway says the whole infernal village speaks of nothing but the merry widow burning her candle with two swains now left without so much as a stub for solace."

He'd expected her to laugh, or at least to grin, at such a village comedy. Even Tway himself had smiled over this Mrs. Hewitt's pretensions to gentility, and how outraged the widow was at getting caught in a stew of her own making. But, instead the girl almost looked ready to weep, her face flushed with misery and her hands twisting together.

"The tale's a farce, pet, not a tragedy," he said kindly. "The widow's hardly worth your tears."

"No, she's not," she said, turning away. "Not at all. But I've kept you from your work long enough, haven't I? I should leave you now, else that splendid new venture in Virginia will never begin."

"You don't have to go," he said quickly, too late reaching for her hand as she darted across the room and away from him. Blast, he *had* offended her, after all. "Besides, you haven't chosen your book yet."

Without looking back at him, she randomly pulled a book from the shelf. *"A History of the Borgias,"* she read from the spine, and gave an odd little laugh. "How appropriate, yes?"

"Only if old Rome was a country village," he said, following her as she began inching toward the open door. Her gown was drifting about her in the breeze, making her seem even more insubstantial and elusive, and he felt as if he were coaxing a pink-winged butterfly to light. "You do not have to go, Corinthia. It's almost time to dine. You can stay. Stay. Please."

"Then I shall see you at table, Brant," she said, clutching the book to her chest. "For now, I wish a bit of time to myself, just to…to *be* myself."

"You can be yourself here, you know," he said, even as he realized how he wasn't brave enough to be entirely himself with her, either.

She only shook her head and slipped through the open door. He went to the window, but did not follow, instead watching her hurry across the gravel paths of the garden,

her skirts fluttering around her slippered feet and her
dark curls bobbing as she passed among the early flowers. She paused for an instant at each crossing in the
paths, considering which way to take; clearly she'd no
definite course in mind except to escape him, and his
own mood darkened.

Here was the real country farce: the idiot duke daring
to reach for the butterfly lady. He'd felt more at ease
with her than he ever had with any other person, yet
once again he'd bumbled and done or said something
that had sent her racing away from him as fast as she
could.

And leaving him, as ever, alone.

Jenny hurried through the bushes and beneath the
trees, her slippers crunching softly into the gravel paths.
She didn't care where she went: it was the running away
that counted more, running from the house and the man,
but most of all from the ever-growing lie that would
swallow her up no matter how fast she tried to run.

For as long as she could recall, the truth had been
something to be bent and molded to serve necessity. It
was never referred to as lying in her family. That
sounded too common, too dishonorable, too willfully
wicked, which, of course, they weren't. And besides,
gentlemen didn't lie. Her father had called it dissembling, a prettier term, or a game of wits, or even a higher
kind of acting where the actor wrote his own lines as
well as spoke them. She'd never had reason to question
his philosophy, and why should she, when she'd known
nothing else?

But in a handful of days, Brant had turned her father's
teachings upside down. A man who lived by truth and
honor wasn't necessarily a dullard who deserved to be

cozened into sharing his wealth; he could just as easily
be an intelligent, thoughtful peer of the realm. To Brant,
idleness was the real sin, not work, and he'd stay up half
the night to prove it. And while her father and Rob
scorned generosity as fit only for old maids and charity-
mongers, Brant seemed determined to spread his good
fortune wherever he could.

Not that he was a saint. Far from it. He gambled for
the highest of stakes, he was prone to moodiness, and
expected his will to be obeyed as quickly as any other
duke would. He was appallingly handsome, and the self-
assured saunter, almost a swagger, with which he entered
a room showed he knew it. He didn't like being crossed
or challenged, Jenny had learned that quickly enough,
though she'd rather liked doing it, being by nature a
challenger herself.

But most unsaintly of all was how Brant had treated
her. There was absolutely no acceptable reason for any
gentleman—even a duke—to have a young lady alone
as his guest in his house, no matter how noble his first
intentions might have been. The minister and his wife
had known it, and by now likely everyone in the county
did, too. The Duke of Strachen had wanted her to stay,
and that had been reason enough for him. But if Jenny
had been a true lady, instead of a pretend one, her reputation would already be in tatters and past redemption
from circumstance alone, despite how innocent she
might be.

But, Gemini, she wasn't innocent. She'd kissed Brant,
and he'd become the first man from which she'd longed
for more. They bantered back and forth, two clever people appreciating one another, with their minds as well as
their bodies. He'd smile at her and she melted inside.
He took her hand and her heart would race and her knees
weaken, she'd be so eager to fall into his arms—his bed,
too, if he'd but show her the way. She liked him, liked

him fine, liked him more than simple liking and more than a woman like her had any right to do.

Yet in return she'd lied to him. Who she was, how she'd come to be there, her lack of memory—none of it had been true, had it? From the moment she'd opened her eyes to find him bending over her, to this very morning, not ten minutes past.

And for the first time in her vagabond life, there among the roses with a book about the Borgias clasped to her chest, Jenny Dell recognized her lies for what they were, and sorrowfully could see the grief they were bound to bring.

What she didn't see, however, was the scruffy boy, some tenant's son in a grass-stained smock, who darted into the path before her.

Startled, she gave a small shriek and raised the heavy book in her hands as a makeshift weapon.

"Hush, hush, lady, don't be flustered!" the boy ordered in a shrill whisper. "I don't mean t'harm you, only t'give you this."

He held a folded paper out to her in his grubby fingers and reluctantly she lowered the book and took the paper. As soon as she did, the boy ran off, vanishing as swiftly as he'd appeared.

Cautiously Jenny unfolded the paper. She'd thought she'd rejoice when she finally read this message. Now, instead, she felt a sick dread growing in the bottom of her stomach as she read the words written in her brother's familiar sprawling hand.

You landed in clover, you Lucky Girl!
    Meet me at the Statue of Jupiter near the fountain, tonight at Eleven and tell me All.

Jenny read the note one more time, to make sure she'd remember the message. Then she tore the paper into as tiny and illegible pieces as she could, and scattered them like snowflakes deep inside the bushes, where no one would find them.

Tell me All, asked Rob, and because he was her dear, only brother, she would. But which All would it be: the truth or the lies?

Chapter Seven

Brant swung down from his horse in the stableyard while three grooms came running, ready to rub down the weary animal. Brant was weary, too, and hot, and he gladly took the pewter mug of water that another groom handed him. The late-afternoon shadows from the Hall's tall chimneys stretched long across the brick-paved yard, showing how long he'd been gone.

Brant hadn't planned to ride out again this afternoon, but when Corinthia hadn't appeared at dinner, pleading a recurrence of her headache, he'd lost his appetite, as well. He'd spent the afternoon riding hard and determinedly trying not to think of her. But all he'd managed to do was exhaust his body, not his mind, and with a tired sigh he watched Tway hurrying across the yard toward him with some kind of urgent business or news. It had to be urgent; nothing less could make Tway move at this ungainly trot, the queue of his wig flopping between his shoulder blades.

"Your Grace," he said, puffing as he bowed. "I must speak with you at once."

"And so you are," said Brant, wiping his handkerchief across his forehead. "What has happened?"

Tway said nothing, pinching his lips together to re-inforce his silence as he glanced pointedly at the nearby grooms tending to the horse. Impatiently, Brant stepped back into the shadow of the stable wall and out of the hearing of the others.

"It's not my brother George, is it?" His younger brother was a much-decorated captain in the Navy, and while over the last year George had been on shore leave during the lull in the wars with France, he was now eagerly expecting to be posted to a new command from the Admiralty. George had done well in the Navy, making a fortune of his own in prize money, but it was a dangerous career that too often ended in an early, grue-some death. Brant would much prefer that George re-mained a landsman, instead, content with his new wife and infant son, at least long enough to see the boy bap-tized here at the Hall. "He hasn't had his blasted letter from the Admiralty yet, has he?"

"No, Your Grace, not as far as I know," said Tway. "I'm afraid this has to do with Miss Corinthia."

Instantly, Brant's concern shifted. "Has she wors-ened? She was complaining of her head earlier. Has Gri-stead been sent for?"

"No, Your Grace," said Tway. "I do not believe Dr. Gristead's services shall help us with this."

He showed Brant the letter in his hand: a crumpled single sheet, sealed with a greasy blob of tallow without a signet. "It would seem the lady has an enemy, Your Grace."

"Read it," ordered Brant curtly, his mind already rac-ing on to a thousand possibilities.

"Very well, Your Grace." Tway cleared his throat before he began. "'Beware the stray bitch you've taken in your house. Her bite is a pox that will poison your soul.'"

Brant swore softly. "No signature, of course?"

"It is signed only by 'a friend,' Your Grace."

"What a lovely friend," said Brant. "How did this rubbish come into my house?"

"By the regular post, Your Grace, with the rest of the day's letters," said Tway. "I would, however, venture to guess that the letters were written in a purposefully coarse hand to deceive, and that from the light touch of the pen, I should also guess that the writer may be another woman."

"Then she is the true bitch, yes?" He took the letter himself, slowly turning it over in his hands as if searching for some other clue or meaning. Though he himself was occasionally attacked in the press—it was impossible to lead as public a life as his without that kind of attention—he'd never received any vile letters like this directly. The obvious hatred behind it both concerned and angered him, and he could not imagine what Corinthia could have done to inspire such an anonymous attack.

Even more threatening was the fact that the writer not only seemed to know Corinthia, but also that she was here in this house. Did she also know of the girl's loss of memory? Was that why she didn't dare be more specific in her message or signature, fearing that Corinthia could identify her? And could she in turn identify Corinthia and unlock the secret of who she was?

He frowned, thinking. From the beginning he'd believed that Corinthia had been struck by a man, but there was no real reason to assume that. She wasn't a large woman, and especially if she were surprised, she could easily have been overwhelmed by another female, then left for dead. Was that what drove the sender of this letter—that the girl still lived?

Or perhaps he was thinking too much. Perhaps the sender was no more than another mean-spirited village puritan, too cowardly to voice her disapproval of the girl's presence in his bachelor house, but too self-righteous to keep her judgment to herself.

Tway delicately cleared his throat. "Shall the lady be shown this, ah, letter, Your Grace?"

"Good God, no," said Brant, handing it back to Tway. "It would only upset her further, particularly if she's not feeling well this afternoon."

"Mrs. Lowe believes Miss Corinthia has not suffered a relapse, Your Grace, but that she is simply feeling the effects of having walked too long in the midday sun, something that delicate young ladies are always warned against."

"Perhaps." Brant sighed. The truth was he didn't know much at all about how delicate young ladies could be, though this particular one seemed spirited enough not to be deterred by any mere warning. Not that he found fault with that spirit—in fact, he found her all the more fascinating for being quick and clever and determined—but he did wish she'd show more regard for her own health.

Unless, of course, this was somehow all his fault, which was entirely possible.

"Do you wish me to ask Mrs. Lowe to keep her indoors, Your Grace?" asked Tway, misreading Brant's silence. "For her own sake?"

"I don't believe that's necessary," said Brant quickly. "I don't want her to feel like she's a prisoner. She's free to go wherever she pleases. But tell the other servants, both in the house and out, to be aware of anything out of the ordinary, or any stranger on the grounds, and come to me at once if there is. I doubt that the writer of this damned letter will do more, but I don't wish us to be surprised if she—or he—does."

He looked up at the house, to the window of her bedchamber. All he wanted was to do what was right. Who would have known it would be such a blasted challenge?

The night was warm, the moonlight muted by a gauze of hazy clouds. Jenny walked quickly, keeping to the grass on the side of the paths. The dewy grass had already soaked through her slippers, but she couldn't risk the sound of her footfalls on the gravel. It was enough that the moonlight seemed to seek out the pale pink of her gown. She'd have preferred, instead, something black and encompassing that would make her blend into the shadows, but the mantua-maker had supplied her only with what was bright and fashionable for a young lady, and not dark disguises made for stealth and skullduggery.

Uneasily she glanced back at the house, where there were still lights in several of the windows. No doubt Brant was awake, and she prayed the lights meant he was once again lost deeply in his American plans, with no stray thoughts to squander on her. When she'd excused herself from supper, too, he'd replied with the most cursory regrets and hopes for her recovery, relayed through a servant.

She supposed she should have been grateful that he had left her alone, the way that would be best for them both. But she hadn't, instead eagerly looking up each time she'd heard a servant in the hall outside her door, even after she'd dowsed her candles and pretended to sleep.

*Oh, Jenny, Jenny, you cannot have it both ways, not
with a man like the duke!*

She found the tall statue of Jupiter easily, his white
marble majesty blotched with gray-green lichen. Obviously, Rob had already been on the grounds to choose
such a spot for their meeting: while the statue made an
unmistakable landmark, the bushes surrounding it were
ancient dense boxwood pruned into fantastical shapes
that were tall and thick enough to hide a regiment from
sight of the house.

Quickly she scanned the boxwood and the paths that
led to the statue, wishing Rob would show himself, and
pulled her shawl higher over her shoulders. She was
shivering, not from cold, but from anxiety. The moonlight was reminding her of that first night when she'd
come across Brant on the terrace and first felt the dangerous pull of the attraction between them.

But Brant had also confided how his restless energy
made him walk these same grounds by night. What
would she say to him if he found her here now? Worse
yet, how would she explain Rob's presence if the duke
found them together?

When she finally heard the owl's muted hoot that had
always been their signal, she gasped with relief and ran
toward the sound. Her brother was waiting for her, grinning as if there'd never been a question that he'd come,
or even that he'd lived.

"Oh, Robbie, Robbie," she cried as she hugged him
fiercely. "You can't know how I missed you, you
wicked rascal!"

"What, Jen, tears for me?" he said, holding her apart
to look fondly into her face. "Silly goose! You knew
I'd find you, didn't you?"

"I knew nothing of the sort!" she said, indignantly

fumbling for her handkerchief to wipe away the tears he didn't deserve. "When we parted last, you were racing away in a rattletrap chaise with a murderous grenadier hot after you!"

"Oh, I dealt with him soon enough," said Rob with airy nonchalance. "He was no trouble, not to me."

"'No trouble,' ha," she said. "I've heard of your performance behind the Black Lion. Likely everyone in the county has. Brawling like any common drunkard in the tavern yard! What would Father had said to such a show? That plum-size bruise there on your jaw, and the other over your eye—such lovely badges of honor those are, Robert Dell!"

He scowled, and drew back to keep her from touching the still-swollen bruises on his handsome face. "I fell from a horse, Jen. The filthy nag was frighted by a nightingale and tossed me into a garden fence. You should be thankful this is all I have to show for it and not a broken neck."

"Oh, Robbie," she said sadly. Before now she hadn't realized how deeply the Dell habit of dissembling ran through her brother, the lies so unthinking that he couldn't tell the truth even to her. "I was worried about you, that's all. When you didn't come for me as you usually do, I was frightened for you. There's nothing wrong with that, is there?"

"I tell you, Jen, I was fine," he assured her with his familiar, engaging smile, the smile that always could set things to rights. "I only needed a day or two to lay low, and, ah, to recover. After my fall, that is. But look at how well you've done without me! Landed in clover, you have, the deepest, sweetest clover imaginable!"

He looked around her up at the Hall, his eyes bright with greedy appreciation. "A bona fide duke, Jenny. A genuine peer of the realm and cousin to the king! We've never reached this far, not even with Father in his prime. So what's your game, Clover Girl? What lure did you use to catch a duke in your snare?''

''I haven't caught him, Rob,'' she said uneasily. ''And I haven't used any lures or snares. All I've done is play at forgetting, pretending that I can't remember who I am.''

''Ah, and he went for it, the stupid old fool!'' said Robbie gleefully. ''I've seen you in that role before, and so prettily, too, that he couldn't help but accept it. There's no duke that's a match for us Dells, is there?''

But Jenny didn't share his amusement. ''He went for it because he is kind, not because he is stupid. He's not, Robbie, not at all. He's very, very intelligent, and if you are not careful, he'll take you so quick you won't know what happened.''

''Because 'he is *kind*'?'' repeated her brother incredulously, overlooking everything else she'd said. ''What kind of prattle is that?''

''It's not prattle,'' insisted Jenny. ''It's the truth. Somehow after *you'd* tossed me out of the chaise, I struck my head and fainted. He found me and he took me back to his house and had a doctor look after me and all the rest, because he didn't wish me to suffer, same as he would for anyone else on his land. He *is* kind.''

''Oh, aye, a right regular good Samaritan, straight from the Bible.'' His gaze had wandered back to the long facade of the Hall, ghostly in the moonlight. ''And that's not a *house,* Jenny. That's a ducal *seat.* Don't you remember anything that poor Father tried to teach us? How many bedchambers, would you guess?''

''I don't know,'' she said, her misery growing. ''I

haven't counted. But I have learned other useful things, Rob, things like how His Grace handles all his financial affairs directly himself. Father would've wished us to know *that*."

"Himself?" repeated Rob with surprise. "Aren't many peers who can claim such a thing. So if he were to decide to make us a smallish loan, even a gift of capital, why, it would be the most simple agreement possible, yes?"

"Yes," she said. She was only doing what she and Rob had always done, looking out for one another. Yet still she felt as if she were betraying Brant's trust and the warmth she'd felt between them as he'd explained his latest ventures. "I suppose it would."

But Rob wasn't listening. "That's not your gown," he said abruptly, "and that's not your shawl, either. I know all your clothes, and besides, I still have your trunk. Is that a sample of His Grace's kindness, then? Pink Indian muslin and a Kashmir shawl and coral beads around your throat?"

Self-consciously she pressed her hand to the necklace. The beads were glass, not coral, and had been sent with the gown, with no special significance beyond that the mantua-maker wished to pad her reckoning. But they were also another little sign of Brant's unthinking generosity, and something she wanted to keep clear of her brother's careless ridicule.

"I had only the one gown I'd been wearing, and that torn and soiled," she said defensively. "So yes, his providing a few new things for me is proof of his kindness and generosity."

"Oh, I'm not complaining," he said, nodding as he thought, which was seldom a good sign with Rob. "It's all part of you being in clover, isn't it? We've only to figure what I should play, to come and force His Grace's hand a bit.''

''It's not that simple,'' she said quickly, ''and that's partly your fault. When I was still waking, I babbled something about the grenadier to the duke—doubtless worrying over you—and that was enough for the duke and his people to find your Mrs. Hewitt and her John Parker and even you, at least the part of you that was fighting behind the Black Lion.''

Rob's eyes widened. ''John Parker, too? Gad.''

''I've done what I can to convince them there's no connections among us,'' she continued, wanting him to understand, ''and I believe they've abandoned the notion at last. They'd thought I might actually *be* Mrs. Hewitt, and at least when His Grace's man of business met the real one, that put an end to that. But if you were to arrive with your face all battered as it is—why, they'd put the pieces together and we'd be done, Robbie, done to a turn.''

''They spoke to the widow herself?'' he asked with fresh surprise. ''Mary Hewitt of Bamfleigh?''

Jenny nodded. ''I told you the duke wasn't a fool.''

''Poor Mary,'' said her brother sadly, sentimentally. ''She's a sweet little honey pot. I'm sorry matters ended as they did between us. If only she'd been honest with me about that grenadier!''

''Oh, yes, then you could have told her all about our parents, too.''

He made a mocking bow over his leg, complete with a fillip of his wrist. ''Honor before honesty, my dear, the way it is for every true gentleman.''

''Rob, be serious,'' she said, her impatience growing. She couldn't begin to imagine what Brant would say to such an outrageous comment from her brother, and with any luck, she'd never have to find out. "This isn't our ordinary game."

"No," he said lightly. "Nor is the duke an ordinary mark, is he?"

"Of course he isn't!"

"Oh, of course." He plucked a sprig of boxwood from the bush behind Jenny and idly twirled it between his fingers, watching the small, glossy leaves spin from the stem. "The question, sister, isn't what the duke is to me, but what he has become to you. Are you warming his bed already? Is that how you know so much of his kindness, eh?"

"Stop it, Rob." Furiously she snatched the twirling sprig from his hand. "I won't hear you speak of me like that."

But just as quickly he seized her wrist, holding her arm awkwardly raised over her shoulder. "Why not, when everyone else in England soon will be saying exactly the same?"

"Because it's not true!" she cried. "Let go, Rob, you're hurting me!"

He didn't, and she asked again the way she had when they'd been children: by kicking him in the shin.

It worked, just as it had then. With a yowl he released her, dropping back to sit on the ledge of Jupiter's base to rub his leg where she'd kicked it.

"What the hell are you doing, Jen?" he demanded indignantly. "We've always worked together, haven't we?"

"Then why are you talking about me as if I were a low, common trollop, instead of your sister?"

"Jen, you could take as many lovers as the Russian queen and I wouldn't care," he said earnestly. "But His Grace here *is* different. Think of it, now. You've been given the best hand any of us have ever had, and I don't want you to spoil it. This could be even better for us than the old *marchesa*. You were little then, I know, but surely even you remember her.''

Of course Jenny remembered. Falling in with the dowager Marchesa di Bartolemeo had been her father's greatest coup, soon after he'd abandoned the traveling theatrical company for good. Father had never confided to Jenny his exact relationship with the *marchesa*, and Jenny had never really wanted to know. But for five glorious years the Dells had lived as favored guests at her villa overlooking the Bay of Naples with Mount Vesuvius in the distance. If the *marchesa* hadn't died, they might be living there still, especially if the elderly lady had included her father in her will, the way he swore she'd promised.

In many ways those five years had been the best and most secure of Jenny's vagabond childhood, but along with the hanging red flowers and the small pet monkeys with silver collars in the garden, Jenny hadn't forgotten the darker side of the old noblewoman's hospitality, either.

The Dells became the *marchesa*'s unquestioning courtiers. She was always to be obeyed and flattered, never to be crossed, no matter how imperious or outrageous her demands had become. There had been one party when she had ordered Jenny, not quite eight, to be suggestively dressed as a half-naked nymph for the amusement of a drunken party of the *marchesa*'s friends. Jenny could still recall their jeering laughter and casually cruel jokes, and the way the men had reached out to fondle her as she'd shivered on her plaster seashell. Yet no matter how terrified Jenny had been, because it was the *marchesa*'s wish, her father had done nothing to stop it.

No. That was not what she wanted with Brant, or anyone else, either. She didn't want any more fawning obligation, or having to please even if the pleasing felt wrong. She wanted love, freely given and taken, and she wanted the truth.

"If this goes well, Jen, then our wandering days could be over for good," Rob was saying. "You're always saying you want a home of your own. Could you ever fancy a more perfect home than this?"

"But it's not mine," she protested. All those vast, echoing rooms, all those servants, were not her idea of a home. "It's Brant's—that is, His Grace's."

"'Brant,'" repeated Rob, not bothering to hide his satisfaction. "That's good. That's fine. He can be your dear Brant. You've saved yourself like a proper Vestal, Jen, and clever women say it's as easy to love a rich man as a poor one."

Unhappily she twisted her hands into the corners of her shawl. She'd longed for Rob to reappear and to take charge, the way he always had before, but not like this. Having been apart from her brother for so many days was making her look at him with fresh eyes. Even without his recent battle scars, he wasn't as young as he'd once been, not so boyishly handsome or lithe. His face was settling into the hard lines of a professional charmer, and to her shock she realized his days of cajoling ladies into doing things they shouldn't for the sake of his smile were rapidly dwindling.

"No more, Rob," she warned, "else I'll kick you again."

"Then listen to me first," he said seriously, his earlier teasing gone. "I do not care whether you are no more than the duke's mistress, or can bargain your way into becoming his wife. Though gad, think of how Father's chest would have puffed to have Dell blood sit beneath a coronet!''

"No, Rob,'' she whispered miserably. "Please don't ask me to—''

"No, you listen to me,'' he ordered, more curtly than she'd ever heard from him before, "and mark well what I say. Do you believe I've always liked what I've had to do, eh? Do you think I've always been in the humor to be charming? No, I have not, I can assure you, Miss Jenny Dell. We're shabby gentry, and always have been, and now on top of it we're poor as dirt.''

"But there's always tomorrow, Robbie,'' she said, quoting their ever-optimistic father. "Tomorrow will be different.''

"Oh, aye, it always was tomorrow for Father, wasn't it?'' he said bitterly. "But fortune never does seem to smile on us, Jenny, no matter how hard we've tried. Until now, here, with you. We'll never have another chance like this, neither or us, and I won't let you squander it for the sake of being missish or overnice. You'll do what the duke wants, when and where and exactly how it amuses him to do it, and together we'll make his pleasure worth our while.''

How had it come down to this? she wondered. This wasn't their old familiar game, with her and Rob matching their wits against the rest of the world. This was something else altogether, so wicked she'd no wish to give it a name. What she felt for Brant—and what she'd dared to hope he might feel for her—didn't deserve to be reduced to this.

Numbly she stared down at the scuffed toes of Rob's riding boots, wondering when he'd become this desperate, or whether she simply hadn't noticed if he'd always been this way.

"You can't come back here like this, Rob," she said, not really answering. "You'll be caught. There are dogs and more servants, indoors and out, than you can imagine, and His Grace himself scarce sleeps but walks his own property by night like a ghost."

"Then I'll watch from a distance, and not interfere," he said, "until you need me to come. I'll send you word when I've come to roost. We need to plot this together."

"But I won't need you, Rob," she said quickly. "This time I can do it myself."

He fell silent, studying her face so closely that her cheeks warmed with a guilty heat.

"You'll do what you must, Jenny," he said finally, "the way I always have for you. That's the way we Dells are, aren't we? You'll do it for us both."

Brant stood at the open widow to his bedchamber, staring out at the moon and the faint stars around it. There was too much of a haze in the sky for true stargazing, but at this time of the night, it was often his habit to look up into the sky, whether the sky cooperated or not. It was his way of clearing his thoughts, of emptying his head of the last scraps of one day before he turned to his bed and prepared for the next—in the same fashion, he supposed, that other men would find solace in a favorite book kept by their pillow for the purpose. Robbed of the comfort of reading, Brant looked to the heavens, breathing deeply of the night air that drifted in through the open window.

Think of the stars and clouds, he ordered himself. *Of how the starlight shines through the shifting blue to change and meld.*

*Think of that, think of that, and not of the girl, how
her blue eyes had brightened while you talked, how unconsciously she'd tugged on that curl and licked her lips
as she'd leaned across your desk toward you, how the
breeze had blown the sheer pink cloth of her gown over
the full curve of her hip. Think instead of the sky and
the stars, and forget her impulsive, impetuous challenge
to be boring....*

Yet when the knock came on the door, his first
thought was of her, that she'd come to him again. He
didn't turn, unwilling to let her see the longing that must
surely be on his face.

"Forgive me for disturbing, Your Grace," came
Tway's even voice, instead. "But you said you wished
to be told of any news as soon as possible."

"So what news is it this time, Tway?" he said wearily, dropping into an armchair beneath the weight of his
foolish disappointment. "How can you possibly top the
Wicked Widow of Bamfleigh?"

"You asked to be notified at once of anything unusual
on your lands, Your Grace," said Tway, managing to be
both dogged and wounded. "One of the footmen was
awake with a toothache and happened to see Miss Corinthia in the garden, not an hour past."

At once Brant thought of how he'd met her on the
terrace in the moonlight. If only he'd looked down at
the path and not up at the stars, he might have seen her
again tonight.

"That's not unusual for her," he said. "She seems to
sleep as seldom as I, and I've come across her out walking myself."

"Yes, Your Grace." Tway hesitated, but only briefly.
"The footman said he thought she'd been meeting with
someone else."

Brant's finger tightened around the arm of the chair. "Did this damned footman see who it was?"

"No, Your Grace. He saw no one, but he believed he heard voices, a heated exchange, and when he saw the lady, he thought she seemed distraught."

"He *thought,* he *believed,* she *seemed.*" Brant forced himself to relax. Damnation, she wasn't meeting anyone else, not in his gardens. She simply wasn't the kind of woman who was sweet on the outside, but rotten with deceit. "Those are not the kind of words to assure me, Tway."

"No, Your Grace." This time Tway gave a small half nod, as close as he would come to a shrug of resignation. "But because the man is reliable and his words seemed true, and you did ask to be notified of any—"

"You don't like her, Tway, do you?"

Tway's impassive expression didn't vary. "It is not my place to have an opinion about the lady, Your Grace."

"Ever the diplomat, Tway," said Brant impatiently. "The king should send you to settle things with the damned French."

"Thank you, Your Grace." He bowed again. "But one thing I have learned in your service, Your Grace, is that things, and people, are often in truth not as they appear to be."

"Meaning Miss Corinthia?"

"Meaning any of us, Your Grace," he said evenly. "We are none of always the same, or even what others might believe us to be. I have told you everything the footman told me, Your Grace. If it pleases you, I shall leave you to your rest."

Only the oldest and most trusted of servants would dare presume to dismiss himself like this, and only the oldest and most trusted would dare offer such a warning to his master.

But Brant understood. He understood everything.

"Leave, Tway," he said softly, "and leave me to myself."

Chapter Eight

The next morning Jenny rose early, or at least early for her. Mrs. Lowe had told her that Brant took his breakfast then, in the small back parlor overlooking the garden. Jenny was determined to join him there, not only because she wished to, but as a way to make up for avoiding him for the last two meals. If she was ever going to be able to balance her brother's wishes with her own dreams regarding Brant—a dangerously swaying tightrope if ever there was one—then it was best for her to begin now.

Without waiting for a servant to help her, she dressed quickly in another of the new gowns, this one pale yellow with tiny green leaves scattered across it and green ribbon pleated into a ruffle around the low, round neckline. She dressed her hair herself, twisting it into a loose knot at the back of her head. As elegant as her hair had been yesterday when one of the servants had arranged and curled it for her, she'd realized that Brant preferred something more simple. She'd thought a duke would like a lady to look grand and fashionable, but then again, Brant wasn't an ordinary duke. She'd only to remember how he'd touched her hair, tangling his fingers in it and teasing the skin on her throat until she'd shivered with pleasure—oh, she'd understood then, hadn't she?

She hurried down the stairs, the small heels of her kidskin slippers clicking on the marble. Nervously she plucked at the green ruffle around the deep, rounded neckline, then lifted her head high and straightened her back, forcing her restless hand to still into graceful, calm repose—the hand of a lady, not an adventuress. No matter how uncertain she was feeling inside, no matter how her brother's words were haunting her, she didn't want Brant to see it in her face or posture.

You can do this, Jenny, you can. You can do anything you want, as long as you keep your head clear and your wits about you.

She could hear the muffled clink of silverware against the china through the open door of the little parlor, the slight scrape of a cup settling into a saucer. This would be how he started each day, with tea or coffee and eggs and a chop and toasted bread, most likely reading his letters or a paper with the latest news and gossip brought down from London, exactly the same as other gentlemen. She knew how he treasured his solitude; she'd hoped he wouldn't reject her company. She made herself relax, smiled, and swept into the doorway in a flutter of ruffles.

"Good day, Brant," she murmured, her pleasure almost achingly genuine at seeing him once again. How could she miss someone so much that she'd only known for a handful of days? He was sitting alone at the head of a long table, dressed in a buff-colored frock coat for riding, and from his instant, delighted smile when he saw her and rose to his feet, she knew she'd been right to join him.

"You've come," he said softly, simple words filled with rich anticipation.

The low morning sun slanting in through the window behind him burnished his golden hair like a bright halo—a halo that was very much at odds with the way he was quite frankly appraising her in the new gown. She hadn't needed her brother to tell her to leave out the modest linen kerchief the mantua-maker had used to fill in the low neckline. Duke or not, Brant was first a man, and men generally did not respond to subtlety in women's dress. Now the green ruffles framed only her palest skin along her throat and the tops of her breasts, and Brant's expression was all she needed to know she'd made the right decision.

"Of course I've come," she said, making an impulsive, mischievous little pirouette, instead of a more proper curtsy. "Breakfast and your company. What more could any lady desire on a June morn?"

"What, indeed?" he asked lightly in return. "Perhaps you can explain as much to Mrs. Potter."

His smile shifted past Jenny to the other end of the long table where she hadn't bothered to look herself. Now she did, and belatedly saw the other woman, sitting stiffly across from Brant and clearly ill at ease. She was not much older than Jenny herself, but that would be all they would have in common. Jenny could tell that instantly. The woman's face was wide and ruddy, her sandy hair barely showing beneath an old-fashioned cap, and her thick-waisted body was obviously restrained by the tight-laced stays that had gone from style years ago. A prosperous farmer's wife, perhaps, or a merchant's, but of the middling sort and definitely not a woman accustomed to sitting at a duke's breakfast table.

But what Jenny noticed first was the woman's disapproval, so strong that Jenny felt it like a tangible force in the room. She disapproved of Jenny, and of Brant, and most especially of them together.

So why, then, was she here, with an untouched dish of tea before her?

"Corinthia," continued Brant. "Let me introduce you to Mrs. Reverend Potter. Her husband is the rector of St. Martin's, not a stone's throw from here. Mrs. Potter, Miss Corinthia."

From the doorway Jenny smiled warily, unsure of what her role was to be in this odd setting. Mrs. Potter merely nodded, unwilling to grant her one iota more of respect than she was entitled to receive—which, with no last name and only a "miss" before the first, wasn't much.

The wife of the rector of St. Martin's. That explained the disapproval readily enough. She was a Good Woman, and what little experience Jenny had with Good Women had not been very pleasant, considering that, in most peoples' judgment, she herself was substantially more Bad than Good.

Jenny dolefully studied the stiff-backed woman and self-consciously tugged the green ruffles a bit higher over her breasts. Could this be the same minister's helpmate who'd wished to take her away from Claremont Hall to preserve her virtue and honor? How quickly Jenny would have regained her memory with such a stern and *Good* Woman to oversee her welfare!

"Mrs. Potter has come calling from concern for you," continued Brant. "She and Reverend Potter are among my most loyal friends here in this parish, and they believe that your situation here at Claremont Hall does not present either you or me in the best light."

"It's the talk, Your Grace," said Mrs. Potter, nodding

urgently. "It's gone beyond the parish, you know, all through the county. Such slander poor Daniel has heard said aloud of you, Your Grace, from most humble cottages to the squire's own parlor."

Nonplussed, Brant smiled politely. "Then those people in their cottages and parlors are in sore need of more interesting topics for discussion than my tedious private life."

"But, Your Grace, you must consider the consequences!" pleaded Mrs. Potter. "Your good works, your kindness and generosity are being forgotten because of...of—"

She didn't have to finish. Jenny knew that she, the Almost-Bad Woman in the doorway, was the reason. She'd never intended to hurt Brant or his good name. But what she couldn't understand was how her lowly self could cause so much havoc to the reputation of an unmarried peer without even trying?

And clearly Brant felt the same. "So all is forgotten because my charity and generosity happened to include this young lady so desperately in need of it," he said wryly. "If only she had been an ancient widow, or a little child, or even a stray dog, anything to keep her safe from my ravening desires!"

"His Grace is not like that, Mrs. Potter," said Jenny warmly, jumping to Brant's defense. "Not at all."

Brant beamed. "No, I am not. I am glad you realize that, Miss Corinthia. Here now, sit by me," he said to Jenny, pointing to the empty chair beside him. "Ask for whatever you please and they'll fetch it from the kitchen for you."

At once one of the footmen—how had Jenny overlooked the pair of them, as well?—stepped forward with silverware and a napkin to set her place.

"Tea will be sufficient, Your Grace, thank you," she said as a footman filled her cup. She hadn't needed any prompting to revert back to using Brant's title; the situation was already beyond awkward. "I'm seldom hungry so soon after rising."

"You should be, miss," declared Mrs. Potter. "That's why you're such a tiny mite, scarce more than a bird. You must fortify yourself for the new day. She'll never remember a thing, Your Grace, until she starts feeding herself proper."

"But I've always been this way, Mrs. Potter," protested Jenny. "It shall make no difference whether I am hungry this particular morning or not."

"Overdainty, miss," said Mrs. Potter darkly. "That's the fashion in London, they say, great ladies risking mortal death so's they will look fine in those scanty gowns."

"But I never have been a large woman," said Jenny indignantly, "nor shall I be, and I do believe it's rather rude of you to advise me like this on such a personal matter."

Mrs. Potter scowled beneath the starched brim of her cap. "I only ask from concern for your health, miss, same as any kindly lady would, and because I know how His Grace is so worried over you."

She sniffed, her way of indicating that His Grace would be better served by placing those worries elsewhere. "But here you've been saying you couldn't recall a scrap of who you are, and yet now you're sure you've always been such and such a way and such and such a size, and I ask you, miss, how can you be so certain if you don't remember?"

"Because she says so, ma'am," answered Brant firmly, finally, leaving no opening for further discussion. "She doesn't have to remember how she was in the cradle, you know. She only need look at the delicacy of her bones to realize she's never been large.''

Mrs. Potter sniffed again, a sniff that this time conveyed her unhappiness with his argument and made Jenny feel another step closer to Bad than Good.

But Brant ignored it all. ''Nor does Miss Corinthia appear to be wasting away for want of food,'' he continued serenely. ''To me she seems quite perfect as she is, wanting no more and no less.''

Jenny gulped her tea from surprise, stopping just short of ungracefully snuffling it up her nose.

Oh, my, he should not be saying such things to her, not in this woman's hearing!

He smiled at her, and she blushed furiously. How could she help it when he looked at her like that?

''You are too kind, Your Grace,'' she managed to say, ''even if you are not being entirely truthful.''

''I tell the truth as I see it,'' he said, his smile widening to an unabashed grin. ''Not as a matter of opinion, but of purest fact.''

''Fact as you see it, Your Grace,'' she answered quickly, ''and truth as you wish it to be, not as in reality it is.''

He chuckled. ''You need no improvements, Miss Corinthia, and that *is* the truth.''

''Thank you, Your Grace,'' she said, the only possible reply left to such flirtatious tomfoolery. Men had often said this kind of nonsense to her before, but they'd never given her such pleasure, nor reduced her to such giddy confusion as Brant's particular nonsense effortlessly seemed able to do.

But then this was more than simple flattery. Despite her blushes, Jenny understood that, too, without another word being spoken aloud between them. He was challenging her to share this peculiar situation with him, to accept that their names were being linked together in the county gossip, the same as she'd challenged him yesterday over his piles of calculations, wanting him to share with her his interests, and therefore himself. As strange as this breakfast was, he was making it clear that they would muddle through it together.

Together. A simple enough word, but one that, for her, seemed to hold a fresh new excitement to it. She'd never done anything *together* with any other man—saving Rob, of course, but since he was her brother, he didn't count.

Together with Brant, and she smiled at him to show she understood.

Almost forgotten, Mrs. Potter loudly cleared her throat.

"As you wish, Your Grace," she said, her frustration evident in every word. "I see that I am too late. Daniel warned me it was so, Your Grace, but I did hope. I came here wanting to help you and this young lady, but I cannot force you to change if you do not wish to do so."

"Oh, ma'am," said Brant sympathetically. Despite how he was openly flirting with Jenny, it was clear enough to her that he bore Mrs. Potter no ill will; in fact, she'd guess that he was rather fond of the woman, and her husband, too.

"To my mind," he continued, "there is nothing *to* change. While I appreciated your kind offer to open your home to this lady, I did tell you before that she was doing well enough here, as you can see with your own eyes."

"What I see, Your Grace, is something else altogether," said Mrs. Potter sternly, pushing her chair back from the table to stand and leave. "What I see is that you have made a—a *plaything* of this unfortunate young woman, for your own amusement!''

At once Brant rose, too, tossing his crumpled napkin on the table. ''Dam—that is, that's not right, ma'am,'' he growled self-consciously, ''not at all, not when—''

''Ask me,'' interrupted Jenny. If they were to face this together, then she couldn't sit by meekly, the worthless little bird that Mrs. Potter had judged her to be. She must speak for herself, and for Brant. ''Instead of asking His Grace how he has treated me, pray, ask me.''

That made Mrs. Potter blink, which in turn pleased Jenny. It was satisfying to know she hadn't lost her gift for surprising others, for keeping them off balance. Bluffing was always a most useful talent.

''Leastways you know I shall tell you the truth, Mrs. Potter,'' Jenny continued, her smile as charming as she could make it. ''Then you and Reverend Potter can in turn tell my version to whomever you please to help counter the scandal.''

Mrs. Potter looked from Jenny to Brant and back again, clearly trying to decide whether to accept her offer or not.

''Go ahead, ma'am,'' said Brant, obviously more entertained than he'd any right to be. ''We can end this nonsense once and for all. Ask her whatever you please, and I'm certain she'll give you the dev—ah, God's own truth. I'll even leave you two alone, if that will make you happier.''

Jenny looked quickly toward Brant, wondering if he truly intended to abandon her. But Mrs. Potter had already seized upon his offer and was nodding vigorously.

''If you do not mind overmuch, Your Grace,'' she said, ''I would appreciate speaking with the young lady in confidence.''

"Very well, then," he said, a bit surprised himself. "Have your hen chatter. Besides, I'm sure Tway is already lying in wait for me. Mrs. Potter, good day."

And as quick as that, he was gone, and Jenny was left standing squarely before Mrs. Potter, face-to-face. The charming smile was much harder to maintain now without Brant there to inspire her; she'd always done much better with gentlemen than other women, anyway.

But how hard could this be? she asked herself. She had seen so much more of the world—she had visited all the grandest cities and sights of the Continent!—than this country parson's wife that she must surely be more clever, more quick. She'd been raised a lady, hadn't she? She could judge fine wines and French suppers, good paintings from bad. Her skin was flawlessly pale, her hair curled into ringlets on its own, and she was wearing an elegant new gown, given her by a duke, that likely cost more than Mrs. Potter's entire functional wardrobe, and her husband's, too. If all that wasn't enough to give her confidence, why, then she wasn't worthy of being Miss Jenny Dell?

"So, ma'am," she began briskly. She didn't sit, for she'd no intention of lingering here any longer than was absolutely necessary. "As you can see, His Grace has been the kindest of hosts to me in my—in my confusion. You know he found me himself, when I was lying insensible beneath a tree. I owe him my very life, Mrs. Potter, and I'd never—"

"What favors has he asked of you in return, miss?" asked Mrs. Potter earnestly. "How has he expected you to pay back what you owe him?"

Jenny had expected that question, though the righteous condemnation she'd expected, too, was missing.

"His Grace has asked for no favors in exchange for his generosity."

"Likely that is true, now that I consider it," said the other woman slowly. "Being a great lord and all. Likely, His Grace doesn't have to ask for much, does he?"

"No, ma'am," said Jenny cautiously. "I expect in London he has his pick of the ladies."

"Oh, I expect he does," agreed Mrs. Potter quickly. "I expect you do, too, wherever you've come from, a fair young lady like you. How hard it must be for you, forgetting everything like you have, your poor head empty as a broken eggshell!"

A broken eggshell was certainly not the analogy that Jenny would have chosen herself, but as she looked down at the other woman's work-roughened hands, she could easily imagine those same hands cracking and beating the eggs for a yellow cake, a treat to grace her husband's dinner, a cozy time for the two of them alone before their hearth fire. No, for their children, too, for surely Mrs. Potter had earned her thickened waist honorably. How many in the Potter family? wondered Jenny. Boys or girls or both?

Where is your mind wandering, Jenny, my girl? You've never been one to coo over babies, or long to wipe the gruel and pudding from their sticky chins. What could turn your thoughts to such sentimental drivel now?

"The hardest part must be having no recollections of your family," continued Mrs. Potter, her sympathy warm and genuine as she spoke of things she understood. "To have no happy thoughts of your home for comfort—ah, miss, how hard that must be for you!"

"It is," said Jenny softly. "It is."

Stop, Jen, stop this at once! The woman's speaking of Corinthia, not of you. She cannot know you've never had

*any home of your own to speak of, no special place
waiting at the end of your travels. She wouldn't understand about Father or even Rob, and she'd never believe
that Mama had abandoned her husband and babies in
gloomy Dublin and run off with another actor to the
always-shining sun of the West Indies, leaving not so
much as a ghost of a memory for her daughter to cher-
ish....*

Mrs. Potter reached out to pat Jenny's arm. "That's
a big hole left inside you, miss, a spot that's aching to
be filled with all the love and kindness that you can't
remember. That's only right, miss. But what's wrongful
is if you're mistaking His Grace's kindness for the sort
that you've forgotten."

Jenny looked up sharply. "You're listening to the gossips yourself, aren't you?" She turned away, pointedly
slipping her arm from the other woman's hand. "There's
nothing wrong with the regard that His Grace and I share
for one another."

Mrs. Potter sighed and shook her head. "Isn't there
now? Not an hour past, I watched how His Grace looked
at you in that strumpety gown he's bought you, and you
making calf's eyes back at him. His Grace is a great
lord, but in his breeches he's the same as any other man.
He'll ruin you, miss, sure as anything, but the worst sin
will be that you didn't save yourself when you could."

"You've listened to too many sermons, ma'am, finding sin where there's none." Jenny forced herself to
laugh, to prove how little effect such talk had upon her,
but the sound, instead came out miserably hollow and
unmerry.

*Jen, Jen, listen to your head, not your heart! Be
strong, not weak! Remember how many times Rob has
suffered for such foolishness, or remember the troubles*

that inevitably followed each new time poor Father imagined himself in love!

"His Grace won't marry you, even if you lie with him." Mrs. Potter's voice was urgent, relentless, determined to make her point. "His Grace will always be kind and generous because that is his way, and he would provide for any bastard child you conceive between you, but he'll never marry you, any more than he'll wed any of those ladies in London."

"I never expected him to," said Jenny, and that much was true. She never dare such a dream for herself, not with a man like Brant.

"That's one bit of sense, then." Mrs. Potter nodded grimly. "Rank and birth matters to such as His Grace. He's worked too hard to come back from his father's shame to settle for anyone less grand than himself. You're pretty and genteel enough to tempt him to take you to bed, but you're not his equal, and he'd never make you his wife."

"You don't know that," said Jenny defensively. "You don't know who I am, any more than I do myself!"

"I know you're no peer's daughter, nor wife, nor sister, neither," answered Mrs. Potter firmly. "If you was, the outcry across this country would have been so great you'd be claimed by now. But not one person's come asking after you, miss, not one, let alone any other great lord. I do not mean to be cruel, miss, but that's the honest truth, no mistake."

There was no good answer to that, and Jenny didn't try. If this plainspoken country woman had figured this bit of impeccable logic for herself, then no doubt Brant had, too. How much longer would Jenny have here at

Claremont Hall before he'd tire of her and send her away and out of his life forever?

But Mrs. Potter misinterpreted her silence for contrition, as if she'd already won the battle for Jenny's wavering soul.

"Come with me, miss," she urged softly, the motherly hand returning to Jenny's arm, "back home to St. Martin's. It's not so grand as the Hall, but you'll be safe and snug. Here there's only certain grief and heartbreak, miss, wishing after him you can't have. Come with me, miss, and behave like the true lady you are by birth. Save yourself and your good name, before it's too late."

But Jenny was no true lady any more than she'd a home of her own, and she'd no real name to squander, let alone a good one. All she could claim was her own small person and her wits, and the few days left to her in the glow of Brant's smile and generosity. Then she would be gone again, leaving before he could tire of her. One night she'd simply melt away with Rob over the next hill and out of Brant's life forever.

Gently, Mrs. Potter shifted her hand from Jenny's arm to her hand to lead her away. "Come, miss," she coaxed. "Come home with me."

But Jenny pulled her hand away, holding it in the other almost as if it had been burned. "No—no, thank you, ma'am," she said. "Thank you, no, but that's not the way for me."

Before Mrs. Potter could try again, Jenny fled, running down the echoing, empty hall. In the space of a few hours she'd heard one argument for her to become Brant's mistress as the only proper thing to do, and now had come the opposite warning: that sharing his bed could lead only to heartache and ruin. As her misery grew, she'd listened to both yet agreed to neither.

But now Jenny realized there was only one other person whose opinion truly mattered, the one who could make her think straight for herself. That, of course, was Brant, and she wanted—*needed*—to find him as fast as she possibly could, with all the urgency of a sinking boat struggling to reach a safe shore.

She'd expected him to be at his desk, but to her surprise, the room was empty, the piles of papers so neatly arranged she knew he'd yet to be there this morning. Trying not to panic, she hurried up the stairs to his bedchamber, guessing that he'd gone to the dressing room to change from his riding clothes, but those rooms, too, were empty, except for a parlor maid sweeping the already-immaculate floor.

"Is it His Grace you be wanting, miss?" asked the girl as she dipped her curtsy, broom in hand like a straw-bottomed partner. "He be out with them dogs, miss, on the lawn beyond the folly."

With a hasty thanks, Jenny was off, racing down the stairs and through the garden door toward the folly and the sounds of the two dogs barking. The folly was exactly that, a tiny whitewashed indulgence of a structure, a perfectly proportioned Ionic temple in miniature surrounded incongruously by English ivy. Jenny hurried along the path and up the little hill to the temple, pausing on the porch between two columns only to catch her breath.

Brant's hat and coat lay across the steps where he'd shed them. In his shirtsleeves, he was racing back and forth across the green lawn with an energy that matched Jetty and Gus. Laughing, he'd hurl a length of leafless branch as far as he could for the dogs to retrieve, then try to worry the branch free from their happily growling jaws when they brought it back to him.

"Come back, you cheating rascal," he roared when Gus dropped the branch then snatched it away as Brant bent to pick it up. "Come back here, I say!"

But the dog darted away, taunting his master just as his master had been taunting him, running loping circles around Brant while Jetty barked encouragement. Suddenly, Gus spied Jenny at the top of the folly's steps and in three leaping bounds he brought the branch to her, dropping the slobbery tribute on the kidskin toes of her slippers.

"You found us, lass!" Laughing, Brant followed the dog to join her, his billowing shirt untucked and grass-stained, his hair damp around his forehead, his grin irresistible. "Swear you won't tell Tway I'm here, or we'll never have any peace."

But it wasn't peace that Jenny sought, not now, and with a little sob she hopped over Gus' branch offering and ran down the last two steps to meet him. She flung her arms around his waist and, taking advantage of the extra height from the step, she leaned forward, closed her eyes and kissed him.

She could sense his surprise even with her eyes shut, and for a terrible instant she though she'd misjudged. But then she felt the his hands at her waist, pulling her closer, and his mouth slanting the exact measure over hers to deepen the kiss. With a shudder of relief, she parted her lips, striving to remember exactly how he'd kissed her before so she could do it back to him. For once she wished she'd more experience, for she wanted to be sure she did this right, to be able to give him at least the same amount of pleasure he'd given her.

Not that she'd much to say about it, anyway. The longer she kissed him, the less she seemed to think and the more she simply seemed to *respond* to him—the musky male scent of him mingled with the grass and warm sun, the feel of his muscles shifting beneath the slightly damp linen of his shirt, the tantalizing taste of his kiss, hot and hard and faintly laced with the coffee he'd had at breakfast. She felt sure she'd never have enough of him. How could she be content, knowing that this much might be all there'd be for the rest of her life?

"Ah, sweetheart," he whispered gruffly when their lips finally parted. "And a good morning to you, too. Whatever Mrs. Potter said to you, I hope she'll come say it every morning."

She tried to smile, and failed miserably, instead looking down at the golden stubble on his chin to avoid meeting his gaze. The dogs were waiting patiently beside them, the sound of their hopeful panting filling the awkward gap.

"She wished me to go back with her to her house," she said softly. "She wished me to leave here, that was all."

"That again?" he growled. "I'm glad to see she didn't change your mind."

And he kissed her again, a darker kiss on this sunny morning that stole away her breath and seemed to echo Mrs. Potter's gravest warnings.

This is your choice, Jen. Remember that. Not your brother's, or Mrs. Potter's, or even Brant's. This is your choice, for good or ill.

"What's this about, eh?" he said, his fingertips gliding over her cheek. "Why the tears, Corinthia?"

Your choice…for good, for ill, forever….

"Not Corinthia, Brant," she said, her voice breaking with the truth. "Jenny. My real name is Jenny."

Chapter Nine

"Jenny," Brant repeated slowly, carefully, as if making sure he wouldn't forget it, either. "Your real name is Jenny."

She nodded, another fat tear sliding down the curve of her cheek.

He took a deep breath, marveling at exactly how fast a perfect morning could go straight to hell. "You remembered this?"

She nodded again, and the tear dripped from her jaw to spot the front of her gown. "This morning, while I was with Mrs. Potter. It came into my head, just like that, and it felt *right,* the way Corinthia never did."

"Jenny." It did feel oddly right; he couldn't disagree. Jenny had the proper sprightliness to suit her.

But remembering even this much was the beginning to remembering everything else, and the end of her staying here with him. Was that the reason for that kiss, then? A farewell before she returned to her other life, a polite thank-you to him for charity rendered?

He sat back against the bench, purposefully trying to distance himself even that little bit from her. "So what's the rest of your name?"

She looked down at her lap, another tear following the trail of the first.

"I don't know," she said, her misery genuine. "I told you, the name popped into my head, but that was all. The rest is still missing—as 'empty as a broken eggshell,' said Mrs. Potter."

"Jenny." Nothing more than that. He frowned, struggling to feel sorry for her and not so selfishly overjoyed. But if she couldn't remember, she wouldn't leave. "Jenny, Miss Jenny."

"Yes." She glanced up, a wobbly smile through the tears. "Hearing you speak it in your voice, I *know* it's mine."

"I don't know whether that's a compliment or not." He let his arm slip back around her shoulders, and she let it stay there, as if it belonged. "Jenny, oh, Jenny. I never did like Corinthia. Corinthia always sounded like a stout elderly aunt wearing scratchy lace and too much lavender scent."

The wobbly smile gave way to a small chuckle, just as he'd hoped. "Did you have an Aunt Corinthia like that?"

"No, but an Aunt Augusta, which was much the same," he said. "A grim-faced harridan who'd sweep in from the north, demanding forced kisses from her terrified young nephews. My brothers and I always looked for her broom in the stable, certain that was how she must travel, instead of in a lowly coach."

She chuckled again, a warm, happy sound that made him happy, too. This wasn't as fine as kissing her had been, but it was certainly pleasant enough, having her nestled here beneath his arm. Though the tears seemed done, it now seemed safe to acknowledge them, and he pulled out his handkerchief and passed it to her.

"She couldn't have been that bad, Brant." She dabbed at the corners of her eyes and sniffled back the rest of the unshed tears. Weeping had made her nose as red as a small strawberry, but it had also magically turned her eyes a brilliant blue, her black lashes as spiky as beaded stars, and he considered the trade a worthwhile one. "Likely you just remember her that way because you were so young."

"Oh, Aunt Augusta was that bad," he answered solemnly. "You can ask either Rev or George, and they'll tell you the same. We drew lots to see who'd have to kiss her first. She used far too much paint, so her cheek was bitter to kiss, and so much powder drifted from her hair that we'd always sneeze, too. But I expect you had an aunt like that, as well. Everyone does."

Her smile faded. "I don't know. I suppose I did."

Damnation, why hadn't he recalled that she couldn't remember? "I'm sorry, Jenny, I shouldn't have—"

"Hush." She twisted around to face him, pressing her fingertips across his lips to stop him. She was also pressing her breasts against his chest, a soft, warm weight through the thin linen of his shirt that silenced him much more effectively. Automatically his hand settled on the small of her back to keep her there, his fingers spreading possessively. "For all you claim this Aunt Augusta was a witch, I can completely understand her wishing to kiss you."

"Oh, but she didn't want to kiss me," he said, his voice sinking deeper. "All she wanted was for me to kiss *her.*"

"Ah," said Jenny softly, settling more closely against him, her mouth so close to his he could feel the little breath of that *ah* on his own lips. "I can sympathize with that, too."

The shifted slightly again, just enough to make him groan as the soft curve of her hip wriggled over the front of his breeches and the hard proof of his interest directly beneath it.

She might not remember, but she sure as hell *understood*.

"Tell me, Brant," she whispered with another of those husky chuckles. "Exactly how did she make you oblige and kiss her?"

"How?" he croaked, the demands of his body turning his head to overcooked mush. "With sweetmeats. She, ah, bribed us with sweetmeats."

"Sweetmeats?" she repeated, her eye widening with incredulous delight at the word. "Oh, Brant, I don't believe I have any—"

"Then think of something else, Jenny," he ordered hoarsely, pulling her mouth down onto his. "Or don't think at all."

If she didn't think, then at least they'd be equal. He seemed to have stopped thinking altogether, or rather to have stopped thinking of anything else other than her: how he could taste her hunger in the heated depths of her mouth, how he could feel the hard crests of her breasts against his chest, how he could hear her startled little moans of wanting lost between them in their kiss.

She twisted again, agile as a kitten, and slipped her arms around the back of his neck. That was easy enough to fathom. But how she'd somehow come to have her legs tucked up and her thighs astride his was more than he could comprehend or question. His hand slid away from her back and pulled her skirts higher, instinctively finding the bare skin of her thigh above her garter.

Higher, higher he roamed, far enough to discover she had yet to adopt the prudish new fashion for women's underdrawers, and higher still to find her wet and ready and open. He touched her gently, stroking her, and she shuddered and lurched against him, whimpering with frustration.

Another blind tug and he'd pulled those green ruffles clear of her breasts, her nipples rising up dark pink and eager to be kissed. Of course he obliged, without any bribery necessary, and felt her shiver with pleasure.

"I don't care what they say," she gasped. "This— this cannot be wrong, Brant, not for us!"

"No, lass," he grunted, not really giving it any further thought. That was the sort of thing women always said at moments like this, great-romantic-our-passion-is-bigger-than-the-world nonsense. As a man, he'd other more important matters to consider, such as why the devil he was having such trouble unfastening the buttons on the fall of his trousers.

And why Jetty and Gus had suddenly flown back to hysterical life, barking and yapping and yowling and growling and charging up and down the steps of the folly like the very hounds from hell.

Which was exactly where they'd be bound if they didn't stop their racketing this instant.

"Jetty, Gus, quiet!" he roared. "Down, now, both of you!"

But the dogs didn't obey, let alone stop, and worse yet, Jenny was making odd noises of her own, not the charming moans and cries, but worried, startled noises as she pushed away from him, frantically pulling her clothes back into place.

"Jenny, lass, Jenny, please!" he called, trying vainly to bring her back to him on the bench. What was the use of knowing her real name if this was all it brought him?

"Brant, look, it's Tway!" she whispered urgently, shoving the damp tangle of her hair back from her flushed face. "I thought you said he'd never find you here!"

Brant looked toward where she was pointing and swore. There on the grassy lawn from the Hall in fact did stand a stern-faced Tway, holding a folded paper high overhead to keep it from the reach of the two black dogs dancing a circle around him.

"Oh, hell," said Brant grimly, his finger turning as clumsy buttoning his trousers as they'd been undoing them. "Hell, hell, *hell.*"

Jenny was standing in the middle of the folly—he'd never look at this place again without thinking how aptly it had been named for today—her gown guiltily rumpled and creased and her palm pressed over her mouth. How beautiful she was, he marveled with fresh frustration, and how blasted close he'd come to making her his!

No wonder it took him another entire moment to realize that, behind her hand, she was laughing.

"I'm glad you find this all so damned amusing," he fumed, raking his hair back with his fingers.

She turned toward him, the sunlight seeming to dance about her graceful, disheveled figure.

"Oh, Brant, but it *is* amusing," she said, her eyes merry and her mouth still wantonly red from his kisses. "There is poor Mr. Tway, being good and hunting you down relentlessly when you tried to hide, exactly as he's supposed to, only to have your dogs hunt him down like a rabbit, while here we were, being—"

"Bad?" he supplied, shoving his untucked shirt back into his breeches. "Not half as bad as I wished to be, lass."

"Oh, not bad, Brant," she said. "I thought, instead, we were together vastly…*good.*"

She grinned so impishly, curling a stray curl around her ear, that he almost—*almost*—was willing to laugh with her. Had she any notion of her effect upon him? No, he could answer that for himself: of course she did, which was why he was finding it, and her, so enticing. He was definitely, painfully still hard, and all her talk about being bad wasn't helping that matter one whit. He grumbled, rubbing his hand along his jaw.

Damnation, he could still smell her scent on his fingers.…

"Your Grace," called Tway plaintively. "If you could please but summon your dogs, Your Grace."

With another oath Brant stalked down the folly steps to rescue Tway.

"Jetty, Gus, down," he ordered crossly. "Down now, I say!"

The dogs could hear his crossness, and for once they instantly obeyed, slinking away from Tway with their tails drooping between their back legs, and looking wistfully back at Brant with contrite longing.

But Brant had already turned his attention to Tway, who was in turn demonstrating his own share of contrition.

"Forgive me for intruding, Your Grace," he began, so pointedly not looking back at Jenny and the folly that he made it worse, not better. "But you said to find you at once with any news, and I'd no notion you were, ah, you were engaged in such—"

"Blast it, Tway, just tell me your news!"

"Yes, Your Grace." Tway cleared his throat as he unfolded the paper he'd brought with him, holding it up to read aloud like a medieval crier.

"You don't have to read it to me," said Brant quickly, taking the sheet from him. He knew Jenny must be watching, and the last thing he wished was for her to guess his secret like this. "It's another poisonous letter, isn't it?"

"It came this morning, Your Grace," said Tway. "Not by the regular post, but tucked inside one of the London papers, where I discovered it."

"So of course no one saw the sender this time, either, despite my orders." He frowned down at the single sheet, the paper and ink the same as before, the message equally brief. The sender had to be clever and quick to be able to slip the letter past his small army of servants. "I assume, too, that the content hasn't changed?"

Tway sighed. "It's the same sort of vile insult directed toward the lady and yourself, Your Grace, though this time there is a definite threat included."

Brant shook his head. There was a world of difference between self-righteous name-calling and threatening harm. "What's the coward threatening to do to us?"

"Nothing is specified, Your Grace. Merely that you and the lady will suffer if you do not change your ways."

"Whatever the hell that means." The ease with which this person had gotten letters into his household worried him nearly as much as the blind hate that filled them.

Yet Claremont Hall was hardly a fortress. This was Sussex in the nineteenth century, after all, and Brant, before now, had never considered it necessary to secure his rambling property from invasion. Oh, there was a gatehouse and a fence that surrounded the lands closest to the house, but any enterprising villain would have little problem entering over the fence and then hiding away among the gardens and outbuildings for as long as he or she pleased. He wasn't concerned overmuch with his own safety—even if he hadn't been born with a peer's supreme sense of invulnerability, he was seldom out-of-doors without the company of the two large dogs—but when he thought of Jenny, his blood turned chill.

"If you please, Your Grace," suggested Tway, "it might be time to show the letters to the magistrate for his opinion."

"And what in blazes would he do? Come bumbling about here, asking foolish questions and setting everyone to seeing ghosts and murderers, and for what purpose?" Brant frowned as he handed the letter back to Tway. "No magistrate. Not yet, anyway. But I promised the lady she'd be safe here as long as she needed a sanctuary, and I intend to see that she does."

"Yes, Your Grace." Tway paused, obviously weighing his next words with care. "And as before, Miss Corinthia is not to be told of the letter or its contents?"

"Miss Jenny," corrected Brant absently, his thoughts elsewhere. "She finally recalled her true given name this morning, exactly as Gristead predicted she would, and it's Jenny, not Corinthia."

"Jenny?" Tway couldn't mask his surprise. "What of the name stitched into her handkerchief, Your Grace?"

"A memento from a sister, perhaps, or her mother or friend. Even an aunt." Brant thought of how he and Jenny had bantered about his own aunt Augusta, and how innocent that now seemed in comparison to this. "It hardly matters now."

He shaded his eyes with his hand and looked back to the folly. Flanked by the two dogs, Jenny was sitting on the top step, between the two pillars. Her arms hugged her bent knees with her fingers linked tightly together, like an impatient child's, and she'd smoothed her rumpled skirts tight over her knees so just the tips of her slippers peeked out from beneath the green-ruffled hem. She caught his eye and smiled with such genuine delight that he felt the joyful warmth of it clear across the lawn.

He smiled in return. He couldn't help it. So what if she'd laughed before? She hadn't been laughing at *him*, after all, only at their shared misadventure. His smile widened, remembering their own folly in the folly, and as he did he felt an unfamiliarly expansive glow growing somewhere deep inside of him. He wasn't exactly sure what the feeling was, but he did realize it had to do with Jenny.

How in blazes had this elf-eyed little woman with the unknown past come to mean so much to him in such a short time? She'd turned his orderly life upside down, she made him laugh over next to nothing, and she made him forget the endless weight of his responsibilities, along with all the tidy rules by which he usually ordered his life. He didn't know why or how it had happened, and he couldn't imagine how much longer it would last.

But for this moment he did know what he'd do to protect her.

"I've changed my mind about going to London, Tway," he announced. "Tell the coachman that I intend to leave tomorrow morning, instead of next week."

He didn't wait for Tway's sputtering reply, which would be that such a hasty departure wasn't possible, just as he was equally certain that, once Tway had calmed himself, he'd do whatever was necessary to have the baggage cart packed, the servants dressed in their livery, the horses groomed and in their traces, and the traveling coach waiting before the front door tomorrow morning.

"Jenny, lass," he said as he bounded up the folly steps to join her. "You knew I'd planned to go to London next week, to meet with the investors regarding my Virginian venture. But I've changed my mind, and shall leave tomorrow, instead."

"Tomorrow?" She gazed up at him, squinting into the sun, and her happiness faltered visibly. "Truly, Brant?"

"Tomorrow, truly," he said. "It won't be a difficult journey. The roads should be dry enough by now."

He dropped down on the step beside her, his legs stretched out before him. He considered reaching out to take her hand, but the way she kept hugging her knees, instead of him, was, well, *discouraging*. Whatever hopes he might have harbored about returning to the shadows of the folly with her seemed doomed, and with real regret he considered once again how differently women regarded such opportunities than men.

"Gemini." She was blinking her eyes very fast, which made Brant wonder uneasily if she were going to begin weeping again. "I thought we'd been happy here, Brant. I thought we'd been happy together."

"We have been," he said evenly, for as far as he was concerned, it was a simple matter of fact. "Now we'll be happy in London, as well."

She stared at him, incredulous. "You wish me to come with you? Clear to London?"

"Of course I wish you to come with me, sweetheart," he said. "And I've no intention of abandoning you in some stableyard halfway there, either."

"Ah," she said softly, not the reaction he'd expected

or wanted. Most ladies were mad to go to London, with all its shops and amusements. "London."

He began ruffling Jetty's ears, making the dog growl with tail-thumping ecstasy. Dogs were easier than women; you always knew where you stood with a dog.

"Claremont House is on the north corner of Grosvenor Square," he said, mainly because he needed to say something. "It's not so big as the Hall, being a town house, but I think you'll find it tolerable enough."

"If it's yours, Brant, I'm sure it's one of the most elegant houses in London. You wouldn't have anything less." She gave her shoulders a little shrug and tried to smile. "But couldn't we stay here another few days, Brant? London seems so large and vast compared to here, especially with my head still so…so confused."

"I don't think that's possible." Now he did take her hand, sliding along the step to sit more closely beside her. He hadn't planned on telling her about the letter, not wanting to upset her, but now it seemed better that she know the truth, or at least part of it.

"I don't wish to frighten you, Jenny," he began, "but since you've been staying here, there has been talk."

"Just as Mrs. Potter said," she said, wrinkling her nose. "You know, I should rather be surprised if there weren't, Brant, given who you are. Not that I shall let any of their gossip bother *me*."

"Yes, but some bastard has decided not only to whisper his slander, but to write it to me," he explained. "I've had letters, Jenny, mean-spirited, cowardly letters without a name to them."

She frowned, her face serious but not frightened. He should have known she'd be brave, his Jenny. "Was it one of these letters that Tway brought to you to read?"

He nodded. "It had to be something damned important, didn't it?"

She opened her mouth to answer, then obviously changed her mind, shaking her head as if to shake away a nonsensical reply. Curiously he wondered what she'd first intended to tell him, what she'd thought Tway's news might have been; likely now he'd never know.

"So tell me, Brant," she said, instead. "Have you any notion of who is writing these letters?"

"If I did, I would have their head," he said, and he meant it. "Tway is convinced from the handwriting that it's a woman, but beyond that, we have no clues."

Her fingers tightened around his. "But will you regard the letters seriously, yes?"

"How can I not?" he asked. "That's why we're going to London, far from this infernal letter-writer. Though I cannot believe the writer will ever cause the harm he or she threatens, I refuse to take that chance with you."

"Nor I with you," she said stubbornly, lifting her chin with determination. "Even if you are a peer, Brant, I will not let you be so wretched *noble*. If you must fuss over me, then I will do the same for you."

"Will you now?" He raised her hand to his lips, kissing her fingertips. All his life he'd looked after himself, and he couldn't recall the last time anyone had promised to fuss over him. He wasn't even precisely sure what her "fussing over" would entail, but he was willing to submit to it by way of experiment. "What if I don't agree?"

"You will," she warned softly, "else I shall have these two fine, large dogs run circles around you until you do, just as they did to poor Mr. Tway."

He laughed. "No mercy, then."

"None at all." She sighed, and he thought he sensed

an unexpected note of sadness in her smile as she rested her head against his shoulder. "So tomorrow you will carry me off to London to keep me safe. You truly are far too good a man for me, Brant, too good by half."

He grunted, perplexed. "I'm sorry, Jenny, but I believe I preferred being good *with* you, instead."

That finally made her chuckle, deep and low, the way he liked best.

"Together to London, then, Your Grace," she whispered as she leaned forward to kiss him. "To London!"

Jenny sat beside the window in her darkened bedchamber, anxiously staring out into the night. The maidservants had packed away her new clothes in the large trunk that now stood in the center of her room, and with many yawns she had ostentatiously announced an early bedtime after supper, citing their morning departure for London.

Fortunately, Brant hadn't objected. From the light shining from his windows, Jenny knew he was working at his desk with Tway and likely would be there until dawn, finishing the last letters and other scraps of business affairs before they left.

At least that was what she hoped as she sat here in the dark, waiting for her brother to come. Earlier this afternoon she'd placed a chair with three white stockings draped over the back near the open window, a sign, for Rob to join her, that they'd used with each other for years.

"Come, Robbie, come!" she whispered urgently, willing him to appear. "You have to come. You *must!*"

And at last, when she'd almost given up hope, came the owl's double hoot, his favorite signal for her. She leaned over the sill and spotted him, a dark-clad figure slipping from one shadow to the next until he'd reached her window and climbed inside.

"For not needing me, Jen," he said, bending over to catch his breath, "you've called me back powerfully quick."

She handed him a tumbler of water. "Did anyone see you?"

"I'm here, aren't I?" He drank from the glass and grimaced. "Water, you goose? Haven't you anything stronger for your darling brother?"

"Since when do I keep anything stronger in my bedchamber?" She pulled the stockings from the back of the chair for him to sit. "That would make a fine impression on His Grace, wouldn't it? The lost lady with a taste for brandy?"

He sprawled in the chair and pulled off his black beaver hat, settling it on his lap so he could wipe the sweat from his forehead with his handkerchief. "So what has changed since last night, Jen? Why the summons?"

"His Grace is taking me to London in the morning," she said, perching on the lid of the large traveling trunk with the stockings still in her hand. "We'll be staying at Claremont House, on Grosvenor Square. I do not know how long we'll be there, but I didn't want to leave without telling you and saying goodbye."

"To London!" Rob shook his head, amazed. "We haven't ventured to London in years, you and I."

"I tried to convince His Grace to remain here, but he insisted." Unconsciously she smoothed the stockings across her knee, matching the toes together. "Father's words did leave their mark on us, didn't they?"

"Because in that regard, the old man was right," said Rob. "London's a precious bright stage for country players like us. We'd be like humble moths that fly too close to the candle and scorch our wings, and quick as that we'd be sitting in the docket at the Old Bailey.''

"Oh, Robbie, how much I feel like that sorry little moth now!" she cried forlornly. "When I'm alone with Br—with the duke, then I do well enough, but when I imagine how it will be in London, with all his grand friends about, I'm sure I'll falter and misspeak, and he'll see me exactly for what I am.''

"He'll see what he wants to see," said Rob easily. "Mind that Father knew that, too. He'd seen enough real ladies in his life to raise you like one, and I doubt the Queen herself could tell the difference. You're a Dell, Jen, and you have the gift for making others believe you're anything you wish to be.''

"But what if I want to just be Jenny Dell?" she asked wistfully. "What if all I want His Grace to see is me, as I truly am?''

"Don't be an ass," snapped Rob bitterly. "You as you are—the penniless and likely bastard daughter of a whoring actress and a gigolo actor, and Irish in the bargain. How much interest do you think His Grace would have in a woman with such a heritage?''

"There's more to me than that," she said defensively. "He wouldn't care about our parents if he liked *me* well enough!''

"Oh, aye, and the painted houri in the sultan's harem knows nothing of pleasing men," he said, his sarcasm unmistakable. "Where's your common sense, Jen? For now you *are* a well-bred English lady suffering from a tragic loss of memory, and if you've any wits at all, that's who'll you'll remain for as long as you can.''

Jenny didn't answer, not wanting to argue with Rob. Maybe she was being a fool, trusting Brant so much.

But deep inside she *knew* she was right, just as she'd known she was right to refuse Mrs. Potter's offer.

Rob finished the water, holding the empty tumbler up to the moonlight to inspect the cut crystal.

"At least he's keeping you well enough," he noted as he began wrapping the tumbler in his handkerchief. "This is first-rate quality."

Horrified, Jenny snatched the tumbler back. "You can't take that, Rob! I won't let you steal from this house!"

"I'm not stealing, Jen," he said lightly, his interest turning to the Chinese dragon, carved from ivory, that sat on the tea table. "I'd merely be shifting things from one place to another, to people who'd appreciate it more. Besides, people as wealthy as this never know what they have in the first place, let alone notice if they go missing."

"His Grace would," said Jenny, quickly moving the dragon to the mantelpiece and out of her brother's reach. "He knows every last teaspoon in this house, because when he came into his title, he had nothing."

Rob laughed. "A duke's version of nothing is a sight different from ours, goose."

"Not for him, it's not," she said warmly. "His father left him nothing but debts, and he's had to remake his fortune himself, through investments and ventures and— and lots of other ways I don't begin to understand."

"That's because it can't be true," scoffed Rob. "Investments? Ventures? That's more a City man's talk than a duke's. What manner of peer would sully his hands with that kind of ha'penny intrigue?"

"Don't mock him, Rob," she insisted, "because he doesn't deserve it. I told you that before, didn't I? His

Grace is a good man, kind and generous and clever and honorable—''

''And you love him,'' said Rob softly.

Instantly she flushed. Love was a word she didn't dare dream let alone speak aloud. ''I didn't say that!''

''You don't have to, Jen,'' he said, almost sadly. ''I've been there so many times myself before that I can recognize all the signs, like all the best physicians of the heart.''

''What, Rob, so now you are a physician, too?'' She tried to bluff, but he wasn't going to be distracted.

''You love him,'' he continued, ''and if he's taking you to his house in London, then he's halfway to loving you, too. If all the man wished was sport, then he'd set you up as his mistress in some convenient little love house elsewhere, but Grosvenor Square proves he's already thinking of you as something finer than his doxie. You're still the Clover Girl, even in town. All the more reason to keep at being a lady, Jen.''

She stared down into her lap, at the tight little ball she'd knotted from the stockings. She had only wanted Rob to know she was going to London and not have him worry that she'd disappeared. But this part of the conversation, this calculated appraisal of her prospects with Brant—that she did not want at all.

''There's another reason for going to London, Rob,'' she said, trying again to change topics. ''Someone nearby has been sending His Grace hateful, threatening letters about my staying here at the Hall. His Grace decided he'll go to London to take me from harm's way.''

''Ha, as if any poor scribbler could hurt a duke,'' he said. ''But how well it's played out for you, eh?''

She frowned at her brother, not quite suspiciously but not free from doubt, either. ''You've nothing to do with those letters, Rob, have you? Not to be hurtful, but to better my situation?''

"Blackmail and threats, evil letters over an anonymous hand?" he asked incredulously. "That's never been my game, Jen, and you know it."

She threw the balled stockings at him, striking him in the chest with a soft thump. "You've never expected me to lie with a gentleman for gain before, either."

"Only a gentleman you already love, which makes for neither hardship nor sin, even for a lady." He settled his hat back on his head and threw the stockings back at her. "You go to London, Jen, and play this game out with your honorable duke as you see fit. I'll follow, and find you, and be there if you need me, amusing myself amongst the joys of the great capital just as you shall be. And let's both of us pray that Father's ghost is looking the other way when we do."

She knew he expected her to smile, but she didn't, and she couldn't even find the heart to pretend. She never could guess what Rob would do next, but in the past she'd always been with him to rescue from his worst inclinations. Now, because she'd be with Brant, she couldn't be her brother's conscience, and the possibilities that lack could present were terrifying.

"Better we should pray that Father is looking and watching over us," she said softly, thinking, too, of her own impetuous actions today with Brant in the folly. "Oh, Rob, please take care, whatever you do. Take care for both our sakes!"

Chapter Ten

"Oh, miss, don't you look fine!"

Mrs. Lowe smiled at Jenny's reflection in the tall looking glass, the housekeeper's round-cheeked face hovering over her shoulder. It was, agreed Jenny with satisfaction, indeed a fine sight.

For the long day in the coach, she was wearing a white petticoat that was a heavier cotton than usual, with an elaborate border of serpentine cord that made the hem stand out from her ankles like a narrow bell. Over this she wore a short double-breasted spencer the same iridescent emerald green as a peacock's tail, with a rolled collar that set off her neck and rows of ruffles on the upper sleeves *à la mameluke*. Peeking out from beneath her petticoat were slippers of green-glazed kid that matched the spencer, with the old-fashioned curving heels she always favored to make her look taller.

But Jenny's favorite part came last. Holding her breath, she lowered the green silk bonnet onto her hair, the three curling black plumes tickling her wrist as she tied the ribbons to one side beneath her chin. The brim of the bonnet flared wide to frame her face, curving away from her brow like an oversize sugar scoop in the newest French manner.

Finally she, too, smiled at her reflection. If the bonnet's stylish brim limited how much Jenny could see on either side, so be it. She'd make that trade to look her best for Brant. She knew the ensemble was all very elegant, very fashionable, the kind of traveling clothes suitable only for ladies whose journeys were made in private coaches—which this morning included Jenny.

"Is His Grace below yet?" she asked, nervously plucking at the bow. She was so excited with anticipation that she'd hardly slept during the night, and had been out of bed long before the maid had appeared with her breakfast. "I don't want to keep him waiting."

"No, miss," said Mrs. Lowe. "He and Mr. Tway are still at His Grace's desk, worrying over some last bits of business like a pair of bulldogs with a mutton bone. But the driver's brought the coach 'round front, if you do wish to go down yourself, miss."

Jenny grinned wickedly. "Gemini, what a rare chance, Mrs. Lowe! Consider the blow I can strike for all us females by being there before His Grace and Mr. Tway, tapping *my* foot while I must wait for them!"

"Oh, my, miss, the very thought!" exclaimed the housekeeper. "But begging pardon, miss, you're the lady to do it, aren't you?"

"Indeed, I am," said Jenny gleefully, reaching for her gloves and bag. It was exactly the sort of jest that Brant would enjoy, and one to make them begin their journey together laughing. "Come, Mrs. Lowe, before His Grace can beat me there!"

"If you please, miss," said the older woman hesitantly, dipping a curtsy, "might I have a word with you first?"

"Of course, Mrs. Lowe," said Jenny promptly, putting the gloves aside again to give her full attention to the other woman's request. She wouldn't forget that the housekeeper had, from the first, been one of her best allies here at Claremont Hall. "What is it?"

"I wanted to wish you well, miss, that is all," said Mrs. Lowe warmly. "His Grace never does bring ladies here to the Hall, and though you didn't come through a proper invitation, you did make a world o' difference to His Grace. You made him smile, miss, and you made him laugh, something His Grace don't do nearly enough. And I thank you for it, indeed I do."

"Oh, Mrs. Lowe, thank you," said Jenny fondly, taking the older woman's hands in her own. "That's so kind of you to say to me!"

"It's nothing you don't deserve, miss," she answered with an extra sniff. "Now I don't expect to see you again, miss, so I'll say thank you here, and may God be with you."

Touched by her words, Jenny didn't pause to consider their significance. "That sounds so grim and final, Mrs. Lowe!"

"Oh, no, miss, it's not meant to be that way!" said Mrs. Lowe quickly. "It's only that your poor head seems so much better now, and once you go to London and see so many more gentry, why, you're certain to find your own people again."

"Yes," said Jenny softly, releasing the other woman's hands. "Yes, I most likely shall. Now I'd best go downstairs if I wish to have any hope of being there before His Grace."

She grabbed her gloves and bag and hurried from the room, praying her expression hadn't betrayed her real thoughts. She must learn not to make that mistake again.

Mrs. Lowe's suggestion was the happiest and most reasonable end to her adventure with Brant, the one most people would expect. Only Jenny herself was foolish enough to want more.

Briefly she stopped on the stairway in the front hall, gazing up one last time at the gods and goddesses frolicking in the painting overhead. If she were to be leaving this house forever, she wanted to remember as much as she could, from those painted deities to the black-and-white-marble-checkerboard floor to the sweet william and early roses in the gardens and, of course, the folly among the glossy green ivy.

It wasn't that Claremont Hall was the largest or most palatial country house that Jenny would likely ever visit that was making every last memory bittersweet. No, it was that she'd been so happy here with Brant that she'd never wished to leave, and with a sigh of regret, she bowed her head and forced herself toward the front door, toward the waiting coach, and London.

"Good day, miss," called the coachman, echoed by the footmen who'd be the outriders on the back of the coach, all resplendent in the duke's midnight-blue livery and all obviously surprised to see her here before His Grace. Unsure of exactly what to do, one of the footman solemnly held open the already open door to the coach, ready to help Jenny enter if she wished.

"Thank you," she said, smiling winningly at the footman as he helped her climb inside. "But please leave the door open for His Grace. I want to be sure I see him as soon as he comes."

Or more importantly, that he saw *her*. Even though her first delight in the plan had faded, she still settled back against the soft leather squabs, arranging her skirts gracefully around her legs. She wanted to look as if she'd been lolling here all morning when Brant finally appeared.

Not that waiting here was any hardship. The windows of the coach were unfastened and the leather curtains rolled and tied out of way to let in the warm morning air. Fragrant roses from the garden hung in silver vases mounted beside the windows, and a small wicker hamper sat between the seats, no doubt filled by the cook with bottled drinks and other refreshments for their journey.

She'd never traveled in such luxury before, and since it could well be the only time she did, she should remember this, too, along with the rest. Certainly she'd reach London faster and in far more comfort than poor Rob would, and guiltily she thought of all the times they'd been forced to flee in dreadful circumstances, often in the night and never in a coach drawn by a team of four matched horses.

There's always tomorrow, Father had promised. No matter what happens today, there's always tomorrow.

But what if today was already so good that there'd be nothing left for another day?

With a sigh, she pulled off the bonnet and tossed it on the seat beside her, no longer in the mood for anything so frivolous. Something poked her elbow and she reached down into the cushions to find a folded sheet of paper, a letter, once sealed with a blob of tallow, instead of proper wax. Because there was no address and the tallow seal had been rubbed open between the cushions, Jenny gave in to her curiosity, and opened the sheet.

The handwriting was crude, but the message was shockingly unmistakable, and she gasped aloud as she read it.

You paid me No Heed, did you? The bitch is still in your house and your bed. Do not Deny she is Your Whore. You will both Burn in Hell for your Sin and be sure I will send you There myself if you do not now Heed My Warning.

When Brant had told her of the unsigned letters and their threats, Jenny hadn't paid particular attention. One more unhappy puritan, judging everyone else by impossibly righteous standards. She'd heard her share of such nonsense before and it had been easy enough to dismiss again when Brant had wanted to warn her.

But holding this letter in her hand made it terrifyingly real. Her fingers tightened on the paper and her heart raced with uncertainty. What had she ever done to make anyone hate her this much? And why, why should the idea of her and Brant together inspire it?

"Jenny!" exclaimed Brant, his smile warm with pleasurable surprise as he stepped into the coach. "I'd never expected to find you here before me!"

It was the perfect opening for her lighthearted jest—a jest she'd now forgotten.

"Here," she said, too upset to say more as she handed him the letter. "This was tucked between the cushions."

She could tell by the expression on his face as he took it that he instantly recognized the letter for what it was.

"Oh, hell," he said grimly. "And in my own carriage, too. How the devil did they get past my people?"

"Read it," she said. "See what it says."

But he scarcely glanced at the sheet. "The same paper, the same hand. I imagine it says the same rubbish, too."

"This…this person wants us dead," she said, her voice shaking. "Read it, and you'll see. The last sentence says that—"

"I won't waste my time," he declared, stuffing the letter into his pocket. "That's exactly what this bastard wants, you know—for us to quiver and quake, wondering when the next letter will come. But I won't do that, Jenny, and I don't want you to do it, either."

"But what if he tries something more?" she asked, too troubled to be so easily reassured. "Oh, Brant, this is all my fault! If this person were to hurt you because of me—"

"Which will absolutely never happen," said Brant firmly. He took her hand, pulling her closer and gently turning her face so she'd no choice but to look directly into his eyes. "I'd hoped it wouldn't come to this, but now I'll have Tway stay and take this letter with the others directly to the magistrate. The mean little zealot who's penning these must be made to stop."

"No!" she cried. The last thing she wished or needed was to have her name—any of them—brought to the attention of a magistrate, even in a roundabout way such as this.

Quickly she swallowed her fears and began again. "That is, won't that cause more trouble for you? As you said yourself, what this wicked person wishes is to cause mischief, and what better way for him to do that than to involve you with the magistrate?"

Brant frowned, touching the pocket where the letter rested. "I won't have you upset or frightened, sweetheart. That's why I didn't tell you of the letters in the first place."

"But isn't that why we are going to London?" she asked swiftly. "To shift us both from harm's way and to let this dreadful person's pen go dry without new inspiration?"

"That, and to keep you safe," he admitted grudgingly. "It's a great deal harder to get into any house on Grosvenor Square than it is here."

"But if you have Tway show the letters to the magistrate," she reasoned, "won't we have to remain here, too, to make statements and testify and such?"

"Damnation, you are right." He sighed restlessly. "But I want this settled, Jenny."

"And it will be," she said, soothing. "You give this last letter to Tway to hold, and if—*if*—another manages to follow us in London, then he can take them all to the magistrate, after you have met with your investors."

"Blast, I'd forgotten clean about them. But you are right. That's how it is with you, isn't it? Wise *and* beautiful." He drew her closer and kissed her lightly on her forehead. "You're a veritable Minerva, sweetheart, my own goddess of wisdom."

"Then better send me to Mt. Olympus directly," she called as he left the coach for his final words with Tway, "where I'll cause no more mischief."

She almost meant it, too. For now she'd escaped, her secret once again safe. But she hated telling tales to Brant, and there had been a moment when she'd very nearly told him the truth, instead, all the truth—a most astounding impulse. Only common sense had grabbed her at the last and stopped her, giving her the glibness to talk her way free one more time.

What was it that Rob had noted last night—that Brant would see what he wanted to? He must have been hearing what he wished, too, for she knew her voice had turned squeaky and rushed and her palms had been as damp as if she'd dipped them in a washbowl, sure signs of a bad liar and the first time she could remember it happening to her.

Was this what came of wanting to tell the truth? That

she'd forgotten the art of how to twist and bend it? Or
had the time she'd spent with Brant somehow made her
into a creature unfit for either life—still too dishonest
and false for a lasting place in his, but without the instincts to survive for long in hers?

Brant returned, the door latched shut behind him, and
finally the impatient horses began and the coach rolled
to life. From the window, Jenny waved at Mrs. Lowe,
watching from the top of the steps. The housekeeper had
seemed certain enough that she'd never return, and as
Jenny watched the great house recede, she couldn't help
but feel miserably that fate was going to agree.

Mary Hewitt sat on the bench in front of the inn, waiting for the arrival of the stage to London. Though it was
not long past dawn, the day was already warm, which
was why she'd finally fled the inn's stale, smoky front
room full of noisy common folk to come outside.

Not that this bench was much of an improvement. A
farmer, his wife and four squabbling children had
crowded onto the narrow bench with her, and as the
shadow from the oak tree behind shrank as the sun rose,
the farm family pushed closer and closer against her,
fighting to claim her dwindling sliver of shade.

But Mary held firm against the dust and indignity,
resolutely staring in the opposite direction with her feet
propped upon her trunk to guard it from thieves. She
would be superior and aloof. She would show them how
the better sort behaved, even as the sweat trickled down
her back between her stays and her shift.

Oh, she did know how to behave, to keep a straight
back and impassive face, no matter what nastiness was
tossed into her path. That had been the cruelest part of
being caught between Richard Farquhar and John Par-

ker. She had always behaved properly, even when the men had been brawling like drovers in that stableyard. She'd never slipped and acted like the wanton slattern the gossips had declared her to be, not once!

Which was far more than could be said for Richard's sister, *Miss* Jane Farquhar. On her way to her sister in London, Mary had gotten off the stage here, in this little village in the shadow of the great Claremont Hall, to see and hear for herself if what that Mr. Tway had told her was true. And, oh, mercy, was it. From the dim-witted scullery maid to the innkeeper's wife to the stage driver himself, no one spoke of anything but how the great Duke of Strachen had become besotted with a mysterious young lady, installing her for all the world to see at Claremont Hall. The duke was popular in the village, so well loved that there was fearful speculation for his sanity.

He'd sent for a mantua-maker to dress her from head to toe like a queen. Some claimed he'd called for a jeweler, as well, draping the girl with rubies and pearls. While no one mentioned a brother for the lady, the way those who'd seen the girl described her—small, pale, with upturned eyes better suited to a fairy than a lady— left no doubt in Mary's mind that this was Jane Farquhar, and that somewhere nearby must be Richard.

All of this had made Mary's first letter easy to compose. Because she didn't want anything traced back to her, she hadn't written much—in truth, she didn't know much—but the slander would be more than enough to make the duke doubt and suspect and look at his little ladybird with new eyes. Whatever Richard had planned would be ruined, and he'd be punished by rumor and suspicion just as Mary had been herself.

It had taken only a handful of coins to find a boy

willing to slip over the walls of Claremont Hall and deliver her letter. Mary had lain awake with excitement the entire night after that, imagining the reaction her words would cause and anticipating the stir when news of them reached the village.

But nothing had happened, no reaction and no stir. Furiously she'd written a second letter, sent by a different boy, and this time she'd had the reaction she'd wanted. The duke's huge household was in an uproar, the staff ordered to watch for intruders night and day, the undermaids would only work in pairs from fear of having their throats slit as they scrubbed the floorboards.

Yet still the girl remained with the duke, her place untouched and her brother unpunished.

And so Mary wrote again, aware of the intoxicating power she now possessed. This time her reward came swiftly: the duke was leaving the country at once, His Grace was finished with his dalliance, the girl would receive a settlement because the duke was generous and kind, not because she'd earned it, and besides, no one had ever even learned her true name or where she'd come from. It wasn't nearly as public or painful an end for Richard as Mary could have wished, but because she knew how much he treasured his wicked little sister, this ignominious ending still must have humiliated him, and Mary found much joyful satisfaction in that.

Now she sat on this hard narrow bench, fanning herself and squinting down the road for the first signs of the stage.

A boy came racing down the road toward the inn waving his hat, an excited dog barking as it followed. On his way into the inn, the boy shouted something that Mary didn't understand, though she thought she'd heard the word "coach." That made sense, and Mary stood in preparation for the coming stage, shaking out her skirts and checking the buckles on her trunk one last time. The farmer and his wife stood, too, their ill-mannered children jumping up and down with anticipation.

Now she could hear a distant rumble from beyond the curve, the mingled sounds of horses' hooves and jingling harnesses and iron-bound wheels rolling over a dirt road. People streamed from the tavern and the stable, drawn by the boy's announcement, and as word spread, more came hurrying from the shops nearby.

With growing dismay, Mary glanced from side to side, trying to gauge exactly how many of them were expecting to climb aboard the same London stage. On such a warm day, she could already imagine how unpleasant the stage's jolting journey was going to be, pressed and packed into the narrow space like so many pieces of salted beef in a barrel. Reluctantly, Mary picked up her trunk with both hands, more than any lady should be expected to do, but she didn't want to be pushed aside without a seat when the coach arrived.

"Ahoy, ahoy!" shouted another boy who'd climbed up the oak tree for a better vantage point. "Here it be now, coming down fast!"

Cheering, the crowd of people surged toward the road, sweeping Mary and her trunk with them.

"I beg your pardon!" she gasped indignantly as she was jostled and jumbled and her hat knocked askew. But no one heard her, let alone replied, with every face turned eagerly toward the road, shouting and cheering as if the king himself were coming.

And as the coach's first horses came into view, at last Mary understood why.

This was no common stage, but a rich man's coach. The four horses in the team were beautifully matched dapple grays, the brasses on their harnesses polished to shine like gold in the sunshine. The gold braid and buttons on the livery of the driver and the footmen glittered, too, while the coach itself gleamed as if made of dark blue enamel, swaying gently on its leather springs to ensure passengers comfort.

As the coach drew closer, the crowd's cheers rose to a happy roar. Now Mary could see coat of arms painted on the door, the rightful symbol of His Grace the Duke of Strachen. Purposefully the coach slowed and the duke himself appeared at one of the open windows. A most handsome gentleman, decided Mary with shock, for she'd been imagining an older man, not one with bright blue eyes and hair the color of gold. He leaned from the window, waving with a very unducal spontaneity, even calling a word or two to people he recognized in the crowd.

Then, too soon, the coach rolled away and the duke was gone in a swirl of dust, lost beyond the next bend in the road. The crowd separated, chatting happily about His Grace and how well he looked, and not at all mad or unwell, and what a good notion it would be now to go raise a tankard of ale together to His Grace's health, just to make sure.

Only Mary remained by the side of the road, too stunned and disbelieving to move, and still holding her trunk in her hands like an offering before her.

Had she really been the only one to look past the duke and into the coach? Had no one else seen what she'd seen there inside, the small dark-haired woman elegantly dressed in the color of emeralds? Hadn't anyone seen how the creature had lounged back against the cushions, indolent and languorous and wanting only for her aristocratic lover to return to her embrace as they journeyed so regally to London?

But Mary Hewitt—Mary Hewitt had seen everything, and forgotten nothing.

As the coach finally came to a stop on the north side of Grosvenor Square, Brant looked at the tall stone block that was his home in London and tried to see it as Jenny would, free of his own associations.

One of the first houses built on the Square nearly eighty years earlier, Claremont House's chilly, regular facade and shutterless windows had somehow always reminded Brant of his father. Perhaps it was because he and his brothers had never been brought here as boys, children having been considered a nuisance and a hindrance to his father's London recreations, or perhaps it was simply because the formal house would never have the trees and gardens to soften it the way Claremont Hall did.

But though Brant had lavished a small fortune on this house's improvements, striving to make the rooms inside less cold and more hospitable, it had always seemed to resist him. He never had determined why. Maybe simply having Jenny here as his guest, with all her ebullient warmth, would help make the difference.

He looked down at her now, curled up in the corner of the seat, one hand cupped beneath her cheek like a napping child's despite the city's ceaseless racket and din. It had been a long, tedious journey, launched with an inauspicious beginning. First she'd found that damned letter in the coach, forcing him to explain to her about the others, and then she'd come close to discovering his own secret when she'd tried to insist he read it for himself. Maybe she already had guessed the truth;

he couldn't say for sure. But he didn't wonder that she'd been moody and lost in her own thoughts, and he hadn't been much better.

"We're here, sweetheart," he said, gently running the backs of his fingers over her cheek to wake her. "Claremont House, in all its glory."

"Glory," she muttered, her voice still thick with sleep, and pushed herself upright just before the footman opened the coach door. "Here, you say."

Brant smiled and took her hand. "Come, I'll help you out."

She yawned and stretched, then let him help her from the coach. "This is your London house, is it?"

"It is," he said, "though I promise it's more agreeable inside than out."

"I should hope so, Brant." She leaned back, looking up at the four severe stories. "I know it's barbarously rude of me to say this, but I already prefer your country house."

"So do I," he admitted wryly as he led her inside. "Claremont Hall is my home, but Claremont House is no more than my house."

Even this late in the evening, there had been people walking in the fenced park in the center of the square, and idly he wondered how long it would take before it was known that he had returned to town. By the time he sat down to his coffee in the morning, he expected there'd be a stack of cards and invitations in the silver salver by the door. Another hour after that and all of the town that cared would know he'd returned, and with an unknown lady as his guest.

"Good day, Your Grace. Miss," said the housekeeper briskly, greeting them in the hall as soon as they entered. She was the kind of housekeeper who specialized in anticipating arrivals and other needs, a tall, more austere version of Mrs. Lowe whose name escaped Brant. "Mr. Tway sent word that you'd be arriving. I'm sure you'll find everything in place, Your Grace, exactly as you have ordered. Miss, I am Mrs. Harper. If you please, I shall now show you to your rooms, so you might dress for supper."

But Jenny, it seemed, had other plans.

"Thank you, no, Mrs. Harper, I do not please, at least not at this exact moment," she said so politely that not even Mrs. Harper could object. "First I should like to speak with His Grace alone."

Surprised, but not foolish enough to say so, Mrs. Harper glanced to Brant for agreement, and when he nodded, she left them alone. They hadn't gotten any further into the house than the front hall, a narrow space that followed the curving staircase three flights up to a skylight overhead. Directly below the skylight, a compass rose had been inlaid into the floor, and now Jenny in her green slippers was standing at the tip of the northwest point.

"So, Jenny," he said as lightly as he could, which, given his present degree of weariness, was as light as a millstone. "I am tired and I am hungry, and we have been alone together today for hours and hours in that infernal carriage. What the devil can you possibly have left to say to me that cannot wait?"

"I won't take long," she promised softly, folding her arms across her chest. "I have one concern, that is all. In this house, things will be different between us. I can sense that already."

"Then you're wrong, Jenny," he said automatically, even though he didn't believe that any more than she did. "Things don't have to change."

"But they have," she said softly, "and they will. You're a gambler, and so, I suppose, am I, to be with you still. But what will become of me now, Brant? This is London at the height of the Season. Everyone knows who you are, and if I am seen with you, then someone in turn is bound to recognize me. And God help me, Brant, I do not know which to wish for—to have someone step forward and claim me, or to be left here with you."

"Damnation, Jenny, do you think I haven't thought of that for myself?" he asked roughly. "What if your husband should—"

"I've told you before I've no husband."

He wished he could be as certain. "Your brother, then. No matter what we say, Jenny, the rest of the world is going to say I ruined you, having you stay at Claremont Hall. Hell, just riding with me in the coach today would do it."

"It's all been my choice, Brant," she said warmly. "Don't try to be so noble and honorable again!"

"If I hadn't been that way," he said, his temper rising to match hers, "I would have left you beneath those wretched trees, instead."

"You didn't force me. *I* wanted things this way."

Damnation, why didn't she *understand?* "But what if your brother were to appear at this door and demand his satisfaction for what I've done to your reputation and honor?"

She laughed, an odd little gurgle. "Oh, Brant, I do not think that will ever happen with any brother of mine."

"You don't know that, and neither do I." He came forward and took her in his arms, there on the compass point, as if it were the most proper thing in the world, which, for that moment, it was. He could tell that by the way her arms curled around him, holding him as tightly as he did her. And when he kissed her, fast and deep, that was right for them, too.

"Look at me, Jen," he ordered, wanting her to open her eyes and see him through the dizzy joy of the kiss. "This is what we have, each day that we seize for our own. Look at me, and tell me what you want."

"From you?" she asked wistfully, searching his face for the same truth he'd wanted from hers. "Oh, Brant, all I really wish for is you, here, and I have that."

"Then wish for something else," he said gruffly, unable to concentrate on anything but the intense desire to kiss her again—on her lips and forehead and eyelids and cheeks and throat and the tip of her nose, wherever he could find. "Say it, and it's yours."

"Anything, Brant?" Her smile was lopsided, her lips bruised from their kiss. "Then give me a name, that is all, a name of my own."

"A name?" He paused, unsure of her meaning. Jewels, gold, silver, ivory fans and silks from China: these were gifts in his power to give her. But a name?

"Give me another name to go with Jenny," she pleaded. "It's foolish, I know, but until I can recall the real name, I'd rather have one from you."

He shook his head, reluctant. "Wouldn't that confuse you more, having to answer to a name different from your own?"

"It wouldn't bother me," she answered quickly. "Not at all."

"I don't know, Jen," he said. "How wise can—"

"That is it!" she cried. "You said before I was your own Minerva. Let me be Jenny Wise for now, Miss Wise. Miss Jenny Wise."

Before he could protest, she was kissing him again, standing up on the toes of her slippers to arch against him, and making him forget whatever it was he wanted to protest, anyway.

She chuckled when she finally broke away and rested her cheek against his shoulder to catch her breath. "Look, Brant," she said. "The compass in the floor is wrong."

"What's that?" He was far more interested in exploring the curve from her waist to her hip than the compass.

"I told you, this compass is wrong," she said. "I remarked where the stars and moon were in the sky when we stood outside the coach, and this—here—is west, not northwest."

It was such a preposterous thing to notice, considering the circumstances, that he laughed. "My sea captain brother has said exactly the same thing. Which means in fact you really are a wise Jenny."

"I am at that," she declared. "A most glorious and wise Jenny."

Yet he couldn't help noticing that despite her brave words, her smile still seemed fragile and uncertain, almost sad.

"Oh, Jenny, Jenny," he said softly. "I can't say for a moment where the devil all this will end, but I do know, hands down, that I've never met another woman like you."

"Of course you haven't, Brant," she whispered, the sadness lingering still. "And if you're very, very lucky, you never shall again."

Chapter Eleven

Much to the surprise of the lady's maid assigned to her, Jenny rose early and dressed herself, determined to join Brant for breakfast. But as early as she'd thought she was, he had already eaten and gone out, leaving her to face the dismal prospect of a long mahogany dining table fit for twenty but set for only one.

"His Grace regrets that he could not linger to join you, Miss Wise," said Mrs. Harper, appearing only half a moment after Jenny herself. "He said that you are to dine without him and amuse yourself however you please within the house. If you please, Miss Wise, tea, chocolate or coffee?"

"Tea, thank you," said Jenny as a footman seated her. She liked the sound of that Miss Wise, and if Brant wanted her to amuse herself, he'd made a splendid start for her by telling the housekeeper her new-minted name. Whenever they'd chose a new name, Father had always encouraged them to select one that not only suited the ruse, but was also agreeable and easy to say, and Jenny Wise had the extra advantage of being a kind of private jest between her and Brant.

Jenny Wise, wise Jenny: oh, yes, that was a first-rate name, made all the better because Brant had created it.

As her tea, a plate of buns and several folded newspapers magically appeared before her, Mrs. Harper went to stand on the other side of the table, her black silk grosgrain skirts rustling around her. She clasped her hands before her and kept her back impeccably straight, ready to recite the rest of Brant's messages.

"While His Grace is away for the day, Miss Wise," she began, "he will return in time this evening to escort you to Covent Garden for the evening's performances."

"The theater?" asked Jenny faintly, unable to contain her dismay. Her parents had both played Covent Garden once they'd left Dublin, and even after her father had taken her and Rob to the Continent to escape his creditors, he'd followed the careers of friends—and enemies—so avidly by way of the papers that she felt as if she'd known them herself, as well.

But what worried her was not how many of the actors and actresses she'd recognize on the stage: it was how many of them would recognize *her,* for Father had always sworn she was the very image of her mother. She hadn't really expected anyone to know her in London, the way she'd said to Brant last night, but at Covent Garden it could be a dreadfully genuine possibility. To be welcomed back as the daughter of Amelia Rose and Edmund "Irish" Dell—oh, how would she ever explain that to Brant?

You could tell him the truth, Jen. Yes, the truth, for the first time in your life. If you care as much for Brant as you want to believe, if you're half as wise—wise!— as you claim to be, then you'll trust him, and give him the truth....

"They say Mrs. Siddons is expected to take the stage

this evening, Miss Wise,'' said Mrs. Harper severely, misreading Jenny's response. "His Grace is taking you to see one of the finest actresses of our time."

"Oh, I am honored, Mrs. Harper," said Jenny quickly. "Everyone has heard of Mrs. Siddons."

"They have, indeed, miss," said Mrs. Harper, mollified enough to continue relaying Brant's messages. "His Grace said that if you have nothing pleasing to wear this evening, you may visit Mrs. Bertram's shop in St. James Street, where His Grace maintains an account. If you do, His Grace asks that a footman accompany you."

Jenny nodded, trying not to consider why Brant would maintain an account at a ladies' shop as famous as Mrs. Bertram's. But what struck her as more peculiar was that he'd given such a complicated message to Mrs. Harper to relay. Why hadn't he simply written a note for her, instead? It wasn't just she'd no little notes from him to reread and give her pleasure; she'd yet to see one letter of his hand.

She frowned as she broke one of the raisin rolls in half to butter it. "Is that all, Mrs. Harper?"

"Yes, Miss Wise," she said. "That is *all*."

Jenny looked up sharply. The housekeeper's expression hadn't changed and her posture remained perfectly deferential, but in that single, final word, Mrs. Harper had made it clear as day that she'd believed Jenny was an interloper, an imposter and a strumpet, deserving of the street and worthy of nothing more than His Grace's scornful contempt.

This is how it will be in London, Jen. As long as you cling to the arm of the Duke of Strachen, the world will smile and bow and jump to please, but the moment you try to stand on your own, that same world will treat you worse than offal in the gutter, and all because you tried to be something you're not.

No wonder that Father would never come back....

Carefully, Jenny spread the pale butter over the roll, back and forth and over the raisins, the small sterling knife reflecting the morning light like a mirror.

"Thank you, Mrs. Harper," she said evenly. "And please have the carriage ready at three."

No, she would not blush, and she would not stammer, and she most definitely would not back down.

Not when the stakes were Brant himself.

From the moment Brant stepped from his door, he'd prepared himself. The only surprise was how long— nearly ninety-seven minutes by his own watch—it took before the question was asked.

He'd gone riding in the park early, when most of the town's bloods and bucks were stumbling toward their beds not onto their horses. He'd had the lanes largely to himself, and as he'd let his thoughts wander, he'd caught himself whistling for Jetty and Gus, left sadly behind in the country, to follow.

He'd just turned his horse's head back toward home when the question finally came, brayed across the lawns by a man he'd knew—barely—from school and cards.

"Claremont!" he called with a cheery, too familiar wave as he guided his horse to fall in alongside Brant's. "You've come back among the living and out of the country, I see."

"Yes," said Brant, and that was all, as unencouraging as possible.

"So who is she, Claremont?" the man persisted eagerly. "Who is your mysterious lady?"

Brant sighed wearily. "If I knew, then she wouldn't be a mystery, would she?"

"But you're not a fellow who's easily tempted," the other man pressed. "She must be a right rare beauty if she's caught your eye."

"You can judge for yourself," said Brant. "I'm taking her to Covent Garden tonight to see La Siddons."

"You'd take her out for all of us to ogle?" The other man whistled low with admiration and more than a little envy. "You're a damned confident rogue, Claremont, to be that sure of the lady."

"I am," he said, and with a curt nod of farewell he turned his horse down another path. He'd no doubt now that he'd see the man again tonight, plus a score of his other acquaintances and a great many others he'd never met. Who would be able to resist a glimpse of his "mystery lady"?

But there was more to this than simply showing Jenny off to his friends. He would take her to the theater, to the pleasure gardens, to the picture galleries and the opera, and everywhere else he could in the short time they were in town. If Jenny had one friend or relation here in London, he wanted that person to have every chance to recognize her and give her back her name and her past.

For Brant it was a terrible risk and, like an inescapable toothache, he thought again of that phantom husband or sweetheart who might have already claimed her heart. She could be gone from him forever before the overture was done tonight, and there'd be not a thing he could do to stop it.

But until Jenny knew exactly who she was and felt

free to leave him, then he in turn would never be free to ask her to stay.

He could only now pray that Fate would give him that chance.

"I should like to see white ostrich plumes," said Jenny to the shop girl at Bertram's. "Tall ones, that I might pin into my hair."

"We have exactly the proper plume, miss." The girl nodded and bowed before she went behind the counter, and yet still managed to notice both the Claremont carriage waiting outside and the liveried footman standing behind Jenny's small gilt chair. But that was enough, even in a store this small and elegant. When the girl returned with a selection of plumes cradled carefully in her arms, Mrs. Bertram herself accompanied her.

"I am honored, Miss Wise," she said, the shop owner's words coming round and soft like a cooing dove, "and most pleased to serve your custom. You will see that our plumes are the finest, languid and graceful in form, yet with strong ferrules. I have them imported directly from Africa, miss, which ensures only the best. Nothing is too fine for my ladies, you see."

She turned the looking glass on the counter toward Jenny and held one of the plumes to one side of Jenny's head.

"I believe you need two, miss," she said critically, adding a second, smaller plume to the first. "Three would overwhelm, but two adds interest. You have chosen your gown, yes?"

Jenny nodded. She would wear the white muslin that had been made for her by the country mantua-maker. Though Mrs. Bertram would likely dismiss it as hopelessly plain and unfashionable, Jenny knew its simplicity flattered her, and besides, she didn't want Brant to think she was taking advantage of his generosity.

"Then I shall have these wrapped, miss, for your footman to take." The shop girl disappeared with the plumes, and Mrs. Bertram leaned closer, her voice turning more confidential. "Now, miss, I have something special to show you. I do not as a rule carry rarities such as this, but when an Italian gentleman in need of funds brought it to me first as a favor, I could not say no."

From a locked drawer behind the counter, she lifted out a flat leather box with the greatest care to increase the anticipation. Jenny leaned forward, curious to see what lay within, but also skeptical; she recognized first-rate showmanship for what it was, having had a lifetime of examples to observe within her own family.

But when Mrs. Bertram finally unlatched the leather box and slowly opened the lid, Jenny gasped aloud. Lying inside was the most magical necklace she'd ever seen: branches of the finest rosy-red coral had been woven together with burnished gold leaves, a kind of garland, scattered all over with tiny diamonds that glittered like drops of morning dew. It wasn't a necklace for St. James, but rather for a fairy queen.

"Here, miss, let me put it 'round your throat for you," said Mrs. Bertram, already fastening the clasp.

Jenny turned back to the looking glass and gasped again, this time with delight. She'd never seen a piece of jewelry that so perfectly suited her, not only from the color of the coral against her skin to the little sparkling flashes of the diamonds, but also how the fancifulness of the design seemed to enhance her own unusual beauty. Other customers were noticing it, too, turning away from their own purchases to admire hers in a rush of appreciative female murmurs.

"As soon as you came through my doorway, miss, I thought of this necklace," said Mrs. Bertram with undeniable satisfaction. "No other woman could wear such a piece with your grace. Perfection, miss, perfection."

Lightly, Jenny touched the coral. The necklace *was* very beautiful, and doubtless very, very dear. Neapolitan coral and rose diamonds did not come cheap, even from impoverished Italian gentlemen.

Not that she'd dare ask the price. In a store like this, where most every customer would simply put their choices on account, no one would be so vulgar as to mention prices. Before Mrs. Bertram had even unlocked the drawer, it was understood by everyone that this would be charged to the Duke of Strachen and that His Grace could most certainly afford it.

But Jenny herself was not as sure. "I shall have to consider it, ma'am," she said as she unclasped the necklace herself. She hadn't wanted to seem greedy to Brant by buying three plumes, instead of two; to buy a necklace such as this went so far beyond lowly greed that she didn't know the right word for it. "I agree that the necklace is most wonderful, but to take such advantage of His Grace's generosity today—today I shouldn't."

"There is always tomorrow," said Mrs. Bertram sympathetically, and with an eerie echo of her father's philosophy. She replaced the necklace in its fitted case, stroking it gently as if it were a pet. "Though if another lady should choose it this afternoon, miss, I cannot refuse her. But you consider it, miss, consider it well. Ah, here's the box with your plumes. Shall I have your footman take it to the carriage for you?"

"Yes, thank you." Mrs. Bertram led the footman away, all the while cooing orders to him and leaving Jenny on her own. Jenny knew well that this was her time for considering, and, if Mrs. Bertram had accurately calculated the necklace's magic, for Jenny to change her mind.

"Why the devil didn't you take the necklace?" asked her brother, suddenly at her side. "We could have lived for half a year on that."

She glanced at him nervously, knowing she had no business talking to him in public, and pretended to admire the French laces displayed inside a glass-front case. "Because it was too dear."

"Too dear!" he exclaimed softly. "What manner of nonsense is this, Jen, refusing gifts? When have you become so squeamish and overnice?"

"Since I began to see the differences in how other people live," she whispered sharply. Though the store was crowded, she was sure that others had noticed them together. At least he'd taken care with his dress, his hair neat and his jaw newly shaved, and he didn't look out of place among the fashionable customers. "Rob, you have to leave. You'll only make trouble here with me. Where are you staying?"

"With a friend," he said, purposefully vague. "Not so grand a friend as yours, to be sure, but it suits. But let us say I shall walk each afternoon between three and four among the fine folks in Grosvenor Square. If you need me, you'll find me there. And as for my lodgings, why—"

"Rob, tell me quickly! I don't want you to be here when the footman—"

"Oh, yes, your personal bully boy," said Rob, looking back over his shoulder for the footman. "You fuss about me with a pistol, when that swaggering fellow's practically carrying a blunderbuss beneath his coat. What a time I've had finding you alone! You must be mightily pleasing His Grace if he feels you must be kept on such a short rein.''

"What do you want, Rob?''

"You shame me, Jen, making me spell it out,'' he said softly, sadly. "But London's an expensive place for a gentleman, and I'm short, damnably short. If you could but share a bit of your good fortune—''

"Rob, I don't have any, not a ha'penny.'' How ironic to be having such a conversation in a place filled with costly, unnecessary indulgences! "His Grace hasn't given me any, and I haven't asked, because I don't need it.''

"Well, I *do*.'' He smiled with his old charm at a young blond woman as she sauntered past, and she smiled freely in return, distracting him for a moment. "Come, Jenny-girl, help me.''

"I won't ask him for money, Rob,'' she warned. It wasn't that Brant wouldn't give it to her if she did. It was how she'd think of herself afterward. "I won't do that, not even for you.''

"Then if you can't—if you won't—I might have to call upon your darling duke myself and ask after my sister.''

"No!'' she exclaimed, barely remembering to keep her voice an urgent whisper. "You can't do that, Rob, please! You'll spoil everything!''

"It's your choice, Jen,'' he said, his gaze wandering past her to the fair-haired girl again, "just as it's mine.''

"Then, here—take this.'' As discretely as possible, she slipped the bracelet, garnets and seed pearls in silver, from her wrist and pressed it into his hand. The bracelet had come with the gowns, another selection from the mantua-maker's to pad her reckoning, and though it was neither a personal gift from Brant, nor of any great value, parting with it under such circumstances made her feel ungrateful and low and dishonest. "That's all I have for now."

"It's something, I suppose." Instantly the bracelet vanished into his pocket, and she knew she'd never see it again. "Mind yourself, Jenny, and remember who you are. We Dells never have been able to afford a single conscience among us, and I don't want you setting yourself up grand with one now."

But with a sick sadness in her heart, Jenny knew such a warning was already too late.

Once again Jenny was ready before Brant and waiting in the hall as the clocks through the house chimed the hour they'd agreed to leave for the theater. She never did take long to dress, no doubt from so many years of hasty departures. It would perhaps have been more appropriate, more ladylike, to remain in her own rooms and make him wait, instead, but she was too eager for the evening to begin to delay even a minute or two more than she had to.

She stood before one of the tall looking glasses and nervously smoothed her hair. She wore it twisted into a knot to give a firm anchor for the two plumes, and with them nodding gently in place, she'd left off any jewelry or extra ribbons. She'd long ago learned that elaborate fabrics and designs overwhelmed her, and that simplicity, like the white gown she was wearing tonight, suited her size and coloring the best. But she wasn't so sure what Brant would say, and she worried that, here in London, he might be expecting more *splendor* from her. She still had time to run upstairs and add something more to—

"Here you are," he said with surprise, coming down the stairs to join her. "How fine you look, Miss Wise!"

But any thought of how *she* looked flew from her head as soon as she saw him. Brant, dressed for evening, was a beautiful sight, indeed; all dark blue velvet across broad shoulders, impeccable linen and a waistcoat embroidered with glittering threads, and that warm, wicked smile that must make women weep when he entered a ballroom—a smile that was now entirely focused upon her.

"Thank you, Your Grace," was all she could manage to say, dropping a curtsy for good measure. "And you do look quite fine yourself."

"Oh, I look as my tailor wishes, that is all." He took her hand and kissed the air over the back of it, not the embrace she'd expected and had been ready to give. Puzzled, she wondered what she'd done, until she finally noticed Tway hovering to one side of the hall, his usual implacable self. How fortunate that she hadn't flung herself at Brant the way she'd wanted!

"So these are the feathers you bought at Mrs. Bertram's?" asked Brant, surveying her plumes. "She must have some wonderfully rare chickens in her henhouse to produce these."

Jenny wrinkled her nose. "They're from African ostriches, not common chickens, which you know perfectly well. And if you don't like them, you'd only to say so, and I'll pull them out."

"No, no, I like them well enough," he said, "though I'll be sure to keep to your left so they don't tickle my nose. Yet as that tailor of mine would say, the overall effect is still somewhat lacking."

"Lacking?" repeated Jenny uneasily, her earlier worries confirmed. "If I have dressed myself wrongly, Brant, then—"

"Hush," he said cheerfully, glancing toward Tway. "It's a small lack, one easily remedied. I understand that you were an arbiter of restraint this afternoon with Mrs. Bertram. She'd never seen anything like it, and I had to agree. Any lady that refuses to open Pandora's box when she's given the keys deserves to be rewarded."

Tway stepped forward with a bow, handing Brant a brown leather-covered box before he left them alone— a brown leather-covered box that Jenny recognized immediately.

"Oh, Gemini," she whispered, stunned, as Brant fastened the coral necklace around her neck. "Oh, Brant, you shouldn't have done this."

"I should, sweetheart, and I did." He smiled, as pleased by her reaction as he was by how well the necklace suited her. "Mrs. Bertram was right. No other lady should wear that necklace but you."

"Thank you," she said softly, lightly running her fingers over the polished coral, still not quite believing he'd made her such a gift.

She thought of what her brother had said, how he'd accused her of having acquired a conscience she couldn't afford. Even two months ago she would have regarded such a gift with cool distance, appraising its value even as she'd thanked its giver. But her brother was right. Since she'd met Brant, she *had* changed. Now when she looked at the necklace, she saw only the generosity and thoughtfulness of the man behind it—a man that had become most dear to her.

"It's lovely, Brant," she began, "and you know I can't say that it's not lovely, because it *is*. But when I think of how expensive—"

"I can afford it."

"But when people see it, they'll *know*," she said, troubled, "and they'll talk. Not so much about me, because I'm not a duke, but about you, because you are."

"Let them," he said firmly. "Jenny, they have spoken about me since I was too little to answer it back. That's part of being who I am, and a part I cannot change. As for the rest—people have been talking about us together since the morning I found you beneath the trees, and nothing we do or say is going to change it."

"But if—"

"Nothing, Jenny," he said, drawing her into his arms. "All that matters is what we say to each other. And I say that I cannot imagine anything more agreeable than having you on my arm tonight."

She sighed, slipping her hands around the back of his neck. He made it all sound so simple, and how much she wanted to believe him that it could be that way! "So no matter what you might hear—"

"I won't be listening," he assured her, "and neither should you. Now come, the carriage is waiting, and if we don't leave now, I'll find a thousand other excuses for staying here to kiss you, instead."

She laughed softly, sliding her hands from around his neck and down the velvet-covered expanse of his chest. "Then I shall simply have to give you a thousand reasons more for coming back to kiss me tonight."

"Don't tempt me, sweetheart," he said, his voice so low it was almost a growl. "I've never been a patient man."

"Nor am I known to be a patient woman, Your Grace," she said, barely dancing out of his reach with her skirts twirling around her ankles. "But as you say, we'd better leave now, and not keep the driver waiting."

Brant groaned, reluctantly following her to the door. "I know how the poor devil feels."

Oh, she might as well be walking barefoot across the hottest coals, she was that close to being burned, yet Jenny didn't care. It had been like this for days between her and Brant, simmering and stewing ever since that morning in the folly. Yet no matter how many times they'd kissed during the day, there remained an unspoken agreement that it was better for them now to pause and wait for the rest, and they'd still managed to go to their separate bedchambers each night.

At least, they had before tonight.

Oh, Jenny, Jenny, you're like a different woman, and not a lady, either. What has become of your resolve to keep from any man's bed? What has happened to your vows to hold your heart safe to yourself? And what could have possibly made you want to abandon a lifetime of cleverness and dissembling for the uncertain path of truth?

But none of those questions was so very difficult. The answer was sitting here in this carriage with her, so close she could feel the heat from his thigh pressing through his breeches and her skirts.

In a single word, what had happened to her was Brant.

Because the famous Sarah Siddons was to perform a tragedy tonight, the theater was full, with nearly every seat taken in both the boxes and the benches below. Brant had purposefully waited until the first ballet was nearly done for him and Jenny to arrive, hoping that they'd be able to make their way to his box more easily if the crush had thinned.

He'd calculated wrong. Even as the usher tried to lead them to their box, it seemed that every man that Brant had ever so much as played a hand of cards with came rushing forward to him, with just as many women around them craning their necks for a glimpse. The evening was warm, and the crowds and lanterns and chandeliers made it warmer still inside the theater. Though Brant wanted Jenny to be seen, this was exactly the kind of crush that he'd hoped to spare her, and he was all too aware of how she was pressing closer to him, her hand tightening anxiously around his arm. He shielded her as much as he could, tersely replying to the other men with single words and merely nodding to the women, and pushed on through after the usher.

At last they reached their box, and as Jenny settled herself in her chair, Brant gave orders to the usher that they were not to be disturbed. The orchestra was playing a limp march as intermission music and the main play had yet to begin, but he'd already had his fill of the theater, and he'd be willing to leave as soon as Jenny wished. *Now* would be fine.

"I'm sorry, sweetheart," he said as he came to sit beside her. "I'd no notion it would be quite so much like Bedlam here tonight."

"Oh, but it's not," she said quickly. "It's *wonderful.*"

As she smiled at him he realized she was excited, not frightened. Her eyes were bright with it, her smile glowing, and even the white plumes in her hair seemed to be quivering with anticipation. The candlelight turned her skin to flawless, rose-tinted ivory, and the diamonds in her necklace winked liked tiny stars around her throat. She'd never looked more vibrant, or more desirable, and glumly Brant knew she'd have every damned man in the place ogling her. He'd have to fight them off.

"All those people we passed," she continued, opening her fan. "Were they your friends?"

"Likely they'd call themselves so," he said, hedging. "I'm not certain I would."

He'd sound like a fool if he tried to explain how he kept his distance around others. It wasn't that he didn't trust them; he didn't trust himself. He could be as witty as the next gentleman, the perfect courtier when he had to wait upon His Majesty, an agreeable bluff companion over the faro table or at the races. But being an actual friend required confidences given and taken, a risk he'd never wanted to take, not with the secret of his own idiocy waiting there to be shamefully discovered.

"You could have spoken to the others if you wished," she continued gently. "You didn't have to be so...so *curt* on my account."

"I wasn't being curt," he said gruffly. "That's just how I am."

"Not with me, you're not," she said, placing her hand on his arm with more understanding than he deserved. "Which is likely why I've grown so monstrous fond of you. Oh, look, they're about to begin!"

Eagerly, Jenny leaned forward, as close to the rail as she could, as the orchestra played the overture to signal the rise of the curtain and the stately entrances of the players. At once she let herself be swallowed up by the magic of the play, unwittingly leaving Brant to stew and worry beside her.

What in blazes does she mean? How much has she learned, how much has she guessed? And exactly how fond is monstrous fond, anyway? Can that begin to match what I feel for her, every time she smiles at me or brushes her hand against mine? Damnation, how much has she guessed of that?

His misery grew as the evening stretched endlessly on. To him even Mrs. Siddons seemed a pasteboard harridan, wielding her make-believe dagger as she killed one poor bastard after another until the stage looked like a veritable charnel house of heaped bodies. Finally, and nary a minute too soon, she plunged the busy dagger into her own drapery, gave one last wordy speech, and grandly expired as the curtain dropped.

And at last Jenny turned to him, tears streaming down her cheeks and her handkerchief a sodden ball in her hands. "Oh, Brant, wasn't that perfection?"

"Perfection," he repeated, the safest—though least true—answer he could think of. "You enjoyed it, then?"

"More than you ever could know." Still lost in the emotion of the performance, she looked back at the stage, where the bloodstained actors had all miraculously recovered in time for their bows. "My father used to take me to plays all the time, even when I was so little I'd have to sit on his knee to see. Afterward I'd beg to learn the parts and then he'd proudly stand me up on a tall stool to recite them for his friends. Medea, Hecuba, Isabella, Lady Macbeth and Juliet—I played them all, with him as my hero."

Stunned, Brant seized her hand. "Your father brought you here, to this theater? You remember that? What was his name, Jenny? What was your father's name?"

She gasped and pressed her hand over her mouth as if as shocked as he by what she'd just said.

"I—I don't know," she whispered miserably. "I remember being here with him, and reciting the parts, but his name—he was only Father."

"Forgive me for interrupting, Your Grace," said the usher, his face twisting unhappily beneath his dusty white-powdered wig. "I know you asked not t'be disturbed, Your Grace, an' I'm sorry as can be, but His Grace the Duke o' Wickford, he's insisting, and I cannot keep—''

''You're damned right you can't keep me waiting, you little monkey,'' declared the old duke as he pushed his way into the box, swinging his walking stick at the hapless usher. ''Here, Claremont, let me have a look at this filly you've found for yourself.''

''Eastover.'' Gritting his teeth, Brant slowly rose, but that was as far as he would go for Richard Eastover, Duke of Wickford. Eastover had been one of his father's friends, a reptilian old man still powerful at Court, with hands that shook from palsy and half his nose eaten away by the pox. Only a pact with the devil must have kept him alive this long, and kept his dissipated habits and personality intact, as well.

''Well, Claremont, introduce the chit to me,'' he said, peering down at Jenny as if he wished to devour her. ''This is the one you found by the side of the road, isn't it?''

''She is the lady whose accident has put her into my care, yes.'' Brant wouldn't blame Jenny if she hid behind him or even bolted entirely, but instead she stood with her head—and plumes—held high as she curtsied the precise degree correct for a duke. A true lady born, he thought with pride. ''Your Grace, Miss Wise. Miss Wise, His Grace the Duke of Wickford. His Grace was a friend of my father's.''

''A fellow whoremonger, you mean.'' Eastover cackled, a rattling, cadaverous sound that echoed over the crowd. With the play on the stage ended, people were eagerly turning and standing on their benches or chairs to gawk at the Duke of Strachen's box, and this other infinitely more fascinating performance.

"Let me see you properly, girl," continued Eastover, using his walking stick to direct Jenny.

"You can see me well enough, Your Grace," said Jenny tartly, even as she looked to Brant for reassurance. "You and the rest of the theater."

"You've looked your fill, Eastover," said Brant sharply. He hated this kind of public display, almost as much as the other duke clearly relished it. "We were just leaving."

"'Twill only take a moment, you young pup. Now turn your face to the candle, girl, don't be pert. Aye, that's the way." He grunted with satisfaction and turned back to Brant. "Your mystery's solved, Claremont. I'd recognize this face anywhere. She's the image of her mother, and damn me if I didn't know *her*."

For the second time this evening, Jenny gasped, but this time she also grew so visibly pale that Brant instantly put his arm around her waist to support her.

"That's it, Claremont, hold her tight," said the old man gleefully. "If she's only half the vixen her mother was, she'll give you the ride of your life."

"Damnation, Eastover, that's enough," ordered Brant sharply. "Don't think because you're looking into your grave that I won't send my second to kick you the rest of the way. If you've nothing decent to say, I'll take the lady away from your filth now."

"You'd take her before I tell her mother's name?" Eastover asked, tantalizing. "You would do that to her, Claremont?"

But Jenny herself was desperately shaking her head, over and over. "No, Your Grace," she whispered. "Don't say it, oh, please, don't!"

The old duke only laughed again. "It's only fair you know, hussy, and so should Claremont. If you're not the daughter of the Marchioness of Bucklin, then the devil can come claim me now.''

"Oh, Gemini, it cannot be true!'' cried Jenny as she sagged against Brant's arm. "It *isn't* true!''

Swiftly, Brant swept her into his arms, cradling her, wishing he knew what else to do or say. "Don't listen to him, Jenny! He's wrong, I know it, and I—''

"Just...just take me home, Brant,'' she whispered as her eyes fluttered shut. "Please, please. Take me home now.''

Chapter Twelve

Jenny stared down at the brandy in her glass, swirling the amber-colored liquid into neat circles inside the crystal.

"Drink it," said Brant. "It's not going to do you one bit of good if it stays in the glass."

Jenny sighed, took a deep breath, and gulped as much as she could. She coughed and sputtered, but kept it down, an instant warmth glowing in the pit of her stomach. Or maybe the feeling was only more shame and mortification, and with a groan she closed her eyes, letting her head drop back against the settee's cushion.

"I should not have fainted, Brant," she said forlornly, staring up at the ceiling. He'd dismissed the sleepy footman who'd answered the door, and brought her here himself to the small upstairs parlor that he served as his town office, because he said he kept the brandy here in the locked corner cabinet.

But Jenny guessed that this was also likely his favorite room in the entire formal house, the only one she'd seen that was cluttered with his belongings and interests: a map of the Virginia wilderness, a box with specimens of glossy coal, a worn, outgrown leather dog collar with

Jetty's name engraved on the tag, white shells from the beach at Brighton and pinecones from the trees near the stables at Claremont Hall. He'd even had to clear away a set of surveyor's tools—he'd been dabbling in learning that, too—from this silk-covered settee before they could sit. All that was missing was Jetty and Gus. Yet still she was honored that he'd brought her to this little sanctuary without a thought, that he trusted her enough to share it with her.

That it was also near midnight and they were alone together in his rooms, scandalously unchaperoned, and only a few steps from his bedchamber—ah, Jenny knew that she and Brant had gone far beyond such niceties, nor did she care.

She sighed. "I should have been stronger than that. Only ninnies faint."

"It was the shock," he said softly, taking the nearly empty glass from her hand. "Being a ninny has nothing to do with it. Are you certain you don't wish me to send for a physician?"

She shook her head. "I'm fine. Truly."

"Good. I still cannot believe that evil old bastard lied to you," he said, his angry resentment not far from the surface. "And just for the sport of it, too."

"But I didn't know he was lying," she said. She tugged the two plumes from her hair and the pins out, too, restlessly combing the rest out with her fingers. "I thought he really *knew*."

Of course what she'd feared most was that the old duke was going to tell Brant was that her real mother had been his mistress. It wasn't impossible. No wonder she'd fainted like a ninny, though from relief, not shock.

Take this as a warning, Jen. He should hear the truth

from you, and no one else. If you care about him as you
claim, then you'll have to do it, and soon....

"The Marchioness of Bucklin has two sons, but no
daughters at all," explained Brant. "The boys were at
school with me. The only truth you'd ever learn from
Eastover is how despicable my own dear father would
be by now, for the two of them were always as alike as
two rotten peas in the same pox-ridden pod."

"I'm sorry," she said softly, reaching out to take his
hand across the settee cushions that separated them. The
window was open, the curtains shivering in the what
little breeze there was from the square. In this neighborhood, at this time of night, London was nearly silent.
Brant had only bothered to light two candles on the table
before them, and the shadowy half-light made the room
smaller, more intimate—the perfect place for confidences.

You could tell him now, Jen, and be done with it. No
more secrets, no more worries, only the truth.

And maybe the end of everything.

"You shouldn't be sorry," said Brant, and the bitterness in his voice made Jenny remember the rumors she'd
heard about the last Duke of Strachen. "You're hardly
to blame for my father. He can claim it all for himself."

"My poor Brant," she said softly. She kicked off her
slippers and curled her legs onto the settee, sliding across
the slippery silk to rest her head against his shoulder.
"Was he truly so bad?"

"That bad, and worse." With a sigh, he slipped his
arm around her, making a nest for her against his side.
He'd taken off his coat and waistcoat, and she could hear
his heartbeat through the soft Holland of his shirt. "He
was a selfish man who thought of nothing beyond his

own wicked pleasures, without any care for those he might wound along the way."

"Which explains why you are so generous now," she suggested fondly. "And you are, so don't say otherwise. With every bit of kindness, you hope to set his wrongs to right."

"No mortal could do that much settling, not in a single lifetime," he said, shrugging away her compliment. "The best I can say of my father is that he took no notice of me or my brothers when we were children. Although there were all sorts of nursemaids and tutors, the three of us boys largely raised ourselves, the wild young animals from the Hall."

"I can imagine," she said, chuckling, and reached up to ruffle his hair. "What boy wouldn't like a childhood like that?"

"Oh, it had its share of black patches, I can assure you," he said with a forced lightness that made Jenny guess sadly at how black those patches must have been. She could recognize them well enough: hadn't she had her own share of black patches, too? "Mind you, the house then was a run-down disaster, the stables were nearly empty and the gardens run to weeds. We often had to fend for ourselves in the kitchen because the cooks always quit when the grocers stopped delivery."

She could only picture Claremont Hall as she'd seen it, beautifully furnished and maintained, with a full, happy staff. "That's hard to imagine, considering how it is now."

"My father was extraordinarily thorough in stripping the estate as clean as he could," he said, the bitterness there again. "You can understand why I have none of the fond memories of my father that you seem to have of yours."

"My father," she repeated quietly, letting her hand drop back against her chest. She'd known that would come back, even though she'd prayed otherwise. She'd never intended to mention her father at all to Brant, let alone to tell him how she'd recited scenes for her father's friends. But somehow the excitement of being in a theater again had made her careless, and without a thought she'd shared it with Brant, as if she hadn't forgotten a thing about her past—which, of course, she hadn't.

"I suppose it was seeing the play tonight that made you remember that much," said Brant, more accurate than he could know. "What a pity it didn't jolt anything else free. Who knows? Perhaps you're really Sarah Siddons' daughter."

He meant it as a jest, but for Jenny the remark came too close to the truth for her. "I do not believe Mrs. Siddons would be of the proper age for that, Brant."

"Oh, silly, silly," he said, smiling indulgently as he curled a lock of her hair around his fingers. "I didn't mean it, Jen."

"Oh." She felt out of step, off balance, even as she tried to smile, too. "Though Mrs. Siddons is said to be a most respectable and refined woman, Brant. Fate could have given me a great many worse for a mother."

"True enough," he said amiably, "though to be honest, I do not think the hand that rocked your cradle was quite so covered in white powder and false blood."

"I don't remember," she said softly, which was, for once, thoroughly true. Her mother had run off when she'd been too little to notice, and all Jenny knew of her was what others had told, and none of that very flattering. "I cannot even say whether she lives or not."

"It will come back to you," said Brant confidently.

226 The Golden Lord

"What happened tonight should assure you of that. If you can recall going to Covent Garden with your father, then you must have visited London before, or even lived here. Tomorrow night, if the weather stays fair, I mean to take you to the gardens at Vauxhall. You can put those feathers back into your hair, and we'll dance and see what the fireworks shall shake loose from your memory."

Oh, it was so hard to keep trying to smile like this! "I believe I liked Claremont Hall better, where the only memories I had were the new ones I've made with you."

"Poor little Jen," he said gently, smoothing her hair back from her forehead. "I've fine memories with you, too. But this has to be done. Somewhere you have family, friends—your father who taught you to recite Lady Macbeth's part—who are wondering what's become of you, grieving for your loss. Who knows? Maybe we'll discover one of them tomorrow at Vauxhall."

"I don't know what we'll discover," she said sadly. On a warm summer night, thousands of merrymakers from every walk of life would cross the river to Vauxhall, and the odds were good that among all those people there'd be at least one, maybe more, that would recognize her face, if not her current name. An innkeeper whose bill she and Rob had neglected to pay, or a jeweler still waiting for the credit he'd granted them to be settled, or a country squire who'd made Rob a gentleman's loan in return for a favor that her brother had long ago forgotten—any of them could be dancing next to her and Brant at Vauxhall, ready to bring this fairy tale crashing down around her.

"Who knows what we'll find about me, Brant," she continued unhappily. "Maybe it's better for us not to know. Maybe memorizing Macbeth is the only good thing to be said of my father. He might be a drunken wastrel, and my mother a gaming harlot.''

''And so your parents would be exactly the same as mine,'' he answered firmly. ''I don't care, Jenny. With a father like mine, how could I possibly blame any sins of your parents upon you?''

Tell him, Jen, tell him the truth now!

''But, Brant,'' she began, ''what if I—''

''Hush,'' he said. ''No more worrying over what you know or don't know, or what might be. I've always known you were a lady from how you've spoken and acted from the moment I found you. That's enough for me, and should be for you, as well.''

He leaned down and kissed her, a kiss that Jenny knew full well was intended to give Brant the final word in this conversation. She kissed him back for the same reason, because that was what a lady would do. Ladies never argued with a gentleman. Instead, a lady would politely, meekly acquiesce, and let the gentleman believe he was omniscient and omnipotent and every other *omni* he wished.

''I've always known you were a lady from how you've acted.'' But what would he say when he learned that acting was all it had ever been?

''Jenny, Jenny,'' said Brant hoarsely as he finally broke their kiss, his breathing ragged. ''I warrant that should end our evening, shouldn't it?''

''Now?'' she asked, more anxiously than she realized. She didn't want to be left alone with her own thoughts, not tonight.

''Now, before we can't,'' he said, gently easing himself free of her to stand. ''Come, sweetheart, I'll take you to your own rooms.''

Gallantly he held his hand out to help her up, as well, but instead she only curled deeper against the cushions.

"No," she said so quietly she wasn't sure he heard.

He had, and he looked at her quizzically, his hand dropping back to his side. "No?"

"No." She knew how she must look, her hair tousled and loose around her shoulders, the diamonds still twinkling around her throat, her narrow muslin skirts twisted up around her green ribbon garters, and her bodice slipping down even lower, all of it lit by the two wavering candles.

At least that was how she hoped she looked to him. And from how his body seemed to have frozen with tension, his expression crossing from open interest to unabashed hunger, she could see her hopes were right.

She glanced up at him from beneath her lashes, her cheek resting on her cupped hand. "I suppose you can leave me here," she said. "But I'd rather you stayed, too."

His eyes were shadowed by the half-light. "Damnation, Jenny. Do you know what you're saying?"

She raised her chin, deliberate and defiant, so there'd be no misunderstanding. Maybe that wasn't what a lady should do, but then maybe there were times when it was better not to be a true lady after all.

"I don't want to go back to my rooms," she said in the same low, quiet voice. "I don't want to spend the night alone, waiting awake until dawn and the sound of the milkmaid to call at the kitchen door. You said we should make each day our own, Brant, because that's all we might have. But I won't wait for the day. I want the night, this night, and I want it with you."

"Ah, Jenny, my Jenny." He came to stand over her where she lay, bracing his hands on the arm of the settee behind her head. "You've said before you were a gambler."

"I am." She might be a virgin, but she wasn't innocent, not with everything she'd seen and heard from Rob and her father. She knew the risk of conceiving a child without the blessing of a wedding, and she knew how often the mother would be left with the responsibility of that child while its father blithely disappeared. She knew that passion and desire could be mistaken for love, but seldom the other way around, and that both could be as fleeting as the morning mist.

And she knew, too, that Brant was a gentleman of the world, with the wealth, power and opportunity to have indulged himself any way he pleased. Gentlemen were expected to have such amorous adventures. He could already be carrying the same kind of pox that had ravaged the Duke of Wickford's face, a disease Brant could now pass along to her.

All these risks she knew. But she would freely gamble with them because it was Brant, because she loved him—*yes, she loved him!*—and because the tomorrow her father had always promised might never come. All that she had for certain with Brant was this night, this hour, this moment.

And that, to her, was no gamble at all.

She reached up and looped her hands around his neck, drawing him slowly down toward her.

"I must be Miss Wise after all," she said as she smiled just before his lips found hers, "because no mere ninny would do be lucky enough for this."

This time when he kissed her, she felt the intensity of it rush over her, making her head dizzy and her heart pound as hard as if she were running a race. He teased her lips with little nips, then before she could answer he deepened the kiss, his tongue making heady pleasure against hers.

Now she realized how much he'd been holding himself back before this, even that morning in the folly. He'd so much more to give, and trusting her instinct to follow his lead, she strived to return that pleasure to him. She heard the creak of the settee's springs as he lowered himself onto her, felt how her own body shifted and her legs parted to welcome him.

Even as they kissed, he was easing her bodice lower, magically unfastening by feel alone the tiny hooks that held it together. Her breasts tightened in the cooler night air, or maybe it was his touch that did that, too. He knew exactly how to tease her inexperienced flesh, rough, then gentle, across the crests of her nipples, making them taut and sensitive. With little cries that were lost between their mouths, she arched beneath him, her body begging for the *more* she anticipated but could not express.

Impatiently she pulled his shirt free from his breeches, sliding her hands up and down the hard, muscled length of his back. She wriggled on the slippery silk, and she felt him groan, a power she'd no notion she had. He was tugging at her skirts, pulling them higher, and she lifted her legs to help him, wanting that thin cotton barrier between them gone, too.

Then he was touching her *there,* in that place between her legs that had been, until the folly, neither interesting or remarkable. Now it seemed both, pulsing and quivering beneath his stroking fingers, making her gasp for air and her whole body tremble.

But if he could touch her so intimately and with such results, then she wished to do the same. She tugged next at his breeches, untying the bow at the back of the waistband and then reaching between their hips for the buttons on the fall. With hands made clumsy by desire, she slowly unfastened one, then two, three, four, and suddenly she'd found his own wanting flesh, hot and velvety-hard.

She touched him tentatively at first, not wanting to hurt him. But the more insistent his fingers became against her, upon her, inside her, the more she'd tightened her grasp of him until, abruptly, he was guiding her hands to put *him* to the place he'd been so divinely tormenting.

Suddenly everything made blinding sense, including a lifetime of bawdy jokes about locks and keys, and hands in gloves. Not that she had much time to consider any jests at all, not when he was pushing into her, thrusting deep and opening her in a way that made her cry out loud, not with pain but pleasure. Instead of pushing him away, her body seemed intent on pulling him deeper. Her knees pulled back and crossed around his waist, holding him there, while her hips moved to meet him.

Slowly the rhythm between them built, their bodies slick with sweat and their groans and cries echoing with a passionate fervor. On and on, higher and higher, until Jenny feared the tension in her body was too great to survive, and then came the release, a dizzying plummet so sudden and so sweet she wept with joy. Another quick thrust from Brant, and then, he, too, groaned and shuddered with his completion, collapsing over her in a sweaty tangle of limbs and damp linen.

"Oh, Brant," she whispered at last, her voice wobbly with the emotion that still seemed to be vibrating through her limbs. Gently she smoothed his hair back to kiss his forehead, and laughed softly when his only an-

swer was an unintelligible growling grunt of male satisfaction. "Miss Wise feels a good deal wiser now."

He pushed himself up on his elbows, their faces close.
One of the candles had guttered out and the flickering
light of the one that remained only added to the magic
that Jenny still felt.

"My own dear Jenny," he said, his voice thick and
low and impossibly seductive to her ears. With his
thumb he gently wiped away the tears that streaked her
face, then kissed her with such tenderness she almost
wept again. "Did I hurt you? Are you all right?"

"Of course I'm all right," she said. "How could I be
anything else after we just did that?"

"You might add that we did it most splendidly, too,"
he said, rolling to one side against the back of the settee,
but keeping his arm loosely but possessively around her
waist. "That was your, ah, your first experience, wasn't
it?"

"I did things correctly?" she asked anxiously. "It
seemed right, but if I—"

"You did it with absolute correctness, sweetheart,"
he said, chuckling as he kissed her again. "But I do
believe we can now safely say no husband will come
claim you."

"I told you that," she said indignantly. "You
wouldn't believe me."

He grunted. "I didn't because I didn't want to have
to choose between pistols and swords on some dismal
foggy morning."

"I *told* you," she said again, then sighed.

What she wanted to do now, more than anything, was
to tell him she loved him. It seemed proper and appropriate, considering the circumstances, and besides, it was
true. She did love him, more than anything. But if she'd

learned one thing from listening to Rob, it was that men did not want to hear the tiniest breath about love afterward. The simple word made them irritable, cross, trapped and threatened, or so Rob had stoutly maintained. She wanted Brant to feel as happy as she was herself, and so she said nothing of what was singing inside of her.

"You're very quiet, sweetheart," he said with concern. "Are you sure you're not hurting?"

"No," she whispered, weaving her fingers into his. "Not at all."

"Good," he said. "Because I love you too much for that, you know."

"What?" Swiftly she twisted about, wanting to see his eyes even by the faint light of the candle.

His eyes were heavy-lidded, but his smile was wide and happy and *truthful.* "Because I love you, dear Jenny. I love you."

She would weep again; there was no help for it. "Oh, Brant, I love you, too! *I love you, too!"*

"A good thing, then." He chuckled, kissing her again. "And if we can find a more comfortable place than this damned bench, I'll gladly show you again how much and how often and in how many ways I can love my own dear Jenny."

It was the sound of worried voices that woke Jenny the next morning. Before she'd even really awakened, she heard their murmur, their confusion, even if she couldn't make out precisely what they were saying. Reluctantly she opened the eye that wasn't pressed into the pillow, and saw beyond the bedcurtains a room she didn't know. With a little gasp, she jolted awake and sat upright, jerking the sheets up over her bare breasts.

Then she saw Brant still sleeping on his back beside her, one arm flung to one side and a blissful smile on his face. She relaxed and smiled, remembering. She was in Brant's bedchamber, in Brant's enormous bed with the Claremont arms carved on the canopy. He loved her, and she loved him, and he'd kept his promise to show her in so many ways she still felt pleasingly exhausted. If he was smiling now, then she was the reason, for what dream could ever rival this night?

But there were the worried voices again, just outside the door to Brant's bedchamber. The querulous man: that was Tway, and the other two, younger and female, must belong to maidservants. Jenny flushed, sinking lower against the pillows with the sheets clutched tight, even though they couldn't see though the closed door to her in the duke's bed.

By now the entire household must know she was here, especially once they'd seen her own bed empty. And it wasn't as if she and Brant had tried to hide what they'd done: she'd left her slippers, her shawl and her plumes in the little parlor, and Brant's evening coat and waistcoat were likely there, too. They'd each shed more of their clothing in a hasty, guilty trail to this bed, and Jenny winced when she realized her gown would be tossed across the chair in the dressing room on the other side of that door.

Now she heard a muted clink of china and silver, and the faint wafting scent of coffee. So that was the worry: what was to be done with the duke's breakfast tray? More voices, then the click of the dressing room door and footsteps receding down the hall.

But the scent of the coffee remained, raising Jenny's hopes that the tray had been left and making her stomach grumble with anticipation, too. She slipped from the bed carefully, not wanting to wake Brant, and pulled a coverlet from the bed to wrap around her. Scurrying barefoot across the room, she listened again at the door for voices before she opened it, just to be sure. The tray was waiting, an enormous silver tray filled with every kind of morning food: clearly the staff thought His Grace would need fortifying, and gleefully Jenny hauled it back into the bedchamber.

"What in blazes are you doing?" demanded Brant sleepily as he sat upright in the bed. "What's that infernal racket?"

"Breakfast," said Jenny cheerfully. Enjoying the rare role of waiting on another, she brought Brant his coffee with a kiss before she perched on the corner of the bed with a thick slice of bread and a pot of strawberry jam. She spread the red jam neatly to the crusts, the way she liked it.

But this time she decided to make it special. With the tip of her knife's blade, she carefully etched a heart into the red jam, followed by a simple message: I Love You.

"Look," she said, proudly holding the bread up for Brant to read. When he looked up, she bit one corner from the crust and grinned wickedly.

He grinned back, but clearly in response to her, not the message in the jam.

"Don't you see it?" she asked, puzzled. "'I love you.'"

"I love you, too, Jenny," he said, leaning back against the pillows like a bare-chested king on his throne. "As I'm perfectly happy to demonstrate again."

But he still didn't seem to see the words on the bread, and with a disappointed frown Jenny bit another chunk from the corner.

"I suppose it does make a better breakfast than a valentine," she said philosophically, licking the jam from her fingers.

He paused, an uneasy expression on his face. "What are you saying, Jen? What about valentines?"

"My sweet heart for my sweetheart," she explained, once again holding the slice of bread up for him to read.

He nodded, his uneasiness obviously growing. "Ah. Now I see it. A heart. *Your* heart, yes?"

"But the rest," she persisted. "I know I've eaten some of the crust, but can't you read the words?"

He looked from the bread to her and back again, clearly as bewildered as if she'd carved the three jammy words in Chinese characters. His reaction didn't make sense, she thought, no sense at all. Suddenly she remembered how she'd never seen him with a book or newspaper, how Tway handled his correspondence, how he'd relay all his messages through servants, instead of writing them himself.

It couldn't be possible. He was clever and funny and intelligent, a man who'd become wealthy by his own wits. He was a peer, a duke. He was her *Brant.*

Swiftly she left the bed, intent on finding something, anything, to prove her guess was wrong.

"Jenny?" he called after her. "Jenny, love, what's wrong?"

There were no books in his bedchamber, not so much as a calling card with a friend's name printed on it. But in the dressing room she found a small booklet of rough paper with a stylus tucked inside that was used to keep track of Brant's shirts as they passed to the laundress and back to the clothespress.

"What the devil are you doing, Jenny?" asked Brant, thrusting his arms into his dressing grown as he joined her. "Why did you go running off that way?"

Hating herself for having to know, she quickly printed the same message—I Love You—on the back page of the laundress' book, and held it out to him.

"Read that," she pleaded softly. "Please, Brant. Prove to me I'm a ninny, and read that."

But he didn't even try, his eyes bleak with a suffering she couldn't understand. "How did you know, Jen? It was the bread, wasn't it? You'd written something there besides the heart, didn't you?"

"'I love you,'" she said, reaching for his hand. "That's what it said. Here, too, on this page. I love you."

"So now you know what a true and noble idiot I am." He turned away sharply, shaking her hand away. "Any child in a dame school can read more than the great Duke of Strachen. Any *child* can look at the marks that are letters and see words, sentences. But not I. To my feeble, dim-witted brain, letters are no more than goose tracks in the mud."

"But you're not an idiot, Brant!" she cried, appalled he could think such a thing of himself. "No one would ever say that of you!"

"I would, and so did Father," he said, facing the window to avoid her. "And I *know.*"

"What of your ventures, your investments?" she said, rushing to stand beside him. "You couldn't be dim-witted and do that. I saw you making calculations, figuring losses and profits to the penny."

"Numbers I can see, and make sense of," he said bitterly. "It's letters my weak mind can't decipher."

"Stop saying such things, Brant, because they're not *true!*" she cried frantically. "How could you have survived school otherwise?"

"I nearly didn't," he admitted. "I was thrashed reg-

ularly by the masters for what they deemed my willful-
ness and my gross stupidity, until I feigned a weakness
of the eyes—that was forgiven—and paid another boy
to read to me. I memorized everything, and fooled them
all, and then I had Tway to do the rest.''

"But your brothers must have known!"

"The hell they did." Absently he tapped his knuckles
against the glass. "I was the eldest, the heir, the only
one between them and Father's rages. I had to be perfect
for them. No one has ever guessed the truth. Until you
did, Jen. I could never fool you, could I?"

"But you don't have to," she insisted, coming around
to stand between him and the window, refusing to let
him push her away. "What I wrote is the truth. I love
you, Brant, and I always will. Didn't you say you'd take
me as I am, and judge me for myself? Why won't you
believe I'd do the same with you?"

He didn't answer at first, staring past her head toward
the square outside. "I believed we belonged together,
you know. You had no memory, and I had no words.
Neither of us are quite as we should be, are we?"

"No," she said with genuine sadness. "No. At least
I'm not."

*Oh, Jen, now look what your tale-telling has wrought!
What will he say when he learns that even your lost
memory was a sham? What will happen to his love for
you when he discovers how badly you've played him
false?*

"Nor I." His laugh was dark, humorless. "The lost
lady and the idiot duke. What a pair we make, eh? Perhaps between our fractured selves we could make a
whole."

"We still can, Brant," she said fiercely. She slipped
her arms around his waist, and to her relief he didn't try

to push her away. "We still *will*. There has always been something between us, something that's bound us together in a way I can't explain. But it's right, Brant, and it's what…what makes me love you so much!"

"Miss Wise speaks." At last he groaned and folded her into his arms. "Oh, Jenny, I love you too much to ever say no to you."

"Then don't," she whispered, her cheek pressed to his chest, over his heart, as she tried to forget how hideously complicated and knotted this all had become. "Because that's how I love you, too, Brant. That's how I love you."

Mary Hewitt sat on the tall stool in the back of her brother-in-law's greengrocer shop, eating an orange and reading the newspaper spread on the counter before her. She did not like her brother-in-law for being common and in trade or for keeping an ancient pistol beneath the counter in case of thieves, and she liked him even less for insisting that she must take her turn keeping the shop for as long as she was a guest in his home above it.

However, Mary had soon learned that few customers visited the shop late in the day, the watch assigned to her, which gave her plenty of time to read the scandal sheets devoted to the doings—and misdeeds—of aristocratic London, with a heady assortment of ne'er-do-wells like jockeys and actresses and politicians added for leavening. Compared to all the trouble and shame these fine folk bumbled into, Mary's own trials seemed slight, indeed, a fact she found great comfort in.

Until, that is, her life and the scandals of high folk collided headfirst into one another.

His Grace the Duke of Strachen was also to be seen in his box, his guest a most mysterious and original young lady. Having suffered from a grievous accident that robbed her of all memory of her true self, she is called Miss Wise by His Grace until her real name is known. But all honored to greet her last evening found her fresh and unaffected, most surely a lost gem worthy of a place in the highest circles and favors of Society. There are some hints she might even be the daughter of the C*****ss of B*****n.

The guest of a duke, the daughter of a countess, while she, Mary, sat here in the back of greengrocer's shop! It was not to be borne, not to be tolerated, and desperately Mary tore through the pages, searching for the address of the paper's offices. She would go there herself and tell the editor the truth about His Grace's doxie and her wastrel brother, too. This would be better than all her letters combined. Surely the duke could be made to see his folly. Surely this would bring the girl to her ruin, and her brother with her.

Surely, at last, the two of them would be punished the way they deserved.

Chapter Thirteen

Three days later Brant sat across from Jenny in his bed, and smiled, happier than he'd any right to be. In this short time they'd fallen into a morning routine worthy of any ancient married couple: they'd wake when they pleased, they'd make love for as long as they pleased, and then they'd have their breakfast here on the bed, with the curtains cozily drawn about them like a tent.

How strange and wonderful it was to have her here with him! It was not only that he loved her and she him, but that she'd discovered his hideous secret and loved him still. All his life he'd suffered alone, dreading the ridicule or pity that must surely come from anyone who learned of his stupidity with words.

But to Jenny it had been next to nothing, with his secret shame far worse than the affliction itself. The real marvel to Brant was not only that he trusted her with this knowledge, confident that she'd never betray it, but also the relief he felt in being able to share his frustrations with another—particularly when that other was a woman he loved more and more each day.

Each morning she'd read him stories from the newspaper while he sipped his coffee, an entirely different experience than when Tway had performed the same service. For one thing, Jenny preferred stories about a marvelous three-headed rooster in Derbyshire, or the fishmonger's baby born speaking church Latin, as well as the breathless cataloging of the Prince's activities, while Tway had dutifully stuck to news of politics and foreign affairs.

There was also the charming sight of Jenny sitting cross-legged on his bed as she was now, wearing strawberry jam on her fingers and lips and not much else as she read to him, that Tway fortunately could never rival.

She was exactly what this chilly house needed, he decided contentedly, laughter and strawberry jam and lying abed until noon. And love, boundless quantities of love. How the devil had he managed to live his life so long without Jenny in it?

"O-oh, Brant, listen to this," she said eagerly. "This is most interesting!"

"What, have you found us some amusement for tonight?" he asked. They'd followed his plan to visit as many public entertainments as possible, from painting galleries to concerts to Vauxhall, in the hope that she'd either remember more or meet someone who'd recognize her. But they'd learned nothing new, and by now he'd almost believed she'd dropped clean from the sky, without a single friend or relative. He knew her lack of a past continued to make Tway uneasy, but all Brant felt was sympathy for Jenny, to be left so alone in the world.

"No, no, no, it's far better than that," she was saying eagerly, leaning over the paper. "Listen. 'Those on their morning promenade through Green Park were astounded to view the M**ch****ss of W*lk dressed entirely in scarlet, as if for a hunt. Perhaps in truth she was hunting, tho' with Cupid's darts, for was not the dashing Sir

H**ry to be seen likewise in the Park that morning?' Can you guess who the marchioness is, Brant? Double-you, blank, el, kay. Do you know who that is?''

"The Marchioness of Walk," he said. "The man's Sir Henry Townsend, and they'd each be well advised to stay clear of the other, for I don't know which is worse. Cupid's pox would be more like it."

"Gemini, Brant, but you're no fun," pouted Jenny, turning back to the papers. "Here's one about a duke who—oh, no, Brant, it's you. It's you and…and me."

"Well, read it, then," he said expansively. "Tell me what sort of darts you're flinging at me."

But she stayed silent, her face growing more and more distraught as she read to herself.

"What is it, Jen?" he asked softly. "Is it cruel?"

"It's…it's very cruel," she said. "It's most unkind about us both."

"Then read it to me only if you wish," he said. There were sometimes distinct advantages to not being able to read, and the scandal sheets were one of them. God only knew that as a wealthy duke who'd had the temerity to remain unwed, his name, with suitable asterisks, likely appeared in them far too often. "I won't care if you simply toss the whole blasted paper directly into the fire, where it belongs."

But she only shook her head, and began reading aloud. "'It has been brought to our attention by a most impeccable private source that the young woman currently presenting herself as an acquaintance of His Grace the D**e of St*****n is not the lady of breeding she pretends to be. We strongly advise His Grace to be wary, and guard his heart and his pocketbook against this clever hussy's advances.'''

She stopped, and bowed her head, letting her hair fall

around her face like a veil to mask her shame. "Oh, Brant, I am so *sorry*."

"There's nothing for you to feel sorry for, not in the least." He plucked the paper from her lap, crumpled it in a ball, and hurled it across the room and into the grate.

"That's what I think of such drivel," he said. "That's what you should think of it, too, Jen. I don't believe a word of it, and neither should you. It's the same as those damnable letters that came to us in the country. Some poor bastard is lonely, or envious, or disapproving, and this is the shallow, slanderous way they amuse themselves."

"But the paper warned you against me," she protested, troubled. "They said I meant to rob you."

"Oh, yes, and whyever else would you have an interest in me?" he asked. "Two days ago those bastards were praising your gown and necklace at the theater, and now they've reduced you to a predatory harpy. No one pays any heed to it, Jen."

"But what if it *is* true?" she asked, her voice wavering. "What if this...this *source* knew me before, and I am that bad?"

"Then they didn't know you very well," he said. "No more fussing over this, Jenny. Better you should find me more news of the three-headed rooster."

"The fabulous Master Cock-crow, you mean." She sighed mightily. "You are certain you'll pay that story no heed?"

"Absolutely," he said, reaching out to pull her across the bed and into his arms. "I have the truth about your motives from a most impeccable private source, which is you yourself. Besides, we haven't much time left in London to amuse the world with our doings."

"We're going back to the Hall?" she asked eagerly. "Oh, I am so glad!"

Her enthusiasm pleased him, for he much preferred the country, too. "Jetty and Gus have missed us barbarously much," he said, "and we can't let them pine away. But other than that, my brothers and their wives are coming to visit, and to see my nephew duly christened in the chapel, like the good little Claremont heir that he is."

"Your family will be there?" she asked, her excitement fading. "Oh, Brant, how shall you explain me?"

He frowned, for he hadn't quite figured that out for himself yet, either. "They'll all like you just fine, I'm sure."

"That's not what I asked," she said slowly. "You don't know what to say, do you? It was one thing before we became lovers, when you could say I was simply your guest and you my charitable host, but now—you can hardly introduce your mistress to your brothers' wives. They'll never forgive you."

"Of course they will, because I'm the oldest brother." He stopped, realizing too late what he'd said. "That is, you're not really my mistress, not in the common sort of way. You're not some little milliner's assistant or actress that I plucked from nowhere for amusement. I don't pay you for your favors, or have you settled in a cottage in Chelsea. You're more my lover."

"Oh, yes, and that will make for easier, more proper introductions with your brothers and their wives." She pulled away from him, sitting apart, and inspecting the ends of her hair to avoid meeting his gaze. "The other ladies will hate me, Brant, and I cannot blame them for it. Perhaps you truly should set me up in that cottage in Chelsea."

"You're a lady, Jenny. You know damned well I'd never do that to you."

"At least that way I'd know what I was and where I belonged," she said unhappily, "even if I didn't know my name. Or perhaps I should simply leave you altogether."

"Without family or friends?" he asked incredulously.

"I would manage," she declared. "I'd find a way. There's plenty of common women who make their own path in the world."

"But, fortunately, they're not you," he said, pushing her hair aside to kiss the back of her neck. He had to remember that things were different for ladies, and especially difficult for Jenny. "Where I hope you belong is with me, because you love me, and I love you, and I cannot imagine us being otherwise."

She sniffed, but at least that showed she was listening.

"And when I go back down to Claremont Hall," he continued, "I hope you'll come with me, as my guest, my friend, my lover. Not because I'll make you do it, but because I wish you to be there with me."

She twisted around to face him, her expression so solemn and determined that he realized to his shock she might very well have left him. "Then I shall. Because I love you, Brant. For no other reason, because that's reason enough, I'll come with you to Claremont Hall."

"I must make this quick, Rob," said Jenny, glancing nervously over her shoulder. "I don't know how long I can be away without being missed."

"Well, and a fine good-day to you, too, sister," said Rob indignantly as he fell into step beside her. They were walking along the square path around the center of Grosvenor Square, keeping beneath the shelter of the decorative trees. "Every afternoon I've been here, regular as German clockwork, and that's the best greeting you can muster, that you must leave before you've said hello?"

Jenny sighed. "I'm sorry, Rob. It's the way things are for me here, that is all."

She knew the odds were very slim that anyone would notice her gone at this hour. Brant was at his meeting with Tway, and because they were not expected back for at least another three hours, the staff was all busily napping or otherwise entertaining themselves below stairs. It wasn't even likely that anyone would glance from a window and see her here, for by Mrs. Harper's strict orders, all curtains and shutters were drawn by day to protect the furniture from fading from the sun.

But Jenny herself hated slipping away alone like this to meet Rob, going against Brant's request for her not to leave the house without a footman. No matter how much she told herself that this was the only safe way to see her brother, she still felt as if she were betraying Brant's trust, and she didn't like herself for doing it.

Yet Rob misunderstood. "Does he use you ill, Jenny-girl?" he asked with concern. "Sometimes it's the men born the highest who treat their women the worst. We can leave now, if you're ready, and I can make sure he'll never find you again."

"Oh, no!" she exclaimed, stunned. "Brant's not like that, not at all!"

"No?" asked Rob, puzzled. "Then what's amiss? Why are you here?"

"Because we're going back to Claremont Hall tomorrow, and I wanted you to know. His brothers are coming, too, for his nephew's baptism." Hurriedly she reached into her reticule and pressed a small knitted purse into his hand. "And here. I know it's not much, but I've kept a bit back from when we've gone to shops and—"

"Keep it, Jen," he said, pushing the money away. "I've found my own game for now."

"Oh." She slipped the purse back into her reticule and snapped it shut. She didn't really want to know what sort of "game" Rob had found, what her name was or where she lived, any more than she liked the implication that what she had with Brant was only her "game," too. "I'm happy for you, then."

He shrugged carelessly, ever Rob. Whoever he was with was looking after him: he was less gaunt, better fed and his linen was once again spotless. "It will do for now. But this going back to the same corner of Sussex— that's not wise for you, Jen. You know better than that. Keep moving, keep moving—that's what Father would say—and never go backward."

"I know," she said unhappily. "I know, I know, I *know*. And yet I cannot help myself from going because of him."

"Ah, the lure of the grand and mighty Duke of Strachen, the great Golden Lord himself," said Rob wryly. "So who are you with him, now that your memory's back?"

"It's not," she confessed. "All I've 'remembered' so far is that my real name is Jenny, not Corinthia, and—"

"You told him your real name?" Rob was appalled, and she knew he'd every right to be. "He knows you're Jenny Dell?"

"Not Dell," she said quickly. "Just the Jenny part. And I did slip once, when we were at Covent Garden, and I told him how Father used to have me recite the lady's roles for his friends."

"I cannot believe this." He dropped onto a nearby bench, as if the effort of listening was simply too much to bear. "What else has the duke guessed by now?"

"Nothing," she said. "He trusts me, Rob, just as I trust him."

"He trusts you because you're warming his bed. No, don't deny it, I saw it in your face the minute we met." He sighed with exasperation. "I don't suppose he's spoken of marriage."

"No." She sat on the bench beside him, her gloved hands clasped contritely on her knees. "But it was my choice to lie with him, Rob. I want you to know that. He didn't force me."

"He didn't have to, did he? Not when you were being so blessed accommodating."

"I love him, Rob," she declared as firmly as she could. "I love him, and he loves me. That's why I'm going with him back to Claremont Hall."

Rob stared at her, just stared, as the blood slowly flooded her cheeks. How could he make everything with Brant seem so foolish without saying a word, as if she were simply one more empty-headed woman who'd sacrificed her best chances in the name of love? On the other side of the square's iron fence an organ-grinder was playing his instrument, the bouncy, cheerful music adding a strange counterpoint to their conversation.

"You know what I'm going to tell you, don't you?" he said finally. "I don't have to say it aloud, do I?"

"I'm not going to give him up, Rob," she said, the steeliness in her voice surprising even herself. "That's what you're going to say, and I won't do it. He's honest and kind and good and generous, and that's what I want from my life now."

"You're going to become a kinder and more honest

woman by being his *mistress?*'' asked her brother incredulously. ''How exactly is that to happen?''

''Rob, I love him,'' she repeated defensively, ''and he loves me as I am!''

''Jenny-girl, look at me,'' he said earnestly, taking her hand. ''He can't love you as you are, because you haven't told him the truth. You can't.''

''Yes, I can!''

''All right, then. You can, but you won't. It's too late for that. You've spun your tale far too long, and you've put yourself at risk by doing it, and you're afraid. You let yourself fall in love with a peer who will never wed you. You've made yourself such a favorite of the scandal sheets that you'll have the devil of a time becoming anyone else. I should never have let you go off on your own for so long, and this is what comes of it.''

''Rob, I'm nineteen years old, and it was *my* choice!''

''Yet you've behaved like the greenest lass alive. Father'd have my head for letting you get into such muck.'' He sighed again, and patted her hand exactly the way their father had so many years before. ''I'll hate to see you hurt, little goose, but it's far better that than the alternative. Collect whatever's of most value tonight, and I'll be waiting for you here before dawn tomorrow.''

She stood at once. ''I'm sorry, Rob, but I won't be there. I'll be going with Brant, instead.''

''Don't be a fool, Jen,'' he said sharply as he stood, too. ''Remember who you really are. There's nothing to be gained by going with a duke, and everything to lose.''

''Then maybe it's time we took different paths,'' she said, kissing him swiftly on the cheek. ''Goodbye, Rob, and good luck wherever you go.''

''Remember who you are, Jenny-girl!'' he called after her. ''I'll be waiting for you tomorrow!''

But she kept on walking and she didn't turn back, and by the time she'd reached the house again, no one would have guessed how hard she'd cried.

Mary Hewitt smoothed the newly published print on the greengrocer's counter and cackled with delight. She hadn't shown it to anyone else, knowing her sister would scold her. "Forget that lying gentleman and find another," was what her sister tartly advised; don't waste your life trying to change what was already done. Better to keep poor Herbert's memory dear than fussing over the rascal that wronged you.

But just as Mary's sister would never share the pain of her humiliation at Richard Faquhar's hands, she'd also never realize the satisfaction that Mary had now discovered. Those cursed Farquhars would be made to suffer now, wouldn't they? For those first wicked seeds Mary had planted with the newspaper's editor had grown and blossomed with a virulence she never could have imagined, here in the splendid cartoon on the counter before her.

The artist had drawn the figures with wicked accuracy. Entitled *The Blind Connoisseur of Beauty,* the caricature showed the Duke of Strachen bending over to admire a flower with a dandy's quizzing glass held up to his blindfolded eyes, while behind him the girl labeled "Jenny," the one that Mary knew as Jane Farquhar, was gleefully picking his watch from the pocket of his brocade coat with a knowing harlot's wink.

In a little bubble over the duke's head, he was saying, "Ah, a Jenny by any name will ever smell as sweet!" while the girl proclaimed, "I do so love a rich man!" To complete the scene, a smirking Cupid floated overhead, waving a banner that read Lust is Blind.

Oh, it was perfect, decided Mary with joy, too, too perfect! Surely the artist must have seen Jenny/Jane at the theater or elsewhere, for he'd captured her sly eyes and smug smile. If he'd also drawn the little creature's breasts far larger than they were, spilling out hugely from the neck of her gown, then that would only make the print a lasting favorite on the walls of taverns and rum shops all across the country.

There'd be no possibility the Duke could miss seeing this print, or escape the embarrassment that was sure to follow him. Even a duke must feel humiliation, and do whatever he must to escape it—and the girl who'd caused it.

Mary's only regret was that there was no mention of the brother, the Richard Farquhar who'd treated her so badly in the first place. But she didn't doubt that the duke would make him suffer along with his sister. Surely there'd be no more diamond necklaces or visits to playhouses after this. Instead, the Farquhars would be lucky to leave London without seeing a magistrate first, or even disappearing into the Thames one dark night with stones tied to their feet. A duke would have the power and resources to decide any vengeance he wished against the pair.

And to think that she, Mrs. Mary Hewitt of Bamfleigh, had begun it all....

With his fingertips pressed lightly together in a little arched tent over his waistcoat, Brant silently studied the other men in the room and waited for their answer. From so much gaming, he was generally good at reading faces, but this stern-faced group wasn't revealing a thing.

God knows he'd done his best. He'd already given them more information about the venture than they could ever want or need, more figures and maps and projections of success. He'd used the eloquence of a poet to describe the Virginian wilderness, the eagerness of a visionary who saw opportunity, the no-nonsense rhetoric of a banker to predict the heady profits to be gained. He'd modestly recounted his own success with similar ventures, and he'd reminded them in a roundabout way of how few other peers would offer City men such an opportunity. And though he hadn't mentioned his ridiculous nickname as the Golden Lord, he was sure there wasn't a man in this room who'd forgotten it.

He'd done all he could, here in this severe meeting room with its long table and uncomfortable chairs, and a fly-specked plaster bust of Plato in the niche between the windows. Now it was up to these nine other men— bankers, merchants, speculators and two minor lords— to decide if he'd been convincing enough to invest their money in his venture.

"If you have any further questions or issues, gentlemen," he said, his voice at once confident yet nonchalant, "you know I shall be happy to address them as best I can."

They nodded, some speaking softly to one another behind their hands. Standing behind Brant's chair, Tway again cleared his throat, far more worried than Brant about the outcome. Jenny had been concerned, too, giving him an extra kiss for good luck at the door as he'd left. He felt himself begin to smile at the memory of her balancing on her bare toes to be tall enough, and barely managed to cover his mouth in time to hide it. Besotted grins, even those inspired by Jenny, had no place in a gathering like this.

Finally one older man in an old-fashioned wig, conservatively dressed in a black suit with knee breeches, pushed his chair back from the table and stood to speak: John Sims, the banker in whose room they were meeting, and the most respected member of this group. He would be speaking on behalf of the others, and Brant fought down his excitement.

"Your Grace, you have presented to us a most intriguing proposition," he began with a bow, the light glittering off the gold watch fob slung across the front of his waistcoat. "We are most appreciative of the effort and thoroughness with which you have conceived this venture, Your Grace, and we thank you most heartily for the honor you have shown us."

The others murmured their agreement, nodding and tapping their palms on the table. There were, thought Brant wryly, few things more content than rich men about to become richer still.

"My thanks to you all, Mr. Sims," said Brant, his smile warm and inclusive. Why shouldn't he smile now, when the agreements must be as good as signed? Jenny was right; he couldn't be an idiot in every way, not to make a presentation like this, and her confidence gave him an extra measure of satisfaction. "It is my great pleasure to meet with such an informed and thoughtful group of gentlemen."

Sims nodded again, but for the first time Brant could see a ripple of uneasiness cross the man's round face. "As I said, Your Grace, your proposal is most intriguing, most thorough. However, before we embark together upon a venture as grand as this one, there remains one troublesome question, Your Grace, a question that I fear only you can address."

Brant smiled again, sweeping his hand graciously through the air. "Ask away, Mr. Sims."

"This is rather difficult, Your Grace." Sims dabbed

at his forehead with his handkerchief and looked to the others around him for reassurance. "As you know perfectly well, Your Grace, the success of this plan depends on persuading the most reliable workers to journey to the American states, often with their wives and families. They will look to the venture's leaders for confidence and inspiration before taking such a step. An example, Your Grace, if you will. As a peer of the realm, Your Grace, you are the most prominent among us, both in this project and in your numerous acts of charity, which are known well to the public."

Brant nodded, acknowledging the compliment, but now he was the one beginning to feel uneasy. What in blazes was Sims avoiding, anyway, circling around and around like this?

Sims coughed delicately. "Yet I believe, Your Grace— yet I fear—that all your good works are being undermined by your, ah, your present *connection,* and the notoriety— doubtless entirely undeserved, of course—with which this connection is besmirching you."

Now Brant frowned, for that didn't make a bit of sense. "Forgive me, Sims, if I do not quite—"

But the lawyer was already sliding a crudely drawn print, the kind sold cheaply along the Strand, across the polished mahogany toward Brant. Sims said nothing more, nor did anyone else, with most of the others staring down at the tabletop from embarrassment, or perhaps, pity.

And as soon as Brant saw the print himself, he understood why.

"Your Grace," said Tway softly, reaching to take the print from Brant's hands as he had countless times before. "If you wish, I shall assist—"

"Thank you, Tway, no," said Brant quietly. "No."

He knew there were words along the borders of the page, but for once he didn't need them read to understand the rest. The crude cartoon made the message clear enough. It had been so easy to tell Jenny to disregard the slanderous cruelty of the scandal sheets, but this— this was something else altogether. He knew he should instantly crumple the print, toss it away, denounce it as the vilest lies imaginable, and yet he couldn't make himself stop staring. He didn't care that the artist had made him out to be a fool, but he hated what had been done to Jenny, his brave, dear, lovely Jenny, turned into a blowsy, thieving harlot.

"Forgive us for distressing you, Your Grace," Sims was saying, "but we have discussed this thoroughly among ourselves, and believe it is—"

"What would you have me do, then?" demanded Brant, emphasizing each word with icy precision. "Have the lady paraded through the streets in sackcloth and ashes to beg your forgiveness?"

"No, no, Your Grace!" exclaimed Sims quickly, again blotting his forehead. "We would not presume to censure your personal affairs, Your Grace!"

Brant let his gaze rake over the faces around the table. "Some small consolation there."

"Rather, Your Grace, we would humbly dare to suggest a course of…ah, ah, discretion until the venture is fairly launched. Yes, that is it. Discretion, Your Grace, for the sake of the venture."

Brant didn't answer. How often over the years he had worried that he'd find himself rejected by a similar group for his inability to read—his stupidity, his scrambled wits—but never once had he dreamed of being chastised for being in love.

"For the sake of the *venture,*" he said finally, "you would wish to dictate the rest of my life, so that your tender sensibilities are not offended."

"'Dictate' would be too strong a word, Your Grace," said Sims quickly. "Rather we would—"

"Who bought this?" He tossed the print back onto the table, the paper fluttering lightly across the polished wood. "Which of you judged this filth as a worthwhile investment and laid your careful pennies out for it?"

"The print was, ah, brought to our attention, Your Grace," said Sims.

Once again Brant glanced at the others around the table, while not one of them would meet his eye. Self-righteous cowards, he thought with disgust. His Jenny was worth more than the entire lot of them.

"So no one will admit to such low tastes in amusements," he said, "or in having subsidized and thereby endorsed the insult to me and this lady. Yet all of you are quick enough to be outraged by my behavior as it is depicted, not how it actually is."

"But we who know you are not outraged, Your Grace, not in the least," protested Sims weakly. "It's others who do not know you as you are who might...ah, ah, might be offended."

But Brant had heard enough. He'd always wanted to keep her safe and from harm, and, instead, his love had left her open to ugly attacks like this and the unsigned letters that had come to him in the country. There was only one way to make things right with Jenny, one way that his own foolish head had been far too slow to realize. But he'd realized it now, here, and he meant to make good on it as soon as he left this room.

"As far as I can see," he said, rising to leave, "the only one who has any real right to be offended isn't in this room, and that is the lady herself. And until you can bring yourself to apologize both to her and to me, then all our discussions are done. Gentlemen, good day, and may your damnable righteous confidences all give you cold comfort in hell.''

Chapter Fourteen

Jenny sat on the bench in the front hall, once again dressed for traveling in her green spencer and matching bonnet, with a new novel to help pass the time on the trip back to Claremont Hall. The clock in the stairwell had chimed the hour scheduled for their departure a good long while ago, and the coach was already outside—Jenny could see the footmen standing beside the horses' heads through the open front door—but, once again, everyone and everything was waiting for Brant.

"Ah, here you are, love," he said, hurrying down the curving stairs with Tway as his shadow behind him. "There were a few matters that needed my attention before we left, that was all. I trust you've not been waiting long?"

"No," she lied as he bent to kiss her. "Not long."

"Good." He smiled briefly at her, then glanced out the door. "Has anything been brought for me while you've been here?"

She shook her head, curious. "What are you expecting?"

"A small package," he said, purposefully vague. "Something I need for the country."

Another time she might have challenged such an answer, and teased or bullied him into telling her more. But Brant had been in an odd humor since last evening when he'd returned from his meeting with his investors. To her shock, he'd told her there had been last-minute difficulties, and the venture had been postponed, perhaps even ended. She'd been horrified, ready to commiserate with him, but he hadn't seemed as disappointed as she'd expected, nor would he tell her the cause of the breach. He'd simply shrugged it off and spoken of something else.

It was not that he was being cruel, or callous, or disinterested in her. He had been his usual charming self at the supper and concert that they'd attended, and in bed afterward he'd seemed even more tender, more attentive than usual.

But subtly, in only a handful of hours, things had changed, and Jenny had no notion why. There was a new distance between her and Brant, a gap that seemed to be yawning ominously before her that she'd no idea how to cross. He had, quite simply, stopped sharing his thoughts with her, and she hadn't realized how much his confidence had meant to her until it was gone.

Miserably she watched him giving orders to Tway, making jests with one of the footmen, listening to Mrs. Harper's last-minute concerns about one of the chimneys. Everyone was receiving more of his time than she, decided Jenny sadly, and she thought of all the worst explanations for his disinterest, especially those that her brother had suggested.

What if Brant truly did want her only in his bed? What if the love he spoke of didn't mean anything more to him but lovemaking, that she'd a place in his bed but not in his heart? Had she really deluded herself that badly, believing the bond between them was greater than that?

She looked down at her lap, at her hands folded over the silver frame of her reticule. Perhaps Brant had somehow discovered the truth about her, or at least enough of it to make him stop trusting her with any but the most banal details of his life. It was certainly possible. Though Brant had told her not to read the gossip in the papers, she'd been unable to stop, and she'd seen how the speculation about her continued to grow each day. By now he could have learned everything there was to know about her.

You could have told him yourself, Jenny, but you didn't, and now it's too late, just as Rob said. You had so many chances to tell Brant the truth, yet you always found a reason not to, and now it's too, too late.

She'd wanted love with a man who cared for her, and a better, more honest life. To try to get it, she'd decided to stay here with Brant, instead of leaving with Rob— but what if by doing so, she'd made her future worse, not better?

"Your Grace," said one of the footman who'd been waiting outside with the coach. "This was just delivered for you."

He bowed, and handed Brant a small package wrapped in brown paper and twine.

"The final piece of my puzzle today," he said with satisfaction, stuffing the package into his pocket without bothering to open it. He turned toward Jenny, holding his hand out to her. "Come, sweetheart, high time we were on our way."

At least this time there were no menacing letters stuffed into the cushions, Jenny thought as she settled herself into the coach. And at least they were beginning the journey cheerfully enough, with Brant sitting closely beside her with his hand linked loosely in hers. The day was clear and warm, the roads would be dry, and they should easily be back at Claremont Hall by nightfall.

Yet as the coach slowly drew away from the house, Jenny couldn't help looking out the window at the green trees and iron fence surrounding the strollers in Grosvenor Square. Had Rob been waiting there this morning for her the way he'd promised? She hadn't seen him earlier from the window of the house, but then Rob was very good at not being seen unless he wished it. Had he been standing there beneath the trees, hoping she'd finally come to her senses?

"A penny for your thoughts, sweetheart," said Brant, and Jenny flushed. He could offer her a hundred guineas, and she still wouldn't tell him about Rob.

"I was thinking of the little package that came for you," she said, instead. "Were you waiting for that before we left? Was it something to do with your venture in Virginia?"

"Yes, I was waiting for the package," he answered, his smile as warm as ever for her. "But no, it's not anything to do with that infernal venture. Is that a new book you've brought with you?"

She nodded, wishing he'd have told her more about the package or the venture. "If you'd like, Brant, I'd be glad to read the newspaper to you, instead. We haven't heard any word of Master Cock-crow's doings in days."

"I imagine he's chasing the hens, same as he was before, and who could fault him for it?" He chuckled and released her hand, lounging back against the cushions with a yawn, his legs stretched out before him. "Amuse yourself as you please, sweetheart. I've thoughts of my own that need considering."

"You are certain, Brant?" she asked wistfully. What had become of the magic that had linked them so closely before?

"Quite," he said with a sigh of contentment that she certainly didn't share. "Enjoy your novel. You can tell me of it later."

Dutifully she opened her book and pretended to read. But the words had no more meaning for her than they would have had for him. Trust and love, honesty and deceit; more words that seemed too difficult for her. Unhappily she wondered one more time if she should have joined her brother this morning, and vanished neatly and forever from the life of the Duke of Strachen.

Brant stood in the empty dining room, dressed for evening. By now the sun had dropped low enough behind the trees that he'd had the candles lit in the silver holders on the table, just so he wouldn't go bumbling about in the dark. He was going to be nervous enough as it was without falling over his own feet, too.

He took the small leather box from his pocket and flipped the lid open with his thumb. The ring inside caught the candlelight, and Brant smiled. The large square-cut ruby in the center, as full of bright fire as Jenny herself, was surrounded by smaller diamond brilliants, all set in gold filigree. The moment he'd seen the ring yesterday, he'd known it would be exactly right for Jenny's hand, and now as he turned the ring this way and that beside the candle, he could already imagine it on her slender finger for the rest of their lives together. The only problem had come when the jeweler had dawdled at making it smaller, and had barely brought it before they'd left this morning. Brant would have waited, but Jenny was already so curious that he wasn't sure he'd have been able to hold off her questions for much longer.

He chuckled as he put the ring back into his pocket, imagining her reaction when he slipped it on her finger. Poor Jenny. She was probably ready to throttle him by now for being so evasive today. She didn't like secrets any more than he did himself, and he couldn't count the times today when he'd forgotten and nearly spoiled this grand surprise. They both preferred things out in the open, for better or worse. It was one more way they were suited to each other, one more reason he loved her as much as he did.

He heard her speaking to a servant in the hall outside, and quickly he took his place behind his chair at the end of the long table.

The door opened, and she stood there, her expression surprised but wary. Only the beginning of the evening, thought Brant with growing anticipation. She was wearing the coral and diamond necklace with his favorite gown, a pale green that reminded him of new shoots in the spring, and he wondered if she'd somehow guessed this night would be special.

"Brant," she said as the footman closed the door behind her. "I thought we were to dine together."

"We are, sweetheart," he said. "With my brothers descending tomorrow, I thought we'd have this last night with just the two of us."

Pointedly she looked at the bare, inhospitable table. "Quite a feast you've planned for us, too."

He laughed, and came around the table to take her hand. "I didn't say we'd dine here, did I?"

Now she narrowed her eyes, unabashedly suspicious. "You've said so little to me today, Brant, that I couldn't begin to guess one way or the other."

He laughed again, and kissed her forehead, making amends without just yet telling her the truth. ''Then let me show you, instead. You will trust your eyes, won't you?''

''I will, as long as you don't tell me first what I must see,'' she said. ''Perhaps I should have Jetty and Gus with me, to keep you in check.''

''They're not invited tonight,'' he said. ''I told you, it's only us.''

She let him lead her from the dining room and out the open doors to the steps and lawns beyond. But despite the feistiness of her words, her fingers curled into his, vulnerable as a child's and slightly damp like a child's, too. Had he really done such a good job of befuddling her today, he wondered, good enough to make her feel so anxious now? He smiled to himself and slipped his arm around her waist to reassure her that much.

''It's a fine night, isn't it?'' he said easily, gazing up at the clear evening sky and the sliver of a new moon. A nightingale had begun to sing in the elms, and from the open windows of the kitchen came the faint sounds of crockery and pans, and servants chatting and laughing as they worked. ''London is all well and good, but I cannot trust a place where most nights I can't see the stars or moon, on account of the chimney pots and coal smoke.''

''And the lights,'' she said. ''It never does grow truly dark there, not even at midnight.''

''Oh, especially not at midnight,'' he said. ''I suppose I'm just an old country squire at heart, one step away from greasy old leather breeches, a snuff wig, and a nose like a turnip.''

For the first time she laughed, softly, almost against her will, but a laugh nonetheless. ''You already let the dogs rule your life. But it won't be until you tether your favorite hunter in the front hall that I'll vow you're lost forever.''

''Don't tempt me, Jen,'' he said as they followed along the turning of the path, ''else I'll—''

''The *folly*,'' she exclaimed, stopping still. ''Oh, Brant, that's where we're going, isn't it? Look, *look* what you've done to it!''

He turned and looked, too, because she'd asked him to. He already knew what he'd see, because he'd dictated every last detail to Tway last night and sent the directions by a rider, so that everything would be ready in time for this. He knew, yet the reality of the folly's transformation—especially through Jenny's eyes—was magical, indeed.

The little temple had been hung with strings of lanterns, lit from within by candles that danced and twinkled on the light, even breeze. Roses and vines of ivy had been wrapped around the white columns and tied there with fluttery silver ribbons. A round table with two chairs had been set for dinner in the center of the folly, with more roses in a silver bowl, and wine waiting to be poured.

''Oh, Brant,'' she said again, this time in a wondering whisper. ''When you said we weren't to dine inside, I never guessed this!''

''You can understand now why I'd left the dogs behind,'' he said.

''They'd make a right royal mess in no time, wouldn't they?'' She smiled, but he'd swear there were tears in her eyes. ''You did this for me, Brant?''

''I did,'' he said, ''because I love you.''

He kissed her then, because he wanted to, but also because he wanted to prolong this moment. He was truly nervous now; he couldn't deny it. What if he abruptly forgot every word he'd planned to say? What if he coughed, or sneezed, or choked at the crucial moment, or even dropped the ring over the rail and into the shrubbery? No, it was better to charge on ahead now, before he could think of anything else that could go wrong. He seized her hand and started up the steps two at a time, starting so fast that she pulled back, laughing.

"Gemini, Brant," she protested breathlessly. "Are you that hungry?"

He didn't answer, but instead swept her up in his arms and carried her, giggling, up the last steps. How could he not want to marry her, loving her as much as he did? He sat her in her chair, poured the wine into her glass himself, and then took a deep breath, and a second one.

"You can sit, too, Brant," she said merrily. "You don't have to stand there, gasping like a fish."

"I cannot help it," he said, and with one last gulp of air, he sank onto his knees before her, fumbling for the box with the ring. She must have guessed what was going to happen—he supposed all young women did in such circumstances—because she'd clapped her hand over her mouth and began making odd little gulping sounds herself from behind her hand. Any other time he would have laughed himself at how foolish they must appear, but now—now he was more serious than he'd ever been in his life.

"Jenny," he said gruffly, clasping her hand. "My dear Jenny. You know how much I love you. I know this has been fast, damned fast, but the truth is, sweetheart, I cannot imagine my life any longer without you in it, and I dare to hope you feel the same about me. Marry me, Jenny. Do me that greatest of all honors, and marry me."

He'd expected her to weep, or laugh, or hug him, or even to shriek, before she accepted him, for Jenny was not by nature a calm and measured woman. He expected any of those reactions, and maybe a few more dramatic. But what he'd never considered was what she did now, pulling her hand free of his and going to stand at the folly's railing with her head bowed and her back to him.

And worst of all, she hadn't said yes.

"Jenny." Maybe she'd been so overwhelmed she hadn't understood properly. Maybe he just needed to say it again. Damnation, he hadn't even shown her the ring. "Jenny, love. Please. Marry me."

"Oh, Brant," she said, still not turning toward him, her misery echoing as deep as the ocean. "Your Grace. You have done me the greatest honor any man can show a woman. You don't even know who I am, yet you've asked me to become your wife, your duchess."

"I don't care," he said swiftly, standing. "What I do know of you is enough. The rest will come."

"But you don't know me," she said sadly. "Brant, you've offered me the world, and I love you more than any other man, and always will. But all I can offer you now in return is the truth. The *truth,* Brant, what you deserved from the beginning."

He rested his hand on her shoulder, but she shook him off, stepping away from without looking back. "Hear me first, Your Grace. Then you can decide what...what you will do with me."

She took a shuddering breath and raised her head, making her voice as clear as she could, so there'd be no misunderstandings. "My true name is Jenny Dell, and I was born in the dressing room of a theater in Dublin while the third act of *Hamlet* played on the stage. My mother abandoned me soon after I was born, preferring

a man other than my father. I do not even know if my
parents ever bothered to wed. I am no more a true lady
than your dog Gus.''

He couldn't believe this, or maybe he simply didn't
want to. ''Jenny, please, I—''

''No, wait until I'm done,'' she said, her voice oddly
hollow. ''My father was chased from the theater by the
bailiff, and he fled to the Continent with my older
brother, Rob, and me. He taught us to do as he did. We
pretended to be what we weren't, we charmed our way
into the regard of our betters, we took from them what
we could, then we left by night and changed our names,
and began again in the next town. I was born to false-
hood, and I've never known any other life, until I met
you.''

It couldn't be true, not his Jenny. ''This nightmare
must have come to you when you struck your head,'' he
said, struggling to find some explanation. ''Surely your
real life—''

''This *is* my real life, Your Grace,'' she said, a little
hiccup of suppressed tears in her voice. ''Do you recall
how, at the theater, I spoke of reciting pieces for my
father? I misspoke, because that was true, but not in the
genteel parlor way you thought. My father's friends were
all other actors, and they were the ones who clapped for
me on the stool.''

*Oh, it all was making sense now, far, far too much
sense....*

''And the handkerchief with 'Corinthia' stitched upon
it, the one that was found in my pocket? That was left
from another game—that is how Rob and I speak of
what we do, as games—last year in Bath. I was Miss
Corinthia Beckham, and my brother was Sir Peter. You

can ask at the assembly rooms if you wish. I'm sure they remember us.''

He shook his head, still refusing to believe what she said. "I won't do that to you."

"Even if this is the first time I've told you the truth about me? I never lost my memory, not for a moment. I did strike my head—a bruise like the one I had cannot be feigned—but as soon as I woke, I saw you not as a gentleman, but as an opportunity. Everything was contrived. Everything was false."

Numb, Brant looked at the leather box with the ring still waiting on the table.

Everything was contrived, everything was false....

The first thing that had bound them together had been her lost memory, her own flaw to match his own, had been a lie—a calculated lie, too. He had tried to protect her, to shelter her. He'd trusted her, and in return all she had done was to lie.

"But you were kind to me, Your Grace," she continued, and he was sure now she was crying. "You taught me that honor and truth and goodness were qualities fit for a gentleman, and not to be ridiculed or mocked. Do you know I left my brother and his ways behind because I believed you offered something better, something finer? You taught me what love was, too. I know that sounds foolish and pat, but it's true."

"How do I know you're not lying again?" he asked, bitterness welling up inside him. He'd loved her like he'd never loved anyone else, and lies and betrayal were what had come of it. "Why the devil should I ever trust anything else you say to me?"

"You're right," she said, reaching back to unhook the fastening on the coral necklace. "You shouldn't. But

I've never stolen from you, and I won't begin now. Here, you take this back.''

She turned and held out the necklace, the diamonds sparkling in the light of the lanterns swaying overhead. She wasn't a tall woman, but now she seemed to have shrunk, with all the joy that had been so much a part of her drained away. Her eyes seemed flat and lifeless, her cheeks wet with tears she didn't bother to wipe away.

''I don't want it.'' No matter what she'd done to him, he still could never imagine that necklace around any other woman's throat. ''Not now.''

''Then leave it for the magpies to brighten their nest.'' She tossed it on the table between them. ''I won't fault you if you call the magistrate to take me away. But if you don't, and show me that last bit of mercy, then I promise I'll be gone tomorrow, before your brothers arrive.''

''If you wish to leave, I'll not stop you.'' He wouldn't, either. He could not imagine asking her to stay after this, not when she so clearly wished to be free of him. ''Send for a carriage when you're ready.''

''I'd rather find my own way.'' She smoothed her hair back behind one ear in a neat, efficient gesture that was so characteristic of her that he almost couldn't bear to watch. ''You needn't worry. I'm very good at vanishing.''

She bowed her head and glided past him, already, it seemed, determined to begin vanishing. She hurried down the steps of the folly, her slippers making no noise.

Is this how it will end, then, without a word of farewell or a kiss to ease your breaking heart? Is this how you'll let her go, as if you'd never loved her, as if you'd never wanted her as your wife?

''Miss Dell,'' he called, his voice much louder,

harsher, than he'd intended. "Miss Dell. Tell me one last thing before you go. Did you ever love me at all, or was that false, too?"

"Love, love." Slowly she turned, her face pale in the moonlight as she gazed up at him. "Did I love you? Yes. Yes. I always did, Your Grace. From the beginning. That was the first true thing I've had in my life, and now I've ruined that, too."

He took one step toward her, then stopped. "Damnation, Jen, it didn't have to be like that!"

"But it did," she said, her voice breaking again. "It did. You're the best person I've ever known, Brant, and you're the only man I'll ever love, and now…now it's done."

And then, before he could think how to answer, she was gone, and he was alone.

Idly, Mary Hewitt turned the pages of the newspaper. It was even more slow than usual in this infernal shop, and the day had grown warm enough that the stench of the onions and greens seemed to press upon her like a moldering weight. She'd had enough of this kind of London life. Scandal or no scandal, she was going back to her own cottage in Bamfleigh tomorrow.

Besides, there was nothing left here to amuse her. After the furor of the print with the duke and his paramour Jane or Jenny or whoever she was, the editor of the paper had shown no more interest in Mary's vindictive tales. Lords and their mistresses were of limited interest, he'd told her as he'd shown her the door to the street, not like a good, solid murder among the titled. She'd seen nothing more of either the duke or the Farquhars, and she could only assume that her work had been successful and the duke had moved on to graze in other pastures.

In a way she was sorry it was over. She missed the power, the excitement, the sense she'd had of righting a terrible wrong against herself. Whatever had become of the Farquhars, she was quite sure they hadn't suffered nearly enough.

She turned the next page, and then she saw it, the breathless item that changed everything.

We have from a source of impeccable reliability that His Grace the D*** of St*****n is known to have purchased a betrothal ring from a certain jeweler in Bond Street. It is also known that he has retreated to his Country Abode with his favorite lady, the beauteous and mysterious Miss J**** W***. Other members of his family are also said to be gathering at his home. Can a ducal wedding be nigh?

A ducal *wedding?* Mary gasped so hard she had to press her palm over her chest to calm her heart. The Duke was supposed to toss the slut out, not marry her! It was wicked and it was wrong, rewarding sin with such a prize. She could not bear it—she would not!—and blindly she groped beneath the counter until she found her brother-in-law's pistol.

Her fingers shaking with the audacity of what she was planning, she found the tin box with the balls, the tinder and the gunpowder. Once, long ago, Herbert had taught her how to load and fire a pistol because it had amused him to do so. She thought she remembered how, at least well enough to do what she must. Cautiously she aimed the gun toward the back of the storeroom, feeling how naturally it sat in her hand. It felt right and proper, the next daring, inexorable step, and she smiled, relishing that same sense of triumph and destiny that she'd felt when she'd first seen the print.

She wrapped the pistol in an old length of toweling and placed it in the bottom of her trunk, beneath her spare stockings and petticoat. She would do it. She would do it.

The stage for Bamfleigh would stop near Claremont Hall. And so, tomorrow, would she.

Chapter Fifteen

Not bothering to stop her tears, Jenny gathered her few belongings and packed them into a heavy old cloth bag that she'd found in the bottom of her clothespress. That, surely, would not be missed, but she wouldn't make the same assumption about the rest of her clothes. Just as she'd left behind the coral and diamond necklace, she was now determined to abandon the muslin gowns and the glazed kid slippers, the ivory-bladed fans and the Holland shifts, and all the other stockings and ribbons and jewelry—even the white ostrich plumes that she'd worn to the theater—everything that had come to her through Brant's generosity. She hadn't deserved any of it, not after what she'd done to him, and she didn't want anyone saying she'd loved him only for what she could take away.

What remained made for a pitifully small bundle, especially after she'd dressed herself in the plain white gown that she'd been wearing when Brant had first found her. For money she'd only the small purse of coins she'd tried to give to Rob, hardly enough for her to return to London to try to find him. Yet somehow she would be resourceful and make do; she was a Dell, wasn't she?

But the thought brought no comfort to her, only a fresh rush of tears. With nothing else left to pack, she curled herself in the armchair near the window to wait for dawn. As much as she longed to be gone from here, she wasn't so foolish as to leave at night, a lone young woman on the road to London. She'd climb from the window, so as not to be seen, and she'd locked the door to her room to avoid Mrs. Lowe and the rest of the servants. And Brant—but no, she'd ended things so badly with him, there'd be no question of him ever coming to find her again now.

She hugged her knees, her whole body knotted with grief. Brant had loved her enough that he'd wanted her for his wife, his duchess, the mother of his children. He had offered her all that, beneath fairy-tale lanterns and roses, and all she'd had to give him in return had been the truth about herself. That had been the terrible irony: for if Brant's love hadn't changed her into a person who cared about honor and all the rest, then she wouldn't have needed to tell him the truth that had destroyed everything.

All she'd left to do now was to cry, reducing her old Corinthia handkerchief to a sodden mess, and to wonder if it truly were possible to die of a broken heart.

Brant went downstairs as soon as he heard the sound of his brother George's coach coming up the drive, and depending on the horses and roads, Revell and his wife Sara would soon be arriving, as well. The brothers always met each other like this, so glad to see one another that there was never any standing on ceremony. But this morning Brant's steps were slow and heavy going to the door for the customary welcome, and with extraordinarily little enthusiasm.

It wasn't only because he'd drunk all the wine brought to the folly last night, and then added brandy on top when he'd finally come back to the house. That would explain the crackling throb of his head and the attractive red tinge to his eyes, but the rest—the emptiness he felt inside, the grim downturn of his mouth, the bleak sorrow he couldn't seem to banish from his expression—those were all Jenny's fault. It wouldn't take George long to see it, either, or gleefully to identify the source—the curse of brothers, decided Brant with gloomy certainty as the footman opened the front door for him.

First from the coach was George's wife Fan, a tall, handsome woman with dark hair and pale gray eyes. In her arms she was proudly carrying their son Jack, who had progressed considerably since Brant had last seen him. Four months ago he had been little more than a tiny round head, swathed in a huge mound of blankets and linen, that existed only to sleep or cry. Now Jack seemed to have doubled in size and energy, kicking and flailing and showing little tolerance for those blankets: a good, strong boy that would likely scream bloody fits when Reverend Potter poured holy water on his forehead. Dutifully, Brant kissed the baby's forehead, as was appropriate for his heir, and then, steeling himself, turned to greet his brother, Captain Lord George Claremont.

"A splendid day for a journey, Brant," boomed George, his voice always at the same volume he used on his quarterdeck at sea. With his dark hair and weathered face, George was the largest of the brothers, the one with a brusque tendency toward taking charge and giving orders, and dressed as he was the splendid uniform of a navy captain, dark blue coat and white breeches and everything liberally doused with gold braid and buttons, few would argue. "The inn last night was well enough, too, even for Jack. Where's your lady, eh?"

Brant winced, as much from the effect his brother's voice was having on his aching head as from his question. "The lady's no longer mine," he said, "and thus not here."

"Not here?" repeated George with disbelief. "Not yours? What the hell is that supposed to mean? Your letters were so full of her name I felt sure we'd find you already wed to her."

"No," said Brant curtly. "She's not, and I'm not, and that's an end to it."

"Oh, Brant," said Fan, sadly disappointed. "We did so wish you to be happy!"

But George was studying Brant's face and finding a great deal more there than Brant wished him to.

"Upstairs, brother," he said, his hand on Brant's shoulder to make sure he didn't try to escape. "Fan needs to settle Jack with the nursemaids anyway. You can tell me your tale and I'll give you sailing orders."

Brant scowled, trying to shrug away his brother's hand. "I don't wish your wretched orders, George."

"No man ever does," George answered cheerfully, "because no man knows what's best for his own useless self. You did the same for me in a similar squall with Fan, and I'll happily repay the favor."

Brant resisted, yet five minutes later he was in his study with George, pouring his loss and misery into his brother's willing ears.

"The worst of it was that I loved and trusted her,

George,'' he said after he'd told his brother everything that Jenny had told him, ''and in return she lied to me.''

George made a sympathetic but noncommittal grunt. ''She told you all of this before you proposed marriage?''

''Afterwards.'' Brant reached for the ring box on his desk and tossed it to his brother. ''Not that she cared.''

George opened the box, and whistled with appreciation. ''That's a handsome bit of sparkle, Brant.''

''She's worth it,'' said Brant automatically. ''Damnation, that is, she *was* worth it.''

''She may still be,'' said George evenly. ''You love her. You don't want to, but you do. That's clear enough. Otherwise you wouldn't be raging on about her now.''

''I'll survive.''

''Of course you will, but why must you do it without her?'' George put the ring box back on the desk, pointedly open and facing toward his brother. ''Brant, you've been with more women than I shall likely ever even meet in my entire lifetime. Yet this Jenny is the first one of all that vast harem that you've genuinely cared for.''

Brant reached out to shut the ring box, not wanting to be reminded again of what it represented. ''How do you know? You never even met her.''

''I didn't have to,'' countered George. ''You've described her so well to me—in your letters, this morning—that I feel as if I know her as well as my own Fan. True, that's all I have to judge, but it seems enough. So what wounds you the most about her great revelations? That she's Irish, not English?''

Brant stared at him. Surely, George knew him better than this. ''What kind of bigoted idiot do you take me for?''

George shrugged elaborately, begging the question.

"Is it that she says her parents were worthless wastrels?"

"Which makes them exactly the same as our own noble father."

"Exactly," repeated George. "So was it that she filled her pockets at your expense? Did she have a taste for jewels like those rubies and diamonds?"

"No," said Brant softly, remembering how her hands had trembled as she'd taken off the coral necklace. "The one decent bauble I bought her she gave back."

"Most honorable, in a woman or a man," said George. "Which forces me to ask another question of you, dear brother. You are so intent on these lies she has told you, but have you asked yourself her reasons?"

"Damnation, George, I—"

"Stow it, Brant, and mind what I say," ordered George. "Consider us, and Revell, too. We're all three of us what Father made us, no matter how hard we've tried to be otherwise. The old bastard branded us well and good. Couldn't your Jenny have done the same? How much of a choice could her father have given her to strike a different course, eh?"

But Brant had no ready answer to that. Instead, he remembered how she'd spoken so fondly of learning parts from her father to recite for his friends, and how easy it had been to imagine her, a tiny girl with elfin eyes, standing proudly on a tall stool to recite her piece in a determined chirp for a father she'd obviously loved.

How could she reject the teachings of her father after that? How could she know right from wrong, if wrong had been the only example she'd ever had?

"You say she lied," continued George. "If she didn't lie for gain, then she must have had another reason for keeping her true self from you."

Because she loved you. The answer came to Brant so
suddenly he swore to himself—no, *at* himself. Because
she feared he'd turn her away, she'd kept trying to be
what he'd told her he expected: an English lady, high-
born and gently raised. He knew himself how hard it
was to pretend to be something one wasn't, increased a
hundredfold from fear his great sham would be discovered.

But what reason had he ever offered Jenny that he'd
value her still if she'd turned out to be something less
than a fine lady? When had he ever told her that he loved
her more for her laughter and her quick mind and how
she'd hold up her jam-covered fingers for him to kiss
one by one in the morning in bed?

None of which, fortunately, George could know.

"Some women can keep a secret tighter than the
grave," he went on. "Why, my Fan didn't see fit to tell
me about her papa's smuggling until we both were
nearly shot by the revenue men. At first I was so damned
furious with her for breaking the same law I'd sworn to
uphold, I could scarce see straight, but with a bit of time
and distance, I could see how much that confidence had
cost her, and how much she'd come to trust me to be
able to share it. But Fan's a rare woman like that. Somehow she made a gift of admitting her father was wanted
for all manner of treasonous crimes."

George laughed, for this memory was now comfortably hidden away in his past, with Fan quite content as
George's wife and the mother of small Jack, and her
days as part of a smuggling family long behind her.

But there was no such peace for Brant. Hadn't Jenny
tried to make the same kind of gift to him? The more
he considered how he'd parted with her, the more selfish
and arrogant his behavior seemed. When he'd confessed

his own blackest secret, his shameful inability to read, she'd been endlessly understanding, ready with kisses and sweet sympathy. She'd lightened his burden and made him feel whole in a way that no one else ever had before.

Yet as soon as she'd tried to share with him, all he'd been able to do was sputter and rage about how she'd lied, with not a word about what she was giving him in the name of love.

"Brant, you've offered me the world, and I love you more than any other man, and always will. But all I can offer you in return is the truth...."

"Where in blazes are you rushing off?" demanded George with surprise as Brant abruptly rose to his feet. "I'm not through giving you my wisdom yet, brother."

"But I am through being the greatest jackass in Britain," said Brant, once again putting the ring box into his coat pocket. "All I must do now is find Jenny, and pray that she'll let me grovel enough to hear me out."

"Find her?" repeated George. "How blessed hard can that be?"

"I do not know." Jenny had promised to be gone by dawn; considering how independent she was, that could mean she was anywhere in the county by now, or even outside it.

"From my own foolishness, I let her slip away from me once, George," he said softly, feeling the bump of the ring in his pocket, "but by God, I won't let it happen twice."

It was the birds that woke her, their cheerful din rising from the branches outside her window. Yet even so, Jenny woke slowly, sleep tugging heavily at her as she tried to wake. On some foggy level she sensed there were things she did not wish to wake and confront, not just yet, and she turned her head, searching for the pillow to bury her face.

But there was no pillow, only the hard back of the chair where she'd slept instead of the bed, and with her face now turned toward the window, she unwillingly forced her tear-swollen eyes to open. The sun was as wickedly cheerful as the birds, bright and high in the sky, and as she tried to straighten her sleep-stiffened limbs, she remembered.

Her last awful conversation with Brant, her promise to leave him and Claremont Hall, her determination to be gone with the first light of dawn: all of it came back with a ferocious clarity. But as she squinted at the window, she realized that the sun was already high in the sky and that she'd long ago slept through dawn and a good piece of the morning. Of course no servant had come to wake her, for she'd locked the door against them last night.

Too late, one bird seemed to be singing. *Too late, too late.*

As quickly as she could, she washed her face and braided her hair, and tied on the old-fashioned flat straw hat, a servant's discard, that would shield her face from both the sun and too curious passersby. This time she didn't allow herself the sentimental indulgence of studying the room to remember it, because now she knew the sooner she could forget everything about this house and its master, the better. She tucked the bag with her belongings beneath her arm, swung her legs out over the windowsill, and dropped to the terrace and then to the grass, and as easily as that, she'd made her farewell to Claremont Hall.

She darted into the shadows of the garden like a startled rabbit, knowing which paths to take and which she should not, to avoid the gardeners. She was counting on most of the servants being busy with the arrival and settling of Brant's two brothers, even so late in the morning.

Her goal was to reach the break in the long fences surrounding the property, a place that her brother had discovered where the fence had been taken down for some improvement yet never replaced. The opening wasn't far from the London road, and once Jenny found it, she'd be able to keep walking north along the road until she could hail the stage to carry her the rest of the way.

The last of the tended gardens was really a small apple orchard, with the rows of trees crisscrossed by neat gravel paths. Jenny slipped through the hedge that bordered it, and stopped short. On an old stone bench dappled with lichen sat an unfamiliar dark-haired woman with a young baby in her lap. The woman held the baby in the crook of one arm while she tickled his plump cheek with a long piece of grass, making him chuckle and wave his arms with such delight that Jenny smiled, too.

"Good day," said the woman, noticing Jenny. "He's a saucy little fellow, isn't he?"

"Yes, ma'am," said Jenny, suddenly shy. She should have slipped away before the woman had seen her, and she would have, too, if not for the fat-cheeked baby. "What's his name?"

"Jack," said the woman proudly. "He has a whole mouthful more beyond that, but Jack's what he is to me. And I am Fan."

"You're George's wife," blurted Jenny, then quickly recovered. "That is, you're Lady George."

"Well, yes," admitted Fan, shifting Jack to her other arm. "And I suspect you're Brant's Jenny. Oh, I can see why he loves you so dearly!"

"But he doesn't, not at all," said Jenny miserably. No one would love her as she was now, her eyes red and her face swollen from crying. "Hasn't he told you? Last night we had...differences, and decided we no longer suit one another."

"Which is why you are leaving now," said Fan, noting the cloth bag under Jenny's arm. "But you're wrong about not suiting one another. I'd say from the look of Brant this morning, he spent all of last night cursing himself for letting you go."

"Not Brant," she said sadly, looking down at the baby, his bright blue eyes and downy blond hair. Even at this age, there was already something about his chubby face that reminded her of his uncle Brant, an undeniable Claremont likeness.

"You know you could already be carrying Brant's child yourself," said Fan, stroking the baby's cheek. "If you did lie with him, then it's possible. No, likely. You should consider that before you vanish from his life. They're a potent lot, those Claremont men."

But that was too much for Jenny.

"I must go," she said hurriedly, turning away so that Fan wouldn't see the raw, bitter longing in her face. To marry Brant and bear his child, to become a true family with a mother and father and baby—to consider such a lost possibility of so much she'd always wanted from life was unbearable to her. "Forgive me, but I must go now."

Why was she always running away? Why couldn't she ever stay in one place long enough to find happiness?

"Jenny, wait!"

Had she truly lost her wits, then, imagining Brant calling her back?

"Jenny, please, wait!"

But she wasn't imagining it, for here were Jetty and Gus loping along with her as if it were all great fun, and she could hear Brant, too, not far behind. With a little sob, she broke into a run. She didn't want to see him again, not to make her poor vulnerable heart suffer all the more.

"Jenny, please!" He caught her arm, pulling her, off balance, against him while the dogs barked happily. "Please listen to me!"

She gulped, pulling back, but not free of his hand. Why should she, when his touch was what she wanted?

"That's—that's—what I said to you last night," she stammered, breathless from running and uncertainty, "and look what came of it."

"Then it's up to me to set things right, if you'll let me." Fan had been right: he *did* look as if he'd spent the night in some terrible, sleepless dilemma, his handsome face haggard and drawn. "I made a damned great ass of myself last night, Jenny, thinking only of me and not of you—no, not of us. There, that's what's most important, isn't it? *Us.* Quiet, Jetty, Gus, you infernal beasts, and let her hear me!"

For once the dogs stopped and sat, giving her no excuse. She gulped again, searching his face. She would not cry again: she would *not*. "But I lied to you, Brant, over and over. You said that, and you were right."

"Jenny, I'm not so perfect that I've any right to stand back and judge you," he said, taking the bag from her hands and dropping it to the ground so she wouldn't be distracted. "What matters more is that you told me the truth, likely the hardest thing you've ever had to do."

"It was," she whispered, unable quite to trust this miraculous twist of fortune. "Oh, Brant, it *was,* but I had to do it because I loved you!"

Carefully he pulled off her broad-brimmed hat, the better to read her face, then frowned and nodded simultaneously, an odd combination that was also uniquely Brant's. "I see that now. I understand. You had your reasons, good reasons, too, only I was too much an idiot to listen."

"You must never say you're an idiot, Brant," she insisted despite the tremor in her voice. "You're not, and you never have been."

"All right, then, Jen, *you* can call me an idiot, and I'll agree," he said, purposefully taking her hand. "Because only an idiot would let you go in the first place. Jenny, marry me. Please. Idiot though I am, marry me."

"You are *not,*" she said automatically.

"Damnation, Jenny, will you marry me or not?"

"I *will!*" She flung her arms around his neck, laughing and crying at the same time and not really certain which came first. The rest was a hazy blur of joy: the way Brant laughed with head thrown back, how George and Fan clapped their hands and baby Jack yowled and Jetty and Gus barked and raced back and forth, the leaves and tiny green apples of the trees overhead tossing gently in the same breeze that was tossing strands of her hair across her face. Somehow Brant was sliding a ring onto her finger, the red stone catching every ray of summer sun, and then he was telling her he loved her and kissing her and she felt sure her life would never again be this fine, this perfect, this—

And it wouldn't.

"Look at you both, shameless in your embrace!" The woman's voice was shrill with outrage and righteous with the edge of madness. "She has ruined you, Your Grace, just as her brother sought to destroy me!"

At once Brant put his arms protectively around Jenny, trying to put his body between her and where the woman must be. He snapped his fingers and the two dogs at once came to his side, the fur bristling on the backs of their necks as they sensed the danger.

"Show yourself, ma'am," ordered Brant. "Show yourself, or I shall send my dogs to find you."

Without any hesitation the woman stepped out of the shadows. "Send your dogs to me, Your Grace," she called with strange relish, "and I shall shoot them dead for their trouble."

Jenny gasped. She'd thought she'd recognized the woman's voice, though she hadn't been able to place it exactly. But now she could see the woman herself, standing in a bright patch of sunlight on the grass: perhaps five years older than herself, with ruddy skin and a nest of frizzy curls on her forehead. It was Mary Hewitt, Rob's widow from Bamfleigh, the one who'd tried to make rivals of her brother and the grenadier.

But why in the name of Heaven should Mary Hewitt be standing here now, an old-fashioned army pistol clutched tightly in her hands and pointed directly at her and Brant?

"Please, Mrs. Hewitt, don't harm the dogs!" she begged, pushing herself around Brant so the woman could see her. "They would never hurt you!"

"So tenderhearted you are!" Mrs. Hewitt laughed scornfully. "I won't hurt your precious dogs unless I must, Miss Jane or Jenny or Jackanapes or whatever you call yourself now. That would be a waste of good lead. I'd rather save the shot for you, you wicked trollop."

Jenny's heart plummeted. She thought she was done

with dishonesty, done with deceit, yet here the old lies
had come back again, impossible to escape.

At once Brant shoved Jenny back behind him. "Is this
the same Mrs. Hewitt that inspired the scuffle at the
Black Lion?" he asked with disbelief. "The widow from
Bamfleigh?"

But Mrs. Hewitt didn't wait for Jenny to answer. "Oh,
yes, Your Grace, I'm the *widow,*" she answered. "And
of course this little hussy knows me. It was her brother
who made me the laughingstock of the county and ruined my good name forever!"

"He did nothing of the sort!" cried Jenny indignantly.
"You were the one who played Rob false with that soldier!"

"Hush, I say!" the widow ordered furiously. "You
see how it is, Your Grace, sister and brother alike, and
both of them lying cheats. I tried to warn you of their
dishonest ways. I wrote to you, didn't I? I tried to tell
you what would happen when you took this creature into
your home."

"Enough, ma'am," said Brant sharply. "I will not
stand here and let you slander this lady any longer. She
has agreed to become my wife, and if you insult her,
you have insulted me, and will suffer the consequences."

But the widow only laughed again. "Or perhaps you
shall suffer them, instead, Your Grace, you and your
harlot wife. How can I let either of you go when you
paid so little heed to my warnings?"

She *is* mad, thought Jenny, her heart racing with fear
as she held tight to Brant's arm. She remembered Mary
Hewitt as being self-righteous and foolish, but this was
different, and Jenny didn't doubt for an instant that the
woman would indeed fire the pistol if pushed. True,

there would be only one ball in the loaded gun—if she'd even loaded it—and there were four of them, plus baby Jack and the two dogs. But the risk to all of them was still too great, the cost too dear.

She curled her hand more tightly around Brant's arm, trying to share his strength. She didn't want her life with him to end here, before it had truly begun. She wanted to be his wife, and she wanted his children, *their* children, the way Fan had predicted. She glanced over at them now, George with his arm around Fan and little Jack, unexpected participants in this whole awful scene. They had what she wanted, what she'd always craved. She'd dared to believe love and happiness were at last to be hers with Brant, but now everything could be gone in the next instant....

"You fire that gun, ma'am," said Brant slowly, "and you will hang."

"Oh, my, my, Your Grace, you shall have to do better than *that*," scoffed the woman, "considering that I have come this far to punish you."

"Why, Mary Hewitt, listen to you rant," said a man's mild voice behind them all. "Here I'd always thought you'd a lady's manner, but now, such drama—how you surprise me, my dear!"

"Rob!" cried Jenny, twisting around to see her brother. He was standing on a slight hill opposite the widow, his usual nonchalant charm tempered by the gun in his hand—the familiar French pistol that, for the first time, Jenny was glad to see.

"I thought you might be needing my help, Jenny-girl," he said wryly, "though, gad, I never expected it to be quite this."

"How *dare* you come show your face to me!"

shrieked Mrs. Hewitt. "How dare you, Richard Farquhar, after what you—"

"Actually, it's not Richard," he said easily, not in the
least distraught. "It's Rob. Robert Dell. If my dear sister
can discover honesty by using her true name, why, I
suppose I shall resolve to do the same."

But the widow only shook her head, the curls on her
forehead bouncing furiously with her rage. "You *lied* to
me, and you *ruined* me! You said you loved me, that
you would love me forever!"

"Mary, Mary." Rob sighed indulgently. "It was
never like that between us, Mary. We had a flirtation, a
dalliance, a merry game of it for a fortnight. I liked you
fine, and I flatter myself that you liked me well enough
in return. But it never was love, Mary. You must not
mistake it for that."

Jenny could see the deep unhappiness twisting Mary's
face beneath her rage, and see, too, how her grip on the
pistol was wavering. Had she truly suffered so deeply
from her brother's attentions? She'd seen Rob with other
women—many, many other women—and though he
could be accused of being a hopeless flirt, he was never
cruel, and because he'd always been perfectly aware of
his own limitations, he never led them on to expect more
than he could give. Surely, Mary must have heard more
than Rob had said, or instead heard what she'd wished
to hear.

But, oh, how much more dangerous was the game that
Rob was playing with Mary now, almost baiting her,
trying to talk the pistol from her hand! With tears in her
eyes, Jenny looked back at her blithe, carefree brother
in a dandy's yellow coat with black braid, the gun with
the elaborate silver inlays almost an accessory in his
hand, and marveled at how without a thought for his

own safety, he'd made a target of himself to save her life and Brant's. Was this how he hoped to right a life of dishonesty and glibness, by sacrificing it for her sake?

Oh, Rob, don't, she prayed silently, *not for me. I know you love me without you having to do this for my sake. Please, Rob, be careful, be* careful!

"But you did love me!" cried Mary, angry and anguished at once. "I know you did, and everyone else did, too! They all were sure you'd marry me!"

"Then everyone was wrong," said Rob softly, his voice turning gentle. "You know the truth, dear Mary, the same as I do. I've yet to find real love myself, lasting love, the love the poets sing about, not with you or anyone else. I've only to look at my sister's face and see her joy and happiness to realize that."

"But you did love me, Richard," she insisted forlornly, her face crumpling with disappointment and misery as the pistol drooped in her hands. "You wouldn't have said such pretty things to me if you hadn't."

"In time you'll find a man who truly loves you as you should be loved, Mary," said Rob in the same coaxing voice. "Another who'll love you like your husband did. All you must do is look, and hope, and wait, and then he'll come to you. But before he can, Mary, you have to drop that ugly pistol, right there on the grass."

But, instead of dropping the gun, Mary stared at it in her hands as if seeing it for the first time.

"Yet Herbert never loved me," she crooned. "He married me, but he never loved me, not the way you say could happen."

"Mary, please, drop it," pleaded Rob. "Please drop the gun now."

Lightly Mary trailed her fingertips along the barrel, studying her reflection in the gunmetal. "Herbert didn't love me, Richard, and neither did you. No one ever loved me, did they? No one did, and no one will.''

Gently she placed the silvery barrel of the pistol to the side of her head, nesting it there among the curls she'd set that morning with sugar water. She squeezed her eyes shut and licked her lips, as if waiting for the true sweetheart's kiss that would never come.

Then, before any of them could stop her, Mary Hewitt pulled the trigger, and ended her life in the name of the love she'd never found.

Swiftly Brant tried to shield Jenny from the sight of Mary's faceless body on the grass, but Jenny was already pulling away, desperate to reach her brother. She'd never seen Rob like this, his animated face blank and frozen and stripped of all emotion, as if all part of his life had fled with Mary's.

''Oh, Rob, I am sorry,'' She cried softly, wrapping her arms around him to comfort him however she could. ''It wasn't your fault that—that she did that. It wasn't your fault at all.''

With a groan, he closed his eyes. ''I tried to save her, Jen. Poor, foolish pigeon! She was wrong in so many ways, but she didn't deserve that. I *tried.*''

''I know you did, Rob,'' whispered Jenny fiercely, ''and I'll never be able to thank you enough times for it. You tried to save her, and me, and Brant, too, when instead you could have been killed yourself. Oh, you were so very brave to do that for us!''

''Ah, consider me a hero.'' He tried to laugh, but there was no humor to the sound, only sorrow. ''I did it for you, lass. For you, and your duke, too.''

''You did it for love, Rob,'' said Jenny, tightening her arms around him. ''For love.''

''Whatever else could make an old rascal like me do

anything so worthwhile?'' he asked, and at least Jenny could hear the warmth coming back to his voice as he hugged her in return.

Over Rob's shoulder Brant caught her eye and smiled, enough to make Jenny's eyes fill with tears. Although Rob was indeed a rascal, on this morning he was also a hero. But first of all he was her brother, and he'd nearly given his life for the sake of her happiness.

''For love, then, Rob,'' she said softly. ''For all of us, and for love.''

Epilogue

Beneath the square tower of St. Martin's church, the Reverend Daniel Potter wed the sixth Duke of Strachen to Miss Jenny Dell on a sunny afternoon in the first week of July. It was a small family ceremony, hardly the grand wedding that Society would have preferred, but exactly the one the bride and groom wanted, complete with a shower of flower petals tossed by the parish's giggling children.

The bride wore a pale green gown that already was the groom's favorite, and in her hair was a wreath she'd woven herself of wild strawberry leaves, in honor of her new status as a duchess. The bride's brother, Mr. Robert Dell, gave her away, and her only attendants were Jetty and Gus, both of whom wore similar wreaths of strawberry leaves around their necks to mark their continuing status as ducal dogs. Those who glimpsed the bride's ruby and diamond betrothal ring swore it was even more magnificent than the scandal sheets had proclaimed, and likely worth a king's ransom.

A king's ransom, or at least a Virginian one. Three days before the wedding, His Grace had come to excellent terms with a group of private investors, and therefore was pleased to announce a new venture west of the American states. Englishmen wishing to begin a new life were encouraged to seize his opportunity to better themselves, and the enterprise was considered so certain to succeed that even His Grace's new brother-in-law Rôbert Dell—a gentleman reputed to be every bit as clever as the duke himself—had asked for a place in the new company. Once again the Golden Lord seemed destined to prosper, though he claimed his continuing good fortune was nothing compared to love he'd found with his Jenny.

"If you are always being called the Golden Lord," asked Jenny after the wedding, "does that mean I must become the Golden Lady, too?"

"Only if you wish it," said Brant. "I must admit I'd never given that much thought at all."

"Oh, Brant," she said, pretending to be vexed as she sat on his lap with his arms around her, which was not an easy thing to do. "By marrying you I now have so many names I cannot begin to remember them all. Duchess of Strachen, Marchioness of Elwes and goodness knows what else."

"I believe you're a baroness, too, as well as Queen of the May and Princess of All That Is Good." He laughed and kissed her where the strawberry leaves still crowned the top of her head. They'd stolen away from the wedding feast to sit here in the folly, and though the raucous sounds of the celebration in their honor still drifted across the lawn toward them, they still felt blissfully alone for the first time in the long day.

"Oh, bother," she said, wrinkling her nose. "I was better off as Miss Jenny Dell."

"I disagree," he said. "But tell me, there was one I especially liked that your brother called you today. Clover Girl, it was. I could picture you as a tiny girl, sitting in a field of purple clover flowers.''

"Not exactly," she hedged, for the truth was hardly as flattering a picture as the one he'd imagined. But she was determined to tell only the truth with him, and tell it now she would. "It's nothing as winsome as that. Rob called me that after you'd first brought me here, on account of landing in so fine and perfect a situation for vagabonds like us—that I'd landed in clover."

"Then he was right," said Brant, nodding sagely. "Absolutely right. You landed in the perfect place for you, Clover Girl, and for me, too."

"*You* are perfect, Brant," she said softly, reaching up to kiss him. "Which is likely why I love you so much."

"Not quite," he said, chuckling. "Being perfect, I mean, not the other. Because I love you more than I can ever tell you, Jen."

She laughed, so happy she could do nothing else. "Clover," she said. "*This* is clover, Your Grace, and don't you forget it."

And she saw to it he never did.

*   *   *   *   *

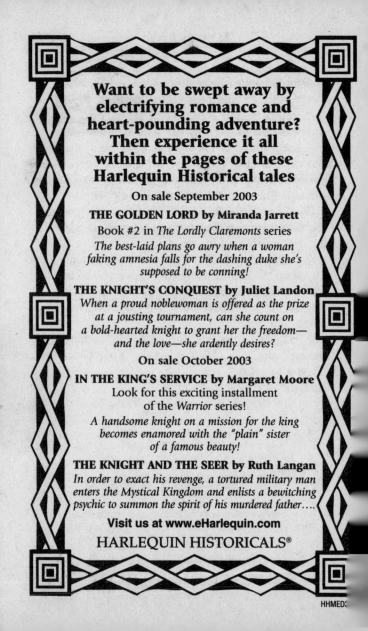

Want to be swept away by electrifying romance and heart-pounding adventure? Then experience it all within the pages of these Harlequin Historical tales

On sale September 2003

THE GOLDEN LORD by Miranda Jarrett

Book #2 in *The Lordly Claremonts* series

The best-laid plans go awry when a woman faking amnesia falls for the dashing duke she's supposed to be conning!

THE KNIGHT'S CONQUEST by Juliet Landon

When a proud noblewoman is offered as the prize at a jousting tournament, can she count on a bold-hearted knight to grant her the freedom— and the love—she ardently desires?

On sale October 2003

IN THE KING'S SERVICE by Margaret Moore

Look for this exciting installment of the *Warrior* series!

A handsome knight on a mission for the king becomes enamored with the "plain" sister of a famous beauty!

THE KNIGHT AND THE SEER by Ruth Langan

In order to exact his revenge, a tortured military man enters the Mystical Kingdom and enlists a bewitching psychic to summon the spirit of his murdered father....

Visit us at www.eHarlequin.com

HARLEQUIN HISTORICALS®

ITCHIN' FOR SOME ROLLICKING ROMANCES SET ON THE AMERICAN FRONTIER? THEN TAKE A GANDER AT THESE TANTALIZING TALES FROM HARLEQUIN HISTORICALS

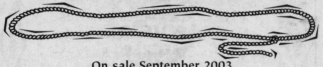

On sale September 2003

WINTER WOMAN by Jenna Kernan
(Colorado, 1835)

After braving the winter alone in the Rockies, a defiant woman is entrusted to the care of a gruff trapper!

THE MATCHMAKER by Lisa Plumley
(Arizona territory, 1882)

Will a confirmed bachelor be bitten by the love bug when he woos a young woman in order to flush out the mysterious Morrow Creek matchmaker?

On sale October 2003

WYOMING WILDCAT by Elizabeth Lane
(Wyoming, 1866)

A blizzard ignites hot-blooded passions between a white medicine woman and an amnesiac man, but an ominous secret looms on the horizon....

THE OTHER GROOM by Lisa Bingham
(Boston and New York, 1870)

When a penniless woman masquerades as the daughter of a powerful marquis, her intended groom risks it all to protect her from harm!

Visit us at www.eHarlequin.com

HARLEQUIN HISTORICALS®

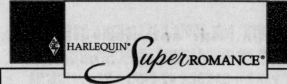

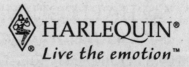

It's romantic comedy with a kick
(in a pair of strappy pink heels)!

Introducing

"It's chick-lit with the romance and happily-ever-
after ending that Harlequin is known for."
—*USA TODAY* bestselling author Millie Criswell,
author of *Staying Single*, October 2003

"Even though our heroine may take a few
false steps while finding her way, she does it
with wit and humor."
—Dorien Kelly, author of *Do-Over*,
November 2003

Launching October 2003.
Make sure you pick one up!

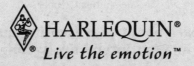

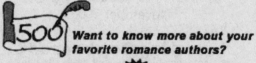

Savor the
breathtaking romances
and thrilling adventures
of Harlequin Historicals®

On sale November 2003

MY LADY'S PRISONER by Ann Elizabeth Cree
To uncover the truth behind her husband's death,
a daring noblewoman kidnaps a handsome viscount!

THE VIRTUOUS KNIGHT by Margo Maguire
While fleeing a nunnery, a feisty noblewoman
becomes embroiled with a handsome knight in a
wild, romantic chase to protect an ancient relic!

On sale December 2003

THE IMPOSTOR'S KISS by Tanya Anne Crosby
On a quest to discover his past, a prince masquerades
as his twin brother and finds the life and the love
he'd always dreamed of....

THE EARL'S PRIZE by Nicola Cornick
An impoverished woman believes an earl is
an unredeemable rake—but when she wins
the lottery will she become the rake's prize?

Visit us at www.eHarlequin.com

HARLEQUIN HISTORICALS®

HHMED33